CROWN OF ICE

THE MIRROR OF IMMORTALITY BOOK 1

VICTORIA GILBERT

License Notes

This book is a work of fiction. Names, characters, places, and incidents are the product of the author's imagination or are used fictitiously. Any resemblance to actual events, locales, or persons, living or dead, is coincidental.

Second, Revised, Edition Copyright © 2017 by Vicki L. Weavil
CROWN OF ICE by Vicki L. Weavil
All rights reserved. Published in the United States of America by Snowy Wings Publishing

Print ISBN: 978-1-948661-38-6
eBook ISBN: 978-1-948661-37-9

No part of this book may be used or reproduced in any manner whatsoever without written permission of the publisher or copyright holder, except in the case of brief quotations embodied in critical articles and reviews.

Published by Snowy Wings Publishing
https://www.snowywingspublishing.com/

Cover Design by Deranged Doctor Design
Formatting by Deranged Doctor Design

Dedicated to the memory of my grandparents:

Ellen and George King
Norma and John Lemp

"The whole world is a series of miracles,
but we're so used to them we call them ordinary things."
Hans Christian Andersen

CHAPTER ONE: SHATTERED REFLECTIONS

MY PARENTS LIE SOMEWHERE BENEATH the snow, buried with my mortal life.

I spend endless days searching for their remains. Tucking a piece of the mirror inside my fur-lined cloak, I harness one of my milk-white ponies to a sledge. Flying over ice and snow, I hold up the shard to catch the rays of the sun.

"Show me," I order the reflective glass. "Show me where they sleep."

The fragment of mirror flashes with prismatic color, but I never catch a glimpse of my parents' icy grave. They are gone—lost to the mountain and the winds. An unfathomable ocean of snow sucked them into its depths, far from even my powers of perception.

I can see much, but never their faces.

I was only five when they were swept from me. When I recall that horror, I remember my tears. I never weep now, but in those days it wasn't unusual for me to cry. My mother claimed I was born with rose-petal skin—too fragile to protect me from the world's thorns. A single harsh word or a sharp look would reduce me to hysterical tears. Seated between my parents in our small sleigh, my father gently admonished me for grabbing at the reins. It was enough. I cried. My parents hushed me, their eyes frantically darting about. But it was too late. My wails echoed through the narrow mountain pass. A roar drowned my cries and a great wave of snow rushed toward us.

My mother lifted me up, as if to wrap me in her arms. A gust of wind tore me from her and bore me aloft, carrying me some distance before tossing me into a snow bank. I didn't see the sleigh disappear, but I heard everything—the screams of the horses, the agonized cries of my parents. Late at night I hear them still.

The villagers always said God took a hand in my life. But it wasn't a deity that snatched me from my parents' icy tomb. It was the hand of master mage Mael Voss, conjuring a wind from the safety of his frozen fortress. Surveying the countryside though the largest fragment of his magic mirror, he spied my plight and saved me. Not from any sense of tenderness, or pity—there were no such emotions clouding his crystalline eyes, even then. He had a use for me. He saved me for himself.

Voss sent the farmer to find me and carry me, shaking and wailing, to the village—an old man who never understood why he was compelled to trudge across his frozen pastures that day, or why he climbed to the pass that led from his village to the greater world. He located me by the sound of my crying. The one time it served me well.

No sounds, even to my enchanted ears, can reveal my parents' resting place. They've been silent far too long. After a while I lay the reins lightly against the pony's neck to turn us from the mountain pass. As darkness creeps over the fields and forests we head to a castle carved of ice. We head home.

At night the palace's crystal halls are tinged sapphire. One of the first bits of magic Voss taught me was to set the carved walls alight so I'm not forced to walk the halls in darkness. I conjure a cold light that glows within the thick walls without melting the ice. I mastered this trick quickly once I knew what those shadows held. If I leave an area in darkness, they come—the girls who reigned as Snow Queen before me.

"I must find it." Their hollow words twist about me like a shroud. "The last piece. I must place it. Give it to me."

They are only shadows—swirling mists that occasionally coalesce to create phantoms of their former selves. So many girls, from so many eras. Some from the far past, their ghostly bodies attired in ancient robes and strange, peaked headdresses, and some dressed in the garb of more recent years. I know there is nothing left of their real nature. A curse has destroyed their minds. All thought is lost to them, except for the memory of their final terror. Of every shape and size and time, they share only one trait—the absolute agony that burns within their hollow eyes.

They suffer a fate that makes ordinary death look like a blessing. It is the loss of so much more than a body—the sacrifice of the soul and the destruction of mind and will.

I would free them if I could. Allow them the respite of a true death. Send them to their rest.

But it does not matter what I might desire to give them, I cannot alter their plight. They thrust their hands at me, but their fingers can neither hold nor grasp. They are not dead, they cannot die. Mael Voss made them immortal when he made them queen.

But the wraiths, deathless as they are, hold no power. They are merely the remnants of girls who failed. They could not accomplish the one thing Voss asks, no, *demands*—that his Snow Queen piece together a shattered looking glass.

He needs the mirror whole for some purpose I cannot determine. I only know it is a magic totem Voss values above all things. Stranger still, Voss requires the assistance of other hands to restore the mirror, despite his own magical prowess.

The wizard constantly foils my attempts to understand the purpose of the looking glass, but I know why I was brought to this cold kingdom. It is simple enough to connect my fate to the stories I heard as a child, told in hushed tones near a brightly burning fire. How, long ago, Voss stole a girl from one of the surrounding towns and transformed her into something the villagers could comprehend, and fear. The embodiment of brutal winters, of ice and death—the Snow Queen.

Voss gave his young queen magic of her own. She never felt the cold that froze others in a breath. Frostbite could not eat into her body. She could call forth blizzards and blighting frosts. She could even slow heartbeats until animals and humans fell into stupors that led to death. But Voss was no fool. He'd create no creature whose power could challenge his own. Aided by the mirror's own magic, he added a draft of poison to his spell. The girl who reigned as queen had to reassemble the magic looking glass before her eighteenth birthday. Fail, and she was transformed into a bodiless wraith, doomed to forever wander the halls of her former palace.

My name is Thyra Winther, and I am seventeen years old. I have five months to restore the mirror or suffer the fate of my predecessors.

I often encounter them in the shadows, their translucent faces frozen into masks of grief, their eyes devoid of memory, of sense. I stride past them. Or through them, if necessary. A disgusting sensation, like walking through a spider's web—light as milkweed floss but clinging to my skin. Still, I'd rather endure such unpleasantness than stay in their company, haunted by a constant reminder of my fate.

"The final piece," they whine. "I have it. I hold it. I will place it correctly. I will remain queen."

They cannot truly speak with me—their words are those burned upon their tongues when their lives were ripped into shreds of mist. Only when they warn of my future, channeling the power of the mirror's curse, do they speak anything other than their foolish, repeated phrases.

"You'll do nothing." I snap at them. "You are smoke and air and unending stupidity."

It does no good for me to show any kindness. They comprehend nothing. Their gaze is turned inward, focused on their memories of horror.

I stalk away to the safety of my bedchamber, where a cold flame fills the icy fireplace and the skins of slaughtered beasts cover the walls and floor.

They failed, all those who came before me. But I will conquer Voss's task. I am no ordinary girl—nothing like the wraiths, although they were once a bit like me. I am brighter than the borealis, sharper than an ice crystal, stronger than the northern winds. I will reassemble the mirror and reign as Snow Queen forever.

Curled upon my bed, I contemplate the leather-bound notebook in my hands. It contains pages of calculations, all the equations I've created to systematically piece together the fragments of the mirror. The looking glass itself does not reside in my rooms. It lies upon a massive wooden table in the Great Hall of the palace. Two-thirds of the mirror now gleams brightly, the fragments perfectly fused together. But I've learned each piece must be placed in the exact position from which it fell. Insert it incorrectly and the mirror will reject the fragment, spinning it off to the opposite corner of the frame.

I keep one piece of the mirror in my chambers, as I know Voss keeps one in his. The final two pieces, to be placed when all the rest is complete—and our protection from one another.

So far, Voss is pleased with me. I've progressed further with the reconstruction than any girl before me. He claims I'm fortunate in my choices, but it's not luck that has gotten me this far. It is logic and mathematics. I wield these skills to piece together the mirror and survive the isolation of Voss's icy fortress.

As I page through the notebook I notice a multiplication sequence and a memory surfaces. I am eleven years old and my foster mother Inga Leth has forced me to accompany her to church. She has no interest in taking me anywhere else, but at church I am her badge of honor, the symbol of her virtue and charity. Everyone else has left, headed home to their Sunday dinners of salted fish and potatoes. But Inga's still chatting with the minister, her hands flying about, punctuating her words.

Scrunched down in a hard wooden pew, I stare at the simple metal cross that hangs over the altar. Two lines that intersect—not centered but balanced. I lose myself in contemplation of the mathematical precision of the figure. My eyes instinctively follow the lines down and up and across. Perfect.

"I can do calculations in my head," says a voice, and I slide around on the varnished seat to face a boy. He is my age or just a bit younger. He has hair the color of walnut shells and eyes as dark as holes cut in an ice-covered lake.

"I can," the boy repeats. He must have read the doubt on my face.

"Who are you?" He doesn't have that look of the others who stare at me. His eyes are bright with curiosity instead of disdain.

"My name's Kai Thorsen. My parents and I are visiting my uncle." He examines me carefully. "What do they call you?"

"Thyra," I reply. "Thyra Winther."

"Oh. You're the orphan rescued from the avalanche."

"Yes." I force myself to stare into his dark eyes. Even visitors to the village have heard my story. "I'm good at sums, my teacher says. Better than most boys."

"I don't think you're better than me." Kai states this as a fact. There's confidence, not arrogance, in his voice.

"Calculate something then." I pull a small notebook and pencil from my skirt pocket as I slide over to allow him to sit next to me.

Kai calls out two large numbers and I write them down. "Multiplied," he says, closing his eyes for a moment before giving the answer. "Divided, smaller into larger." This answer takes a little longer.

I stare at my notebook, where I've figured with pencil and paper. Kai's answers are correct. "You aren't bad."

"Now you," commands the boy.

I hand him my notebook and pencil. "You call out the numbers." I twirl a strand of my curly hair around my finger. "Make it difficult."

He gives me a complicated series of numbers to add. After a moment I provide the answer.

"You got it right." Kai looks up from the paper and smiles for the first time. "Now multiply the first two, if you remember."

I concentrate and provide the answer. Kai scratches the pencil across the paper and whistles loudly.

"Not in church," says a girl who has wandered up to our pew. She looks a few years younger than Kai. Her hair, the color of aspen leaves in autumn, is tightly braided and wound about her head. Her cheeks are blushed pink as a ripening apple and her eyes are light blue and clear as water in a mountain stream. "No whistling in God's house. You know better, Kai." The girl places her plump fingers on Kai's thin forearm.

"Gerda, this is Thyra and she can calculate"—Kai shakes off her hand—"almost as well as me."

"As well," I say. The girl stares at me. I lift my chin and glare back.

"You have strange hair," says Gerda. "It's almost white. And your eyes are clear as ice."

"My eyes are gray," I say with a sniff. "And it's not polite to comment on other people's appearances."

"But you're beautiful." Gerda smiles and I realize as her face lights up that she's the pretty one. I'm unusual, odd, peculiar. Or so I've been told, many times, by my foster sister Begitte and her friends.

"Is this your sister, Kai?" I take back my notebook and pencil.

"No." Kai gives a dismissive shake of his head. "Her name is Gerda Lund. My parents and her parents are friends. They traveled with us. They know my uncle too."

"And we are friends." Gerda reaches for the hand Kai has draped over the arm of the pew. "Right, Kai?"

"I guess," mumbles the boy.

Gerda giggles and clutches Kai's hand. "Of course we are. Best friends. Now, it's time to go. Grandmother's waiting for us outside. And it's a bit cold out."

Kai shoots me a little smirk. "Gerda's my shadow—she follows me everywhere."

"Oh." I tap the pencil against my palm. "Well, you'd better run along then. Don't want to lose your shadow."

They depart, Gerda clinging to Kai's hand. As they head down the aisle Kai turns to glance back at me. "Calculate this." He calls out two numbers. "Divide. Larger into smaller."

After a moment I yell back the answer. I catch sight of his smile before he leaves the church.

"What is all this racket?" snaps Inga, bustling up to me.

I stand and slip the notebook and pencil back into my pocket. I compose my face and steel myself against the slap I'll receive when we step outside.

Kai, I think. *Kai Thorsen*. A most unusual boy.

I stare at my notebook. I've run every equation I can imagine at least twice. I've done well so far, but I know I'll never complete the mirror on my own. Not in five months. Not before my fateful birthday.

I never spoke to Kai again after that day in the church, although I heard his family moved to the village to inherit the mill after his uncle died. With them came their closest friends, the Lunds. When Gerda's father died unexpectedly, Kai's father took over the business, but the Thorsens made sure Gerda's family continued to receive an equal share of the profits.

These events occurred after I was taken away by Mael Voss. Ripped from my mortal life to survive in a palace of ice, I live alone except for the servants Voss conjures from lesser creatures. I only return to the village in the winter, the wind and snow swirling about my sleigh, disguising my true form. But I always notice Kai and Gerda—Kai, tall and slim, a mathematical genius, destined for the university, for greatness. Gerda, plump and merry, fair as a summer morning, destined—everyone says— for motherhood, for love.

I have five months to consider every variable and reassemble the final portion of the mirror. I have my intellect, and will, and an unquenchable desire to survive at any cost. But logic informs me I can't complete this puzzle on my own.

I need someone to assist me. Someone whose ability to understand complicated equations will allow me to triumph over Voss and the mirror. A human who can provide the one thing I require for my survival.

I do not need a lover, or even a friend. I have survived this long without such blessings. But I do need someone—a very special someone. A mortal with a mind to match my own.

Kai Thorsen.

The boy who can calculate almost as well as me.

CHAPTER TWO: STALKING PREY

IT WON'T BE EASY TO lure Kai Thorsen to my palace. He has a logical mind, not given to fancies. He won't be dazzled by magic alone. I spend several days, disguised by a swirling robe of snow flurries, observing Kai as he attends school or assists his father at the mill. He's a quiet, level-headed boy. Little seems to distract him, but I note his special affinity for animals. As I watch him play with a litter of pups, his face bright with delight, I realize I've discovered my lure.

Early one morning I cloak myself in furs and head for the stables. As I pass by a dark hallway, a wisp of smoke gathers into the form of a girl. Her large eyes are as black as the sockets in a skull.

"Burning," the wraith howls, "always burning." She rubs her translucent hands over her arms as if to erase the memory, but her fingers merely slide through her vaporous skin.

I pause, leaning against the icy wall of the corridor for support. I can guess her story. She must have died during her transformation from girl into Snow Queen. I know not all Voss's creations survive the awful force of his magic. I have glimpsed them amidst the wraiths—the most pitiful of all, their final agonizing memory their constant torment.

"Burning." The wraith extends her filmy hands.

"Leave me." In her ghostly face I spy my future, if I do not prevail over Voss and the mirror. "You have no power here."

The wraith wails, reminding me of cries that released an avalanche. I clench my fist, creating a spear of ice to throw toward the creature. A foolish gesture. The wraiths feel nothing, or at least nothing outside their tortured minds.

I hurry into the stables and hitch my favorite pony to a sledge. I don't need my sleigh today. I'm not yet ready to capture Kai. I'm after smaller game.

As we fly over mountain peaks and valleys, I scan the ground, searching for any movement against the jagged planes of snow and ice. A herd of shaggy reindeer and a few lumbering bears cross below me before I spy a solitary dark form streaking toward a small cave. I call to my pony, slowing his pace and directing him to the ground. We land just outside the cave.

I leap from the sledge, dropping the reins into a snow bank. I know the pony won't bolt. He, like all our horses, is trained to remain still when any part of his harness touches the earth. No moose or bear can spook this pony—he's far more afraid of me.

I stride toward an opening in a large outcropping of rock, my boots not breaking the crust on the snow. At the mouth of the cave I call forth a ball of cold light and hold it before me, cupped in my ungloved hands. It illuminates the interior of the cave, showing me what I've come to see—a female wolf and her pups.

The wolf bares her teeth as a low growl resonates through her lair. I fix my gaze upon her face. She stares back, her golden eyes scarcely blinking. I draw upon one of the powers I possess—magic Mael Voss has granted me. The wolf's eyes glaze as I slow her heartbeat. She lowers her head with a sigh that seems to expel all the air from her lungs. She gives one of the pups a final, gentle, lick as her eyelids flutter and close.

The wolf pups whimper, immediately sensing something's wrong. They crawl over their mother, nuzzling her still form with their snouts. I lean in and grab the smallest of the pups and thrust it, wriggling and whining, beneath my cloak. The others I leave with their mother. I'm not certain the wolf will wake. One curse of this power is that I can't always determine the line between life and death. With any luck, the mother will shake off the effects of my magic after I've gone. But I cannot be sure. If she dies, I know the pups will starve, if they don't freeze first.

I clutch my prize to my breast and regulate my uneven breathing. I've no desire to harm these creatures, but I only need one pup. I cannot risk the wolf attacking me, and I certainly can't care for all the pups. There's nothing to be done. It's the way of things.

With my squirming baggage bundled in a bearskin wrap, I take up the reins and urge the pony into the pearly gray sky. We head back to the palace, swift as the eagles circling us, the pup's whimpering drowned in the rush of the wind.

I don't release the wolf from his bindings until I reach my chambers. By this point he's soiled the white fur wrap and gnawed a hole through one of the leather straps. I ball up the bearskin and throw it into a corner of the room. One of our servants will collect it later.

The pup bounds away, racing across the stone floor so fast his legs slide out from under him. He skids into a wall, yelps, and nips at the reindeer hide hanging above his head.

"So"—I throw off my cloak and sit on my bed, staring at the wolf— "I suppose I must find you something to eat."

The pup's gaze pierces me like a shard of ice. He waddles toward me, but stops and sits in the middle of the chamber. His eyes never leave my face.

"I imagine reindeer milk might do." I eye the animal. Although Voss has enchanted many creatures to do our bidding, he's never brought a wolf into the palace. He claims they are far too intelligent to imbue with any magical powers.

I am not concerned. This pup won't live here long, and I have no intention of conjuring him into anything. He isn't a work animal or a pet. He is merely bait.

"Come along, then." I rise to my feet and cross the room in a few strides, opening the heavy wooden door that seals my chambers. I step into the hall and illuminate the icy blocks of the walls. Glancing back, I notice the pup is trailing me. A smile twitches the corners of my mouth.

It's almost too easy, I muse as I make my way to the kitchens. The pup pads along behind me. To my surprise he doesn't run off when one of the wraiths attempts to block our path. He stands his ground and yips sharply until the wraith whimpers and wafts back into the shadows.

"Good boy." I give him an approving nod before I stride into the larder. Its wooden shelves bend under the weight of stone crocks and tin boxes. Barrels line the walls. It reassures me that there's plenty of food stored for the winter. There should be enough, even if I bring another human into the palace. The stores will only be needed for two of us as Voss has long since abandoned the need to eat, and the wraiths require no such sustenance. "Come now, I'll give you some dinner. We must keep up your strength. Tomorrow we travel far."

The pup looks up into my face and cocks his head. Of course he can't speak, but those clear eyes are bright with some form of comprehension.

"You're my lure," I tell him, reaching for a heavy crock that holds reindeer milk. I pour the milk into a small bowl carved from ice. When I sit the bowl on the floor the pup sniffs the air before inching forward to lap a few mouthfuls.

"You'll draw Kai to me." I touch the pup on the head as he buries his nose into the milk. His fur is soft as feathers, and warm. Warmer than anything I've felt in many years. I yank back my hand and press it against the icy surface of the kitchen table. "And with Kai's help, I will survive."

The following morning I feed the pup before bundling him in a clean fur wrap. I carry him to the stables and place him on the floor of the sleigh to wait while I harness the ponies. When I climb into the sleigh he doesn't wiggle or whimper, but rather drops his head upon one of my reindeer hide boots and sighs gustily. He rolls his eyes so he can stare up into my face.

"Yes, you're being good," I say. This seems to satisfy him. He gives one sharp yelp, closes his eyes, and falls asleep.

We travel across my kingdom, over a country devoid of any human habitation, finally reaching the mountain pass that leads to Kai's village. I call up a light drift of snow to hide my sleigh as we land and speed across the frozen ground.

At the edge of the village I slow the ponies to a trot. Anyone viewing my arrival would see an ordinary gray sleigh, its only occupant a slight figure swallowed up in white furs. Just a stranger passing through. Always careful, I conjure snow flurries to whirl about my face and blur my features.

It's merely a precaution, as no one in the village will recognize me. Even when I lived with them they did their best to avoid me. They called me cursed—some even claimed I might draw a blight upon them. Whenever I sail over the thatched rooftops, I observe the village where I spent my childhood with barely repressed anger. The place holds no fond memories except for my earliest recollections, before my parents died.

This does not touch me, let it fall away.

No, not one of them will recognize me. I've been transformed from that young girl who lived among them, yet never lived as one of them. My hair, always pale, is now white as mist. My once gray eyes are clear as new ice. Gerda saw it, that day in the church, what I would become. But even Gerda won't recognize my features now—every curve chiseled into an angle, every angle sharpened by time and necessity. She can't possibly glimpse that young girl in my beautiful and terrifying mask of a face.

I halt the sleigh behind the mill owned by Kai and Gerda's families. The wooden walls of the mill, weathered a pale silver, rise above a foundation of large stones. The great wheel sits silent, its bottom third sunk into the frozen lake, stalactites of ice decorating its paddles. I glance over the lake and observe a group of people skating on its crystalline surface. I know, from previous scouting missions, that Kai and Gerda are likely to be part of the crowd.

The wolf pup stirs at my feet. I lean down and open his fur blanket, then lift him into my lap. "Now's the time for you to do me some good." He yawns and stretches before flopping over on his back, his paws flailing. I lay my hand against the downy fur of his belly to keep him still.

"Enough of that," I say, as he nuzzles my fingers. I thrust him beneath my heavy cloak, one hand cradling him against my breast as I climb from the sleigh. It won't do for anyone to see the pup before my plan is put into action. I walk to the edge of the lake, near the water wheel. A tumble of grasses, desiccated and tipped with ice, clutters the shore between the mill and the wheel. I watch the skaters until I spy Kai and Gerda gliding in my direction. In one swift movement I pull the wolf pup from beneath my cloak and deposit him in the tall stalks of dead grass, then turn on my heel and flee to my sleigh.

The pup's howls ring through the clear air, but he can't follow me. I've employed a touch of magic to freeze him in place, preventing him from moving from his grassy nest. Standing by the head of one of my ponies, I spin a whirlwind of snow about my sleigh and watch as Kai skates closer, drawn by the wolf pup's cries. Gerda doesn't follow him—I make sure of this, sending a gust of wind to blow her backward. She calls out to Kai but he tells her to return to the others while he investigates the source of the noise.

As Kai approaches I step forward, moving closer as he pushes aside the weeds to uncover the wolf pup.

"What have you found?" I ask, adjusting the hood of my cloak until it shadows my face.

"A wolf." Kai turns and I'm astonished by the wonder in his dark eyes. "Just a baby. All alone, poor thing." He bends down and picks up the pup, cradling it gently against his felted wool coat.

The wolf lifts his head and looks into my eyes. He whimpers and strains against Kai's arms.

"He seems interested in you." Kai checks me over for the first time. "I'm sorry, I don't think I know you, miss." His eyes narrow. "And I know everyone in this town."

"I'm just passing through." I turn my head to avoid Kai's direct gaze. "What should we do with him, do you think? The pup, I mean. It seems a pity to leave him here on his own."

"Well, I'd take him home, but my father would have my hide." Kai strokes the pup's head. "We've a few sheep, you know, and chickens. Our dogs would probably try to kill it, anyway. They're pretty territorial—don't like other dogs about, and as for a wolf … "

"Yes, that might be a problem." I move a little closer to Kai. "I may be able to help."

"How's that?" Kai's voice radiates suspicion.

"I have a sleigh. Rather fast, and quite capable of crossing the fields beyond the village. If you came with me—you and the wolf pup, I mean—I could take you somewhere he'd be safe."

"On his own? This little guy?" Kai clutches the pup tighter. "I don't think he'd survive out in the wild."

I close my eyes for a moment, calling upon my reserves of magic. "I know where there's a pack that might take him in. High up in the mountains." I push back my hood and stare directly into Kai's eyes.

He gasps, almost dropping the pup. The wolf yips and bites at the air.

"Who are you?" Kai's eyes are glazed.

I sigh. So it is with every human who looks upon my face when I wield my magic. They forget what they're doing and where they are. Some even forget who they are.

Kai's not so weak-minded. "Do you really know the whereabouts of a wolf pack?"

"Yes, I do." I lay my gloved fingers on his heavily padded arm.

He shivers. The magic still coursing through my body renders my touch like ice, even through my gloves. "And you can carry us there?"

"I can." I slip my hand through the crook of his elbow. "My sleigh's just over there, behind the mill." I gesture with my other hand as I lead him from the lake.

As we reach the ponies the wolf squirms and breaks from Kai's hold. Leaping to the ground, the pup bounds into the sleigh.

"You see"—I tighten my grip on Kai's arm—"he wants to go." I turn my gaze upon Kai's face. "And you—you want to come with us."

"Yes, I … " Kai rubs at his forehead with his free hand. "I do, I think. But it doesn't make sense, really."

"You do want to save the pup, don't you?" I pull off one glove and touch Kai's face with my bare fingers. The remnants of my magic make his lips tremble and turn blue.

"Of course." Kai grabs my hand and drops it as if burned, even through his heavy mittens. He may suffer a touch of frostbite, but I can heal that easily when we reach the palace.

"Kai! Kai, where are you?" Gerda's voice shatters the stillness.

I back away, slumping against the side of the sleigh. Kai's head swivels at the sound of Gerda's voice, and I know he's lost to me, at least for now.

"I'm here." He speaks softly but his next words are louder and firmer. "For some reason, I'm here." He stares at me as I pull up my hood to shadow my face. "Will you still take him, the pup? Will you find little Luki a home?"

"Luki?" I fight the sarcasm that threatens to edge my tone.

"His name. It's Luki. At least it should be." Kai smiles. His face has regained its usual color.

I bite the inside of my cheek in frustration. "Very well, Luki it is. And I shall find him a home, never fear."

Gerda calls for Kai once more. He turns from me, following the sound of her voice.

Not wanting Gerda to see me, I grab the reins and slap them hard against the ponies' flanks. We speed away as Kai spares me one last glance. He can see nothing, of course, but whiteness. I have conjured a blinding drift of snow in this small corner of the world, obscuring everything from view.

I have failed today—a failure that may cost me all my tomorrows. But I won't allow that to happen. I must design a better plan, that's all.

The wolf pup stirs at my feet. I glance down at him, meeting his unblinking gaze. "So, Luki, I suppose you must live with me, at least for a while. I may have a use for you yet."

The pup jumps into my lap and I allow him to remain, curled within the folds of my heavy fur cloak. When I shift the reins into one hand and drop my other hand beside me Luki sniffs it, sensing the freezing power has left my body before licking my bare fingers.

CHAPTER THREE:
THE MAGE AND THE MIRROR

MAEL VOSS IS SELDOM IN the palace. I never know where he goes or why he travels so often. He won't tell me anything of his life, or of the world beyond these icy walls. It's one of the reasons anger burns like hoar frost in my heart. Bound to the cold and snow, I can't venture beyond northern realms.

I don't understand why, but I know Voss chose me when I was a child. I was his property from the moment my parents' sleigh disappeared beneath that roaring tide of snow. While I grew from a toddler to a young woman there must have been many other girls who tried, and failed, to reassemble his precious mirror. Yet I know his hand was always on me—his plans and schemes ruled my life. I have never fathomed why I should be so important to him. It is surely not because he feels any affection for me.

I sigh and roll over in bed, staring at an embroidered bell pull hanging on the far wall. When I was first dragged to this icy fortress I found the tapestry buried in a trunk in one of Voss's storerooms. It shows a young mother surrounded by her children. Her face is alight with love as she watches the children play amidst a verdant garden. All is green and blooming about this happy family. The needlework trees brim with the vivid colors of ripe fruit. I sigh and drape my arm over my eyes.

When I was orphaned, only one person stepped forward to take me in—Inga Leth, a widow with two children of her own. Most of the villagers marveled that this woman would take on another mouth to feed, and praised her kindness and charity. But I was uneasy as I stood outside the bakery, clutching a soft roll the baker's wife had thrust at me.

Inga was as broad as she was tall, her dark hair pulled tightly up under a white linen cap. Her face was ruddy and her eyes blue as chips of delftware. It should have been a merry face, but I spied shadows in the bright eyes and shivered.

Inga looked me over as if she were buying a calf at market.

"Come along then." She turned and strode off, her boots ringing on the cobbled streets. I scrambled to keep up with her

Wiping my eyes, I trailed Inga into her small, snug cottage. She brusquely introduced me to her children—a tall boy named Nels who was already too old to spare me any attention and a scrawny girl named Begitte who eyed me with suspicion.

"You will sleep up there," said Inga, pointing to the loft. I gazed at the ladder that leaned precariously against the rough wooden beams and burst into tears.

"Enough of that." Inga slapped me hard across my backside. "Stop blubbering or I'll give you something to cry about."

My bouts of weeping did not disappear overnight. But Inga's threats and well-placed slaps convinced me, over time, to hide my tears. I learned to swallow them until I was safely tucked up in the loft. Far from prying eyes and hard hands, I could draw them up, like water from a well. I'd bury my face in the scratchy folds of my straw-filled mattress and allow the tears to soak the cotton ticking. Silently, of course. It wouldn't do for anyone in that cottage to hear me.

Over time I trained myself to stop crying altogether, even when alone.

Lingering in Inga's garden, which was mysteriously never touched by frost until far into November, I'd stare into the heart of the roses. The exquisitely layered construction of their petals diverted my thoughts from a daily barrage of harsh commands and snide comments. By the time I was eight I allowed such words to swarm about me like bees, never settling upon my skin. "This does not touch me," I told myself. "Such words hold no power. Let them fade. Let them fall away."

When I learned to hide my emotions Inga was more indulgent, allowing me to eat dinner with her children rather than sending me to the corner stool with my bowl of stew. But she still treated me like the pigs she raised, with a care never quite touched with kindness. "Can't get too close to them," she'd say, yanking me away from the pen as I tried to pet the tiny, squealing, piglets. "One day they must be carted away and slaughtered."

I later understood why she kept her distance. Inga knew that one day I too would be taken away. A knock would rattle the cottage and as the door opened my true master would be revealed. Inga had made a deal—not with the devil, but with a being just as evil. In exchange for a protective spell that shielded her garden from early frosts, Inga had promised me to Mael Voss.

When I was younger I made a few feeble attempts to talk to my new master about his journeys, his work, or anything at all. I was alone, and desperate to hear another voice. But Voss brushed me aside, his cold disdain crueler than any slap. So I learned to talk to myself and the animals that roam the halls of the palace—bear and fox, owl and rabbit and reindeer. All of them conjured into creatures that can perform simple tasks. Paws transformed into hands, hooves into claws. Yet despite their presence my conversations are one-sided. Voss never grants these creatures the power of speech. They understand my commands but can't respond.

I sit upright as a hare hops onto my bed, a slip of paper in his hand-like paws. He drops the paper onto my bearskin coverlet and leaps away, racing through the small opening Voss insisted on carving into my door. He wants his messengers to reach me, whatever the hour.

I glance at the paper with blurry eyes, registering Voss's command. I must meet him in the Great Hall. I've slept later than usual and know it's due to my failed attempt to kidnap Kai. I've yet to design a new plan to lure him to the palace, and sleep offers escape from my darker thoughts.

Dressing swiftly, I hear a noise and turn to see Luki bounding from his bed of furs. He approaches me, his eyes bright with expectation.

"I suppose you're wanting breakfast." I pull on my boots. "First we must see what Voss demands of me. But come along—we'll stop by the kitchens on our return."

The pup follows me down passageways of glittering ice. My inside boots, stitched of soft leather, make no sound on the stone floors. The palace is built inside a mountain and maintains the architecture of its great caverns and meandering tunnels. I was often lost that first year after Voss brought me to the palace, but eventually learned to navigate every inch of the frozen rooms and corridors.

"This way," I say, although I assume the pup will trail me wherever I go. I drag open the heavy doors leading into the Great Hall. They clang against the walls and a fissure runs through one large block of ice. It's of no concern. I flick my hand and the ice repairs itself as I stride into the hall, Luki padding behind me. I feel the pup creep upon the train of my robes when I stop short just inside the door.

The Great Hall does justice to its name. No ice blocks line its walls—this room is built in a cave that opens upon the world. A row of tall, arched windows marches along the stone outer wall, providing a view across a wide expanse of snow-clad lands. The thick glass set in the windows is clear enough to display the jagged ridge of mountains rising against the far horizon. A domed ceiling soars above the chamber, braced by rafters boasting the breadth of towering trees. In the center of the room stands a wooden table so large a small boat could dock upon its surface.

The mirror lies flat upon this table. My task. My challenge. My nemesis.

Voss's enchanted looking glass possesses a rustic frame of dark wood, thick as the span of a man's hand. The graceful lines of the vaulted ceiling are reflected in the lower portion of the mirror. The upper third, though, remains dark. I have yet to fit all the shards in place upon the oak backing board.

"Ah, Thyra." Voss gazes out one of the windows. "Prompt as always. One of your more endearing traits."

He turns, swirling his black velvet robes about his tall, spindly, figure. He never wears anything like the fur cloaks and woolen gowns he provides for me. His clothing reflects the grandeur of some ancient court. I suspect he has preserved his garments along with his body.

As I lift my chin to stare into his face, I am taken aback, as always, by the ferocity that blazes from his gray eyes. "You commanded my presence, Master?"

Voss's smile flashes like a knife slicing his smooth face. His skin is as unlined and pale as a sculpture carved from packed snow. He could pass for a young man, if one did not look into his eyes, or examine his strangely aged hands. "Yes. It has come to my attention that only five months remain for you to complete the mirror. And yet, yesterday you flew off to some village to gawk at skaters. This does not seem like a sensible approach to completing your assigned task, my queen." The last word is spoken, as always, with mockery.

"All part of my plan." My voice is calm. I place my hands behind my back before I clench them into fists. Memories of the pain I endured when Voss imbued me with magic always threaten to overwhelm me when I'm in his presence. But I've trained myself to never show anger, or fear. "I've done well, as even you must admit. But my calculations reveal I need another pair of hands to meet our goal. I've recently discovered someone who I believe can help me."

"Ah, the young man." Voss moves closer to me, gliding over the stone floor in a way that makes me question the state of his lower body. "So you'd bring a human to the palace, Thyra? Did I ever give you leave to do so?"

I clasp my hands tightly. "I'm still human." This is true, despite my magical prowess, at least for five more months. "And I thought you'd applaud any measure that recreates your precious mirror."

Voss's angular face might have been sculpted from snow, for all the color highlighting his sharp cheekbones. "You think this boy will do your bidding? I have given you many powers, but such command is not among them."

"Then perhaps you should grant me that ability." I don't drop my gaze. One can't look away from a demon and live.

"I could, but what then what would stop you from controlling me? No, my queen, you must find another way."

"There is no other way." I note the cruel curve of his thin lips before taking a gamble. "You have never explained to me why the mirror is so important to you. Perhaps knowing its purpose might aid me in my work."

Voss waves aside my query with one narrow hand. "It has nothing to do with you, Snow Queen."

"The mirror's curse has everything to do with me. It will reduce me to a wraith if I do not complete my task in time."

"True. And that is all you need to know, Thyra Winther." Voss's eyes glitter like the scales of a snake.

"I just find it strange. I didn't think you so vain you would put so much stock in a looking glass."

Voss's lips pull back, baring his sharp white teeth. "Am I not worthy of such vanity? I am old, Thyra. Older than you know." Voss runs a hand through his long white hair. "Yet I will look young while your average village beauty ages into a wrinkled crone. You possess the same power."

"If I complete the mirror in time." I step forward and feel the pull of Luki's weight upon my train. Flicking the bottom of my robe with one hand, I dislodge the pup, who tumbles out from behind me.

"And what is this?" Voss's crystalline eyes narrow. "I've warned you never to bring a wolf into this palace."

"He's part of my plan." I bend and lift Luki into my arms before Voss can move toward him. "He's my bait. The boy, Kai Thorsen, loves animals. I'm using this pup to draw him to me."

"It did not work yesterday. Do not look shocked. I have ways to watch over you." Voss crosses to the mirror and presses his hand against the empty portion. "Perhaps I should convert him. The wolf, I mean. Give him fingers and see if he can assist you in your task."

"No, no." I clutch Luki so tightly he yelps. "You've said it yourself—wolves are too intelligent to conjure into servants. Leave him be. He may still prove a useful lure."

Voss caresses the completed surface of the mirror. "Perhaps. And I do give you leave to bring the boy here, if you can. Whatever is required to finish your work. You are my best hope, and for that reason I am willing to make allowances." He turns and leans against the edge of the table, staring at me. "Did you never question why I chose you as my latest queen?"

I lower Luki to the floor. He spins around twice before pressing his body against the soft leather of my boots. "I assumed it was because I was an orphan. Easy to bargain with someone like Inga for my life, and no one to miss me when you spirited me away."

"That was part of it, yes. And I sensed your cleverness, even as a child, even from afar. The wind that blew you from certain death was sent by me."

"I know." I also know he could have saved my parents, if he'd wished. "I'm not always certain I should thank you for that."

"You should bless me." Voss whips his cloak closer about his body. "I have given you life, and great power, and immortality."

"If I complete the mirror before my birthday."

"Regardless, you still have eternal life." Voss examines me like some potion whose ingredients elude him.

"As a wraith. Hardly my idea of a blessing."

"Yes, that would be unfortunate. You see, Thyra, I have a special interest in you beyond my desire for the mirror's magic. I should like"—

he turns his head slightly so I can no longer see his eyes—"the final, everlasting, Snow Queen to be of my lineage."

A river of ice rushes through my veins, freezing a body that should not feel the cold. "What do you mean?"

"Look at yourself, my queen. Do you not see the resemblance? Oh, many, many decades separate us, it is true. But you are my descendent, born from the line my nephew established when I disappeared from his village, and his life, forever."

"That can't be true." I clench my leg muscles until Luki whimpers, obviously sensing the tension radiating through my boots.

"It is. I selected you the day you were born. Your parents suspected this. Your father caught me once, watching you. It was a tale long told in his family—the old man of the mountains, the wizard of the storms. The thief who would come in the night to steal children from their beds. Somehow he sensed the danger to you. Why else do you think they were fleeing that day? What else could compel your parents to take that mountain pass in the dead of winter?"

I sense the truth in his words and vow, were our destinies not linked, I would kill him where he stands. I'd strike him with one of the shards piled in a wooden box upon the table. A piece of his own mirror to pierce his heart. I'd do it, if I'd merely die. But I know from the unfortunate fates of some of the wraiths that Voss's death won't break the mirror's hold on me. His spell may have trapped me initially, but now even he can't alter the consequences of my failure. My mortal death would simply hasten my transformation into a wraith.

"So you see, Thyra, why I have such a fondness for you. Enough to allow you to follow your foolish plan to lure that boy here. Enough to resist harming the wolf pup you should never have brought into my presence."

"You have no fondness." I forge steel to edge my voice. "Not for me or any living creature, besides yourself. And as for allowing me anything—you still need my hands and mind to fulfill your dearest desire. I'd not harm anything of mine, not if you wish to live."

Voss eyes me coldly. "To live? What makes you think you can do anything to kill me? You possess no such power."

"No? Then why do I detect a glimmer of fear in your eyes?" I smile. Like my master, my smile does nothing to warm my expression. I have confirmed this in my own, quite ordinary, mirror.

"That is your imagination, playing tricks on you." Voss turns aside and gazes out the window. "Well, my queen, since you have denied me the joy of transforming this wolf, perhaps I should have you bring me another creature to conjure. I feel like exercising my powers today. A reindeer, I think. That should not be difficult." He spins around, his robes swirling like smoke. "Bring it to the stables by this afternoon or I shall find a way to rid this palace of that pup."

I stand for a moment, staring at his expressionless face. I know I've been dismissed.

"Come, Luki." I turn and stride to the door.

"You've named it?" Voss's voice bores into my brain. "A foolish whim, Thyra, from one who cannot afford such luxuries."

I simply stalk off down the hall, Luki trotting in my wake.

Back in my chambers I clothe myself in a tunic and breeches of tanned reindeer hide and toss on a brown bearskin cloak. I've not hunted reindeer for some time, and then only to kill for food. To capture such a creature and bring it safely to the palace will require considerable craft and cunning.

Luki attempts to follow me when I leave my chambers but I close the door in his face, knowing he can't squeeze through the opening used by the rabbit. He's too young to be of any use to me today. He's more likely to scare off prey than provide any assistance.

I hitch one of our reindeer to the sledge. Like all herd animals, it will be easier to manage another of its kind if it has a companion, even a domesticated one.

We glide over the icy landscape for many miles before I spy a herd of reindeer in the distance. I ease the sledge to a stop and climb off. Creeping over the hard-packed snow I crouch low, a length of rope coiled about my arm. One of the reindeer lifts its head and peers in my direction, instantly alerting the others. They wheel about, forming a tight pack. Every shaggy brown head is turned toward me, though I don't believe they can see me through the swirl of snow I've spun about my body. But I've no powers over scent, and that's their alarm. They thunder off in the opposite direction—a great mass of flanks and hooves flying away from me.

All but one. An older creature, by his grizzled muzzle. He's been caught in the storm I've sent too late to halt the herd. Thrusting his head against the wind, he tries to rejoin his fellows, but the force is too much for him. He's trapped, unable to move in any direction.

I approach him slowly, uncoiling my rope. As I reach his head his eyes roll until the whites show and I jump back to avoid his slashing hooves. There's nothing for it then. I take a deep breath and concentrate, slowing his heartbeat just enough to cause his head to droop. As his eyes close I toss the rope about his neck and pull it tight. He jerks his head back, but he's fallen into too deep a stupor to fight me. I expel a breath, hoping this allows his heart to regain a more normal rhythm. I don't want him dead, merely docile.

I guide the reindeer along the path I've already trod in the snow and tie him firmly to the hitch on the back of the sledge. Jumping onto the wooden planks, I slap the reins hard against my tame reindeer's flank. She takes off at a fast trot. The captured reindeer runs behind us. It pulls against the rope but is sensible enough to keep up to avoid falling. No such creature will risk a broken leg, even to escape.

Back at the stables I unhitch my domesticated animal and dry her steaming flanks before I release her into the paddock. I then turn my attention to my prize, who's still attached to the sledge. His head hangs low, but I can see life and vigor returning to his dark eyes. I quickly tie him between two hitching rings and whistle a sparrow to me. It perches on my finger, a small cylinder attached to its tiny leg. I breathe into my hand, creating a perfect ice crystal I place in the container, then flick my finger to send the bird on its way. I know Voss will receive and understand my message.

He appears several minutes later, wearing a crimson cloak over his black robes. His clear eyes shine with an expression I know only too well. I have seen that look—it is carved into my soul. When he laid hands on me to imbue me with the magic I needed as Snow Queen, I stared into his ageless face far too long while pain wracked my body. Burning, yes, like liquid fire. And he smiled then, just as now.

"I see you've fulfilled my demand. Very good." Voss checks over the reindeer, who trembles violently at his touch. "You may go now, my queen. My work is best accomplished alone."

I depart swiftly, not meeting the reindeer's eyes.

Later I steal out of the palace and make my way back to the stables. I want to see what changes Voss has wrought upon the unsuspecting beast, if only to prepare myself for the first time it's presented to me. I don't want to give Voss the satisfaction of viewing my shock over his latest creation.

The scent of hay and the sound of grain ground between broad teeth permeate the stables. The heat of animal bodies causes a mist to cloud the cold air. I make my way to a corner stall. The reindeer stands with his head pressed in the corner, far from the trough holding his feed and water.

"You must eat and drink." I can discern no obvious physical changes in the animal, but I haven't yet seen its face.

"Bah-h-h … " A noise erupts from the reindeer's throat and I jump back. It doesn't resemble the sounds I've heard from any animal.

"What's this?" I move forward cautiously, gripping the iron bar that tops the heavy wooden stall door. "What did Voss do to you?"

"Bae," the reindeer croaks. He wheels about to face me. "My name is Bae."

I stare at the creature, wondering why Voss has granted him, among all creatures, the power of speech.

"I do not know why I am here." There is a strange glint in the dark eyes fixed on my face, like the blue light at the heart of a flame. "I am meant to run free across the glittering snow. Why am I trapped in this dark place?"

I find my voice at last. "It's the will of the master mage, Mael Voss. This is his palace, and mine. I am the Snow Queen."

"I know. I have seen you before. Once, many years ago, I watched your sleigh cross the sky like a shooting star. A great storm followed in its wake. Many reindeer lost their lives in that blizzard."

I consider telling Bae the queen he witnessed was one of my predecessors, but think better of it.

"It's the way of things," I say with a shrug.

Bae lowers his shaggy head. "So it is, Snow Queen. I have seen worse, over many years, in the natural flow of the seasons." He snorts and shakes his head. "But this is nothing natural, I think."

"No," I agree, "it isn't. Yet Voss has allowed you to live. It's likely he has a use for you, but I'm afraid I can't tell you what that is."

The reindeer gazes at me mournfully. "It is nothing good, I am afraid. But"—he presses his muzzle against the iron bar, brushing my fingers—"I sense things may change. There is a scent in the air like spring, though we have yet to survive the winter."

"Don't wish time away." I speak sharply, thinking of the few months before winter ends, before my birthday.

"The thaw will come, Snow Queen." Bae backs away from the door. "And neither you nor your Master Voss can prevent its arrival."

I turn on my heel and stalk away. The change of seasons means only one thing—the end of my existence. While others long for green buds to unfurl into fluttering leaves, I tremble, knowing a terrible fate awaits me, clothed in the deceptive beauty of spring.

This does not touch me. Such words hold no power. Make them fade. Let them fall away.

Back in my chambers I review my calculations. As the numbers fill my mind, I resolve to develop a plan that will halt any thaw, at least in my kingdom. If I complete the mirror I'll reign as Snow Queen forever and nothing, not even spring, can touch me ever again.

CHAPTER FOUR:
MASTERING THE STORM

SOMETHING COOL PRESSES AGAINST MY hand. I roll over in bed, and I'm nose to nose with Luki. I stare into his golden eyes for a moment, then glance about my chamber. Although there aren't any windows in my rooms, my heightened senses tell me it's still dark outside.

"Go out if you must," I mumble to the wolf. After the first few weeks, when I had to drag Luki outside several times a night, I'd taken to leaving my door ajar, knowing the possible presence of the wolf would keep the wraiths at bay. Luki soon learned to go out on his own, making his way through the concealed cave opening used by our servant animals. I hesitated at first, certain once Luki left the palace his instincts would call him away to the wild, but decided to take that risk. It was unlikely he could help me lure Kai again, at any rate.

But Luki never leaves me.

"Just go," I say, rolling away from him and pulling the fur coverlet over my head. I'm tired from a late night excursion to the Great Hall. During last evening's review of my calculations I discovered I'd foolishly overlooked a wrinkle in one equation. Anxious to correct my error, I raced to the Hall to place five more pieces of the mirror. In my haste I forgot to illuminate all the walls and the wraiths trailed me right to the double doors, barring my entry. I sucked in my breath and plowed through them, dashing inside and slamming the door behind me. The wraiths are forbidden to enter any room that holds the mirror, but their eerie cries slipped under the door and filled the stone chamber

"Be quiet!" I yelled at the door, before focusing my mind on my task. Once I successfully reintegrated the fragments into the mirror I strode out of the Hall, stepping into a cluster of wraiths. I called them *idiots* and *worthless whiners* as I beat my way past their clinging vapors.

"Soon." A threadbare voice whistled past my ears. "Soon you will be one of us."

"Never," I spat at them. Stalking back to my chambers, I reassured myself. *This does not touch me.* The words matched the rhythm of my boots. *Let it fall away.*

When I reached my room I spent two hours reviewing my calculations before I fell asleep.

This morning I'm traveling back to the village. If I can't collect Kai Thorsen any other way, I'll conjure a blizzard that will bury the town. I'll save only Kai from the tidal drifts of snow. Let the other villagers' bodies freeze to match their hearts.

I don't recall much from my first days in that town—just rough hands and nodding heads and lies. I do remember the stories the villagers told about my family, as well as the beatings I received when I protested the truth of their words. My parents weren't fleeing from anything. We were leaving the village to begin life in another land. That's what my father told me. A new beginning, far from frost-blighted fields and summers wafting in and out in a day.

But I can't dwell on such memories today. Dressed in my white furs, I hurry to the stables. Luki outruns me—he's grown large enough to lope faster than I can walk.

I harness two pale ponies to my sleigh. "You aren't quite as adorable a lure as before," I tell Luki as he jumps into the sleigh.

He swivels his head to gaze at me, his expressive eyes opening wide.

"But perhaps you'll do." I lay my gloved fingers on his head and take up the reins with my other hand.

We reach the village as the sun's sailing high in the sky, a pale golden disk swaddled in wisps of cloud. I survey the town from my vantage point above, locating Kai at the mill before I command the ponies to set the sleigh upon the ground. Whipping snow about me, I step from the sleigh. As Luki leaps out, I tell him to stay at my side. It's strange for a wild creature to obey me without any touch of magic, but I recall my father speaking of wolves while I huddled by the fire as a little girl. "They follow their pack leader, whatever the situation," Father told me. "It's loyalty without question."

I suppose Luki views me as his leader now. Wherever he runs, across whatever wild vistas, he always returns to me.

Work at the mill continues in winter, even though the wheel can't turn the grindstone. I watch Kai load sacks of previously ground grain upon a farmer's cart. He's strong, this boy, and sings tunelessly as he works. He's wearing his felted wool coat and dark leather gloves. His knitted cap glows like a drift of snow against his dark hair.

Kai glances upward as he strolls away from the cart, frowning as he notices how white the sky has gone. Luki trembles under my fingers. He remembers Kai, of course. He recalls the boy's scent and the touch of his hands.

I wait until the farmer's reindeer team pulls the laden cart away from the mill. Kai is alone. He locks the door to the mill and glances about before striding down the rutted path that leads to the village.

This is my opportunity. I follow Kai at a distance, Luki padding soundlessly at my side. I've no fear of discovery. If Kai looks in my direction he'll see a swirl of white, as if the wind has taught the snow to dance.

I was prepared to conjure a storm, if necessary, but the elements are on my side. A quite natural blizzard sweeps from the mountains like a rushing tide, wind and snow whipped into a freezing frenzy.

Kai lengthens his stride, but he can't outpace this storm. The wind bends him double and tears his cap from his head. He makes a frantic grab but it's whisked from his flailing hands. He stops walking and glances about, holding his gloved hand over his eyes to protect them from the stinging snow. He's trembling now, though not from an irrational fear of the storm. It's logic that strikes terror in his heart. He knows the price to be paid for a bare head in the killing cold.

It's almost time for me to approach him, his cap in my hands. I glide through the blizzard as if skating over a frozen lake. Instead of forcing me to battle its currents the wind lifts each step of my pale leather boots. Luki, trotting at my side, is wrapped in my magic and suffers no damage from snow or gale.

As I move closer to Kai I spy another figure pushing its way through the blizzard, struggling to meet the boy. I swear to myself when I realize who it is. Of course, his shadow—Gerda.

She's clutching a woolen sack that must contain Kai's lunch. The sack bangs against her thigh as she fights the brutal winds. Her lips move, but the sound is ripped away as soon as it leaves her mouth.

Kai sees her too. He stumbles forward and they fall into each other's arms. I clench my fingers inside my gloves as Gerda whips the scarf from her neck and wraps it about Kai's head.

Always Gerda intervenes. I cast Kai's woolen cap to the winds and stalk after them as they make their way down the path, clinging tightly to one another. I could harness the power of the storm to kill them both in an instant, but that's foolishness. I still have need of Kai.

They spy the old cattle shed as soon as I do. Heads down, bracing their shoulders against the wind, they make their way to the shed and crawl inside. I follow not far behind, my presence disguised by driving snow. Leaning on the outer wall of the shed, I peer through one open window.

Kai and Gerda are huddled together, covered in a deep mound of straw. Their faces are pale with cold, but a blush of color rises in Gerda's cheeks as Kai clutches her tighter. Safe from the worst of the wind and warmed by the straw bedding, they won't freeze. Kai whispers something in Gerda's ear and she sighs and drops her head upon his shoulder.

I whirl away, striding off into the driving snow, Luki at my heels. "Let the storm rise," I shout to the wind. "Let it spin snow into mountains. Let it roar."

The blizzard roils into a killing frenzy as Luki and I climb back into the sleigh. I crack the reins against the ponies' flanks, driving them into the white sky. Speeding away, I glimpse another figure crawling along the mill path. Someone has ventured out in the storm, someone from the village. The dark form staggers and falls, face first, into a great drift of snow.

I can return, and save that person, if I wish. But to do so might betray me to the villagers. It's a risk I cannot take—Voss will sense any action that reveals my true nature, and his vengeance on me will be swift, and deadly.

Hopefully, the fallen mortal will rise and go on his way without my help. I'm not sure if that's possible, but if I want to survive, I must leave this stranger to his fate. It's the way of things.

Another slap of the reins and the ponies gallop away, carrying me far from the village. Back to the palace, and my doom.

I pace the floor of my bedroom, clasping and unclasping my hands. Waking this morning, my certainty of Kai and Gerda's survival faded and I fear the repercussions of my fury. It's bad enough I haven't yet captured Kai. Far worse if he's died when I could have rescued him.

Whistling for Luki, I make my way to the stables. This time I pause at the reindeer's stall. "Will you carry me, Bae, to see what's become of Kai?" I ask, staring into the creature's sad eyes.

"I will, if it may save a life," Bae replies. He's surprisingly docile as I harness him to my sledge.

Luki leaps up beside me and we set off, Bae pulling the load as if it's a pile of feathers. We swiftly reach the village and I order Bae to land the sledge behind an abandoned cottage. I must hide from the villagers, who will question a stranger in their midst.

"Go," I say, unhitching Bae. "Walk the streets. It's not so strange to see a reindeer wandering about this village. Go and discover if Kai Thorsen lives, and report back to me."

The reindeer bows his head and trots into the center of the town. I know he won't flee. I've spun magic that will tether him to me.

Luki and I stand perfectly still, hidden behind the fallen walls of the old cottage. I pass the time watching a solitary lynx stalk a covey of white-furred rabbits. The cat captures one at last and slinks away, his prize writhing in his jaws. "See—this is the way of things," I tell Luki, who cocks his head and stares at me with his bright eyes.

After a while Bae lumbers back into view. He walks to me and bumps my shoulder with his muzzle. "I have returned, Snow Queen, with your news."

"Yes?" I grasp his bridle and pull his face closer to mine. "Does Kai Thorsen live?"

"He does." The reindeer throws his head to the side, yanking my arm. "Kai lives, and his friend Gerda too. But there is great sadness in their homes, for Kai's father has suffered terribly in your storm."

"It was not of my making," I say, although I know I did nothing to mitigate its power.

It was a father then, struggling to find his missing son, who was lost in the drifting snow. The memory of my father's strong fingers, curled about my small hand … *No, let that fade. Let it fall away.*

"Kai and Gerda found him this morning," continues Bae, "lying along the edge of the mill path. He still lives, but is nothing more than an insensible husk. Kai is inconsolable. He was not supposed to have gone to work that day, but desired to make some money of his own and so opened the mill for a farmer wanting grain. His father's body and mind were destroyed trying to save Kai from the storm, and now the boy blames himself. Poor Kai." The reindeer dips his head.

I grasp the bridle again. "If Kai's inconsolable"—I hitch Bae back to the sledge—"and guilt clouds his mind, perhaps he'll be glad to leave his home, at least for a time." I allow myself a little smile. This turn of events might prove beneficial to my plan.

Logic tells me Kai will stay at his father's side, surrounded by family and friends. There'll be no chance for me to approach him for some time. "For now," I tell Bae and Luki, "we return to the palace." I gather up the reins and command Bae to carry us home. Luki's gaze follows the lynx as it races across the snowy fields beneath us.

CHAPTER FIVE:
A NEW EQUATION

AT MY COMMAND BAE HAS returned to the village several times to observe Kai. The reindeer's reports are heartening. Kai's fallen into a deep melancholy no one can lighten, not even Gerda.

"He's only interested in his figuring now," Bae tells me as I rub him down with a bundle of straw. He's just returned from a swift flight to the village and steam rises from his flanks, misting the cold stable air. "Working puzzles and writing out equations. He hardly sleeps and doesn't care to eat. The little miss tempts him with his favorite foods, but he simply pushes the plates away."

"This is good. I think perhaps it's time"—I step out of the stall and grab a bale of hay—"I paid Master Kai another visit."

Bae's eyes are so glossy I could swear they hold unshed tears. "He suffers enough, Snow Queen. Can you not leave him be?"

I dump several flakes of the hay into his trough. "Not if I want to live. And, trust me, Bae, there's nothing I desire more."

Leaving Bae with a scoopful of oats and a bucket of water, I harness the ponies to the sleigh and whistle for Luki. I don't concern myself with my appearance this time—my chamois tunic and breeches must suffice. I pull on a thick wool cloak and throw a reindeer hide blanket across my legs, allowing it to lap over the seat beside me. Luki jumps onto the seat and curls up in the folds of the blanket, his head resting on my knee.

I scout Kai's location from the air before directing the ponies to land behind the mill. Kai's sitting on the edge of the open loft, his feet dangling high above the frozen ground. His dark head is bent over his lap and his right hand moves swiftly across the pages of a leather-bound notebook. He's calculating, of course. I smile slightly. I understand the comfort of equations.

He glances up when he hears the sound of my boots on the hard-packed ground. His eyes widen, but he doesn't move. I've cast no snow spells to hide my form. It's time to face him without disguise.

"You," Kai says, with wonderment in his voice. He glances from my face to Luki. "And this is the wolf pup I found? You kept him with you?"

"Yes." I move closer, until I'm standing beneath his feet. I tilt my head to look up at him. "Luki. You named him, remember?"

"I did, didn't I?" Kai swings his feet onto the edge of the loft beam, drawing his knees to his chest. "Is he tame now?"

"Tame? No. But he obeys my commands, by his choice."

Kai's dark eyes settle upon my face. "I know we met only once, but there's something familiar about you, something that makes me remember … " He rubs at his forehead with one hand. "Where do you come from, anyway?"

"Far from here, yet less than a day's journey as I travel."

"You travel fast?"

"Very." I throw back the hood of my cloak, allowing my tumble of snowy curls to spring free and halo my pale face.

"Alone?" Kai examines every inch of me. Dispassionately, as if calculating my mass.

"Except for Luki. Although"—I turn the full force of my icy glare upon Kai—"there's room for one more in my sleigh, if you're interested."

He meets my gaze with a cool stare of his own. "To go where?"

"Anywhere away from here. Isn't that what you want, Kai?"

"You know my name." He rises to his feet, clutching his notebook to his chest.

"I know a great deal about you. I know you're the smartest boy in this village. Or any surrounding village, for that matter. I know your mind seeks greater challenges than this little place can offer."

"I plan to go to the university. In the city—not so very far from here as the crow flies, but distant as the stars from this backwards village." Kai's eyes light up at this thought.

I purse my lips. I've studied drawings of that university in Voss's library—along with sketches of the ancient walled town where it resides—but I've never set foot in the city's bustling streets. Nor am I likely to ever do so. Kai may believe he is trapped. I know I am.

"Do you? Now that your father lies prostrate, like one dead, who'll run the mill?"

Kai turns his face away. "My mother and Gerda's family, I suppose."

"Will they allow it, Kai?" I slip a little magic in my voice, just to draw his attention. "Will they actually let you go?"

"I don't know!" Kai swears and dashes into the shadows of the building.

I'm afraid I've pushed too hard. That I've lost him. But he was merely climbing down the ladder from the loft. He steps out of the lower level of the mill and strides up to me, his dark eyes flashing.

"I ask you again, who are you?" He makes a grab for my arm but jumps back when Luki bares his teeth and growls.

"I'm the person who can provide a puzzle to test your mind to its limits." I lay my hand on Luki's head to calm him. "I can offer you a challenge that will absorb you, day and night, for months on end."

Kai's face crumples. He looks like a broken little boy. "Can it make me forget? Can it take away memories I can't live with? Can it mask the pain?"

"I believe so." I speak softly, with no magic lacing my voice. I no longer need it. I have triumphed. Kai Thorsen is mine.

Kai trails me, shuffling his boots through the deeper snow behind the mill. He stares at the sleigh for a moment before climbing in. Still clutching his notebook in his gloved hands, he appears dazed.

I wait for Luki to leap in between Kai and me before I take up the reins. Reaching across the wolf's back, I lay my hand on Kai's arm. "I know you're tired," I say, wrapping my words about the boy like silken ropes. "Rest yourself while we travel. Sleep now."

Kai's head bobs and droops. He drops his chin to his chest. I shoot a swift glance his way to make sure his eyes are closed before I urge the ponies to carry us into the stone-gray sky.

My magic keeps Kai asleep until we land at the palace. Drawing up beside the stable doors, I touch his arm to wake him.

"We're here," I say, shaking him slightly.

He blinks and gazes about, then rubs his eyes and stares at me.

"Where are we?"

"At my palace." I step from the sleigh and Luki bounds after me. "Don't worry. You're safe here, no matter how strange things appear."

I toss the reins to a waiting groom—a polar bear whose paws look like furred human hands. Kai blanches at the sight of the bear, but I simply take the boy by the arm and lead him to a set of iron-clad wooden doors that open upon the kitchens. Another bear, smaller and brown-furred, rushes forward to throw back the heavy doors, allowing us to stumble through.

"Palace?" Kai's voice breaks on the word. "Bears with hands?" He glances at me. "What are you?"

I release his arm and step away. "I am the Snow Queen."

"There's no such thing." Kai falls back against a kitchen table, his fingers scrambling against the battered wood.

"There is. She stands before you. Don't you believe the evidence of your own eyes?"

Kai grips the edge of the table until his knuckles whiten. "I believe in logic, in calculations, in equations."

"As do I."

"But this place, those creatures—surely this is some enchantment."

"It is, but reason still prevails. What do you think lies at the heart of magic, Kai, if not the perfection of logic?"

He shakes his head and a lock of his dark hair falls into his eyes. "Why did you bring me here? What do you need from me, if you have such power?" He brushes the hair back and clutches at his skull, as if to contain his frantic thoughts.

"I need your mind." I cross to the counter where a reindeer haunch lies covered in burlap. "You must help me solve a puzzle." I slide out a bone still bearing shreds of meat and toss it to Luki.

"What sort of puzzle?" Kai's fingers relax. This is something he understands.

"One that will surely occupy your mind," I reply. "Now, come with me, Kai Thorsen, and I'll show you my challenge."

I stride from the kitchens, glancing back once or twice to ensure Kai's trailing me. Luki, occupied with his bone, doesn't follow. I'm careful to brightly illuminate all the walls as we traverse the icy corridors. It's far too soon to introduce Kai to the wraiths.

When I open the doors to the Great Hall I sense Kai's right upon my heels. I cross to the mirror, throwing out my hands. "Here's your puzzle. You'll find no greater."

Kai wanders into the chamber, his eyes flitting from the vista revealed by the windows to the domed ceiling and the massive table. At last his gaze lights upon the mirror and he steps forward to stand beside me, staring into its reflective surface.

"It's broken." Kai strokes the smooth surface of the glass.

"Yes, but it can be restored." I lay my fingers across his hand. "With your help."

My touch galvanizes him into action. He springs away, striding to the windows in the far wall. "I know nothing of mirrors." He stands straight as a spear, his dark form silhouetted against the backdrop of my snow-clad kingdom.

"You know mathematics. You can calculate and create equations to solve problems. These are the skills I need."

"And why would I assist you?" Kai turns. His eyes shine like those of our bears—dark, bright, and cold. "It appears you've put me under some enchantment and kidnapped me. Why should I help you with anything?"

I lean back against the table, surveying his frigid face. I must calculate the odds this boy will be able to resist my magic long enough to destroy my hopes. Consider all the variables. Evaluate the possibilities. Find a logical means to persuade him to stay willingly, to aid me of his own free will. If I must hold him under an enchantment it will weaken me as well as him, and neither of us will be able to employ our minds to their full potential.

"This mirror," I say slowly, as an idea blossoms in my mind, "holds a powerful enchantment. Restored, it can grant great magic to my master, Mael Voss. It's he who set me to this task, several years ago. But I've learned"—I allow my fingers to glide across the mirror's surface—"of its other power."

"Yes," says Kai, interested, I suspect, in spite of himself. "What is that?"

The lie slips easily off my tongue. "It can restore health to the ailing, even those that lie near death."

Kai doesn't move, or blink, but I know by his breathing that I've ensnared him.

"How's that possible?" He takes two steps toward me.

"It holds very old, very great magic." This, of course, is true.

Kai closes his eyes for a moment. He mouths numbers, calculating something in his head. "If I help you reassemble the mirror you must promise me one thing."

"Yes, what is that?" I know what it is, but the game must be played.

"After your master achieves whatever it is he desires, you must grant me use of the mirror." Kai takes a deep breath and fixes his dark eyes upon my face. "You must promise."

"Very well, I promise. But what use do you have, Kai Thorsen, for a magic mirror?"

"The only use that would make me help you with anything. I will heal my father. I will bring him back to a full, healthy life."

The trap springs shut, my lie the bait. "Of course," I reply lightly. "You and I will restore the mirror, and you'll restore your father to your family. A logical trade."

Kai crosses to the table and walks its perimeter, examining every inch of Voss's looking glass. He lifts one shard from the table and stares at it for a moment. "I assume, to have gotten this far, you've written some equations?" He waves the shard at me.

"Yes, I've a notebook full."

"Show me." He lays down the shard.

"Wouldn't you like something to eat first?" I think of our recent journey and the lateness of the hour.

"No." Kai's voice is as cold as the walls of my palace. "We've work to do."

I have to force Kai to rest, to spend any time in the chambers I've had the servants arrange for him. His every thought is the mirror. He sits huddled under the windows of the Great Hall, writing equations in his leather-bound notebook.

"You must eat," I say, kneeling before him. "You're no use to me, or your father, dead."

"Did you figure this one already?" He thrusts the notebook under my nose.

I sigh and take the book from his hands, scanning his new equation. "Yes, I'm afraid so."

Kai swears and bangs his head against the stones behind him. "This is impossible."

"Nothing's impossible. Not when two minds like ours are involved." I stare at the equation once more. "If you were to change this variable … " I grab the pencil Kai hands me and scribble another figure onto the paper. "See here—it changes everything."

Kai yanks the notebook from my fingers and eagerly scans the page. "Yes, that's it." He looks into my eyes, his face alight.

"I knew you'd see it." I sit back on my heels when I realize Kai's expression has changed.

"You." His dark eyes bore into me. "I remember you. The girl in the church. The only one who could ever calculate as well as me."

"I'm the Snow Queen." I rise swiftly to my feet.

Kai stands to face me. "Thyra, that was your name. Thyra Winther."

I draw myself up to my full height. "I am the Snow Queen. You've experienced my power."

"You're that girl. A girl no different than any other in our village. Well, except for the calculating part." A faint smile tugs at the corners of Kai's mouth.

"I *was* that girl." I realize I might as well admit the truth, this once. "But the years, and Voss's magic, have changed me. Don't think I'm simply a human girl you can ignore, Kai Thorsen."

The boy whose mind I need, whose equations might save me from an eternity of torment, smiles more broadly. "I doubt it's possible to ignore you, Thyra Winther. Snow Queen or not."

"You need to eat," I say, turning on my heel. "If you'll follow me to the kitchens, I'll see what I can find."

Kai strides forward until he's by my side. "The wolf pup—he's your pet now, isn't he?"

"Pet?" I walk faster. "I don't have pets. Luki is useful as a protector, nothing more."

"Really? Is that why he sleeps in your rooms? And follows you everywhere?"

"Whatever Luki does," I say, remembering to illuminate the walls when I hear a faint wail echoing through the corridor, "he does of his own free will."

"As will I," says Kai.

CHAPTER SIX:
MISSING PIECES

IT'S ODD, LIVING WITH ANOTHER human being again. I constantly encounter Kai in passageways or the kitchens as well as in the Great Hall. He prowls the icy corridors as I once did, obviously determined to catalog every inch of the palace. He's locating escape routes, I think, and concern flashes in my brain. But then I see him huddled over his calculations, his brow furrowed in concentration, and I remember he wants to reassemble the mirror as desperately as I do.

My lie has given him a goal he'll not easily abandon.

I walk into the Great Hall, Luki at my heels. Kai's bent over the mirror, the remaining shards spread out along the edge of the table. He's thinner than the day I brought him to the palace. I make a mental note to remind him to eat.

Kai glances up as I enter the chamber. "There are three pieces missing."

"Two," I say, crossing to stand beside him. "I told you. I have one, Voss keeps the other."

"No." Shadows blue as bruises ring Kai's eyes. "I mean there are three other pieces unaccounted for."

"Are you sure?" I stare at the row of glittering shards.

"Yes, I'm sure." Kai holds up his notebook. "I've reviewed my calculations multiple times. According to my figures, there should be three more shards, beyond what we have and the two you and Voss hold."

I swallow a swear word along with my fear. "Voss told me he'd collected them all."

Kai shrugs. "Then he lied. The question is—does he possess any knowledge of their whereabouts?'

"But that makes no sense." I pick up one of the pieces and examine it from all sides. "He's desperate for me to complete the mirror. Why would he lie about such a thing?"

"Perhaps he simply forgot." The boy bends down to pat Luki, who allows such caresses only from me or Kai. The wolf won't permit Voss to approach him. "You told me it's been ages since he collected the fragments. He may have realized it once, but over time his memory of such things could've slipped."

"Perhaps." I carefully place the piece of reflective glass on the tabletop. "It might be in his notes, if he ever knew some shards were missing."

"And his notes would be, where?" Kai turns the full force of his gaze on me. His lips are drawn into a sharp line and his face is all angles and planes. He looks nothing like the ruddy-cheeked boy I watched skating across a frozen lake.

I've done this—transformed Kai into another creature just as Voss transmuted me. But in this instance it didn't require magic, only a lie.

"In his chambers, I suppose."

Kai collects the shards and gently places them in the wooden box. "I've located his rooms, but the door's always locked."

"He allows no one entry." I think of that heavy door. It's covered in silver, with strange symbols embossed into the metal. "I've never glimpsed inside, all the years I've lived here."

"The two of us might be able to find a way. If we put our minds to it." Kai gives me one of those appraising looks that make me bite the inside of my cheek.

I am the Snow Queen. He's nothing but an ordinary village boy. An ordinary boy with an extraordinary mind, but nonetheless—not my equal.

"Voss left this morning," continues Kai, looking away. "I watched him go. Will he return soon, do you think?"

"Not before nightfall." I turn and walk to the windows. "Kai," I gaze out at the white and gray landscape, "I haven't told you yet, what the mirror means to me." I don't know why I feel the need to explain this now, but the words tumble out, spilling from my lips like water over stones. I tell him of my deadline, of the horror of my eighteenth birthday, of what will happen if I fail to restore Voss's enchanted looking glass.

"A wraith?" Kai asks. I realize while I've been speaking, staring blindly out the window, he's moved close to me. "Like those creatures in the dark halls?"

"You've seen them?" I turn and bump into his elbow. His face is only inches from mine.

"Seen them, heard them, beat them back." Kai's brown eyes have softened. They remind me, for a moment, of Bae. "So they were the Snow Queens who came before you? And they all failed in their task?"

"Yes." I lift my chin and meet Kai's stare without flinching. "But I refuse to become a wraith. Whatever it takes, I won't fail. I intend to remain Snow Queen forever. "

"No, you won't fail. Not with my help." Kai touches the back of my hand with his fingertips. "It seems we both have much at stake."

A gentle human touch. Something I haven't felt in years. I tighten my fingers as my hand trembles slightly

Luki slides in between us, breaking Kai's contact with my skin. I pat the wolf absently and glance outside. Over that distant mountain ridge, across valleys, past the rise of mountains beyond, is another world. A world I may never see. Yet I can, at least, hold what is mine.

"Let's consider, then"—I whirl about to face Kai—"how to break into a wizard's lair."

He smiles. It's a smile that does nothing to warm his expression.

The door to Voss's chambers has no knobs or obvious clasps. Kai runs his hands over every symbol, feeling with his fingers for any hidden latches. We study the door for some time. After a while I give Luki leave to depart for his daily run, a necessity if I want to avoid him dashing recklessly down the palace halls in the middle of the night.

Kai argues with me, claiming we might need the wolf. "Who knows what's behind these doors? He could provide valuable protection."

"We have to pass through the doors before we need to worry about that." I narrow my eyes as I stare at the recalcitrant portal. "There's obviously magic at work here. Stand off and allow me to concentrate."

"Very well, my queen." Kai executes a sketchy bow as he backs away.

I shoot him a fierce glance. "It's in your best interests to follow my lead."

"No doubt." Kai leans against the icy wall next to the door. The magic I've wrapped about him is obviously working. He never shivers anymore, not even when dressed in only a woolen tunic and breeches, as he is now.

I close my eyes for a moment, concentrating on nothing but openings. A tendril of heat tickles the back of my neck—the echo of the spell holding the door tight. The sense of warmth reminds me of growing things, like green vines curling about the hidden, hard buds of new fruit. I reach for that vine and grasp it with my mind. A simple incantation, in the end. It's clear Voss doesn't hold my powers in high regard.

A swooshing sound fills my ears, and I open my eyes. The door stands ajar and Kai's staring at me. It's a look I remember from that day in the church, when he first recognized my mathematical abilities.

"I keep forgetting that you're no longer simply Thyra Winther."

"Wiser for you to remember," I reply as we step through the doorway.

"Can you conjure some light?" Kai's hands are stretched out before him, exploring the thick darkness.

I call forth a ball of cold flame. Stretching out my cupped hands, I spy tapestries draped over rods running along the opposite wall of the room. "I think there may be windows."

Kai's already several steps ahead of me. He reaches the stone wall and drags back the heavy drapes with both hands. Sunlight pours into the chamber, illuminating every corner.

It's a large room, but buried by objects. Every inch of space is filled with shelves and counters, which are, in turn, groaning under the weight of ceramic urns, wooden boxes, tin pails, and glass vessels filled with liquids of every hue and viscosity.

"This isn't going to be easy." Kai crosses to the tall wooden table that divides the room. "Forget a needle in a haystack. This is like looking for one snowflake in a blizzard."

"Rather my specialty," I say, joining him at the counter. I lift an odd tangle of roots tied into a bundle. "I think we need to concentrate on papers, or notebooks, that type of thing."

Kai's gaze sweeps the room. "Why don't I search those two walls? You can investigate this table and the third wall. There appears to be nothing of interest on that side." He points to the windows.

"Very well, but remember we're dealing with a mage of great power. Be careful what you touch."

Kai nods, his expression suddenly solemn. "He may have laid traps?"

"Possibly. More likely just left remnants of his magic." I stare at the table, scanning the clutter for any evidence of paper. I spy a notebook and grab it, knocking over a small, enamel box. The box clatters to the floor, spilling its contents—a large, yellowed, tooth.

Kai looks up from his examination of the north wall. "Careful," he says, with a swift grin. As he lifts a jug from a shelf the tooth vibrates and skitters across the uneven stone floor.

"Watch out!" I shout as the tooth bounces off Kai's heel. He turns in time to see a column of amber smoke rise from the floor. It spins like a dusty whirlwind. Kai falls back against the shelving.

A form coalesces within the smoke. Something broad, and bulky, and covered in fur. A paw slashes out, claws like curved knives slicing the air. It's a bear, I realize, yet not a bear. One of Voss's creations.

"Kai!" I toss him the metal lid I've snatched off a wooden barrel. He grabs the make-shift shield and scrambles to his feet as I clench my fist to form an ice crystal. I toss the icy spear at the bear-thing, piercing its flank. It turns swiftly on its flickering, smoke-wreathed paws. I conjure another crystal to hurl into its massive chest.

"Behind you!" shouts Kai as he rushes toward the bear's back, clutching a jagged piece of wood ripped from the shelving. I spin about to see an undulating form rise from the open barrel.

A great snake lifts its heavy head, its glittering body twisting in the air. It's clear as mountain water, its scales an overlay of ice crystals. Fangs sharp as stalactites drip from its hissing mouth. I swear and call forth a ball of fire that singes my fingers. I try never to handle real fire, but this is an extremity. As I throw the flaming orb at the snake I hear heavy footfalls behind me.

Kai leaps between me and the bear, swinging the make-shift spear like a pike. He drives the creature back as I hurl another ball of flame at the snake.

I barely have time to observe the icy reptile quiver and melt into the barrel before whirling about to discover the bear advancing on Kai, claws slicing at the air.

"Quick, throw me the lid."

Kai sweeps up the metal disk and slings it at me. I slam the lid onto the rim of the barrel, keeping my eyes on the bear's shifting bulk. I draw on my magic until I feel my fingers tingle.

"Got any ideas?" Kai shouts, still standing his ground with only a slender piece of wood blocking the bear from reaching us.

I rub my hands together, spinning a long spear of ice out of nothingness. "Duck!" I yell and hurl the spear at the bear's chest.

The smoke creature staggers backward.

"Magic to fight magic," I tell Kai. "You've held him off long enough. Now get behind me."

I glimpse reluctance in Kai's eyes, but his logic overwhelms his pride. He jumps back as I leap forward, a massive ball of fire blooming in my hands. I rush the bear. Not expecting an attack, it stumbles and falls to all fours.

I slam my hands down upon the bear's massive head, releasing the fiery orb. It pierces the bear's misty skull and explodes.

"Now!" I shout to Kai, "Stab it! Pin it to the ground!"

Kai rushes forward and jams his make-shift weapon into the bear's back. As the light of my fire illuminates the bear's head from the inside out, its body shreds, fur and bone dissolving into mist. Swallowed in the evaporating cloud, Kai releases the wooden pike. It totters and clatters to the flagstones as the creature dissolves in a final swirl of smoke.

We clutch hands and stumble backward, collapsing against the edge of the tall worktable, both breathing heavily.

"Well"—Kai wipes his damp forehead with the back of his free hand—"I see what you mean about the magic part. Perhaps we'd better not touch anything unless it resembles a book."

I release my grip on his fingers. "Even that might not be safe." I glance at the notebook I'd grabbed earlier. It lay on the edge of the table, innocently still. "But I suppose we must take our chances."

"I told you we should've kept Luki with us." Kai brushes off his dusty breeches. He glances at me. "Your powers come in handy in a crisis, I must confess, Snow Queen."

"As does your quick thinking." I catch his brief smile before he turns back to study the wall of shelving.

I flip open the notebook, ready to draw upon my magic for defense, but the pages lie flat, covered with nothing but figures. Voss must have tried calculating the reconstruction of the mirror, long ago. The ink on the pages has faded to a pale violet, and the paper is brittle, crumbling at my touch. I toss aside the notebook and resume my examination of the objects piled upon the table.

After a time I exhaust my study of the table and stride to the third wall of shelving. Kai hasn't spoken since the incident with Voss's magical creatures. I glance at him, observing his methodical search of the other walls. He's careful to open nothing that can't possibly contain papers or a book.

I rummage through several piles of fabric, obviously remnants of ancient, elegant, clothing. There are velvets and satins and silks, each garment bearing traces of exquisite needlework, the ragged collars and cuffs embroidered with silver and gold. On a tattered bodice, a single pearl still dangles from one loose thread. I lift a soft scrap to my cheek. It feels like the brush of a rose petal against my skin, evoking a recollection of flowers, and warmth, and grass beneath my feet. I toss the fabric to the floor and continue my search.

Kai whistles loudly. He's holding up a book, its pages bound between covers of finely worked metal. I cross the room in several long strides and rip the book from Kai's hands. It's a thick volume, the rippled edges of its pages tipped in gold. I rub my hand over the filigree surface of its binding, realizing the powdery black finish is tarnish on silver. Golden straps and hasps lock the book shut.

"This looks promising." Kai wipes his grimy hands on his tunic.

"Yes, but opening it could prove dangerous." I meet Kai's implacable stare. "Remember what happened earlier."

"Carry it over to the windows. Let's put some distance between the book and the rest of Voss's enchantments." Kai crosses swiftly to the far wall, motioning for me to follow.

Laying the book on the window ledge I stare at it for some time, my palm pressed against its cold metal cover. "I don't sense any magic," I say at last.

"So we open it." Kai fingers the clasps. "I don't suppose we've a key."

"We need no key." I slide my fingers beneath the locks and rub the smooth gold between forefinger and thumb until the clasps spring open. "Simple magic," I say, meeting Kai's approving gaze.

I flip back the cover, revealing creamy pages illustrated with brilliant designs; interlocking squares and circles, linked by a delicate embroidery of curling spirals. Within each shape are finely drawn scenes of strange figures and impossible animals.

Kai whistles again. "It's stunning. It's like mathematics brought to life. Such precision." He touches one of the drawings with the tip of his finger. "Who could create such a thing?"

"I don't know, but I doubt it was Voss. His powers are strong, but far cruder than this." I carefully turn the pages, marveling at each new design. "It's letters, Kai. Illustrated words."

"So it is." Kai moves to stand behind me. I can feel his breath upon my cheek as he leans over my shoulder to study the book. "Unfortunately, lovely as it is, we won't find Voss's notes in this book."

I continue to turn pages. The vibrant designs leap out at me, reminding me there's more color to the world than the somber hues of winter. As I press back the center page a scrap of paper slides out and sails toward the floor.

Kai grabs it before it hits the ground. He unfolds the page and holds it to the light.

"What is it?" I snap shut the book and place it on the window ledge.

"Notes." Kai looks over at me, his dark eyes brighter than I've seen them in some time. "Take a look." He hands me the crumbling piece of paper.

I scan the page, deciphering the scrawled handwriting. "It's Voss's hand. I've seen it before." I continue reading. "He mentions a shard … Yes!"

I don't realize I've yelled until Kai grips my forearm. "The missing fragments?"

"I believe so. He writes they're in a cave, somewhere in the mountains that ring our lands. Of course—there must have been so many pieces when the mirror shattered, Voss may have missed a few."

Kai releases my arm and leans back against the stone windowsill. "This means something?"

"If Voss found the mirror in a cave, that's the first place he'd suspect if a few shards were missing when he carried the rest to the palace. I don't know why he never went in search of pieces back then, but perhaps he intended to, and the years made him forget."

"It was broken when he found it?" Kai shoots a sharp glance my way.

"I suppose. He won't tell me anything more." I wave the paper in Kai's face. "There's a description of the cave, and the surrounding landscape. We should be able to find it easily."

Kai raises his eyebrows. "After decades?"

"Little changes in these lands." I fold the paper and tuck it inside the bodice of my simple woolen gown. "We should leave. I'd rather not take any more chances, not with what we unleashed earlier."

"Well, cast the magic that lights up your hands, then, while I pull these drapes. I suppose we should leave things as we found them, as much as possible."

"Yes." I glance about. "I don't think we disturbed too much."

"Voss might be lacking one enchanted bear, but perhaps he won't notice for some time."

"And this." I grab the illuminated book and clutch it to my breast. "I'm keeping this."

"That, Voss might miss," observes Kai, as he takes hold of one end of the tapestry drapes.

I call forth a globe of light in one hand and grip the book in the other. "Let him. He owes me."

Kai drags the drapes across the windows, plunging the room into darkness. I hold my conjured light before me and guide us to the door. As we step over the threshold, the door slams shut behind us.

"So—we travel tomorrow?" Kai walks forward to greet Luki, who's bounding down the hall. The wolf leaps up, his snow-caked paws leaving damp imprints on Kai's tan breeches. Kai gently eases the animal to the ground, giving him a few gentle pats.

"Perhaps," I say, as Luki presses up against me.

Kai frowns. "We need those fragments."

"I can't decide that now. I'm waiting for a message." It's time to reassert my authority. "I'll tell you in the morning."

Kai looks me up and down. "Very well, my queen." He imbues the last word with almost as much irony as Voss. "I'll await your command." He turns on his heel and stalks away.

It doesn't matter. Whatever he thinks of me, Kai Thorsen won't abandon our work on the mirror. My lie ensures his dedication. So let him think himself as clever as me. I know the truth.

"Come, Luki." I watch Kai disappear down the corridor leading to his rooms. "We must see what news Bae has brought us."

I make my way to the stables, Luki at my heels. The scent of steaming animal hide assaults my nostrils. It seems Bae has returned from his mission. Early this morning I sent the reindeer to the village to discover how people are dealing with Kai's disappearance.

Two horses are tied to the hitching rings. One of the mutated bears rubs down their heaving flanks. So—Voss has returned to the palace.

"Snow Queen." Bae dips his head as I reach his stall. Another transformed bear scuttles off at my approach, clutching a curry comb and brush in his peculiar, hand-like paws.

"You've news for me?" I glance into Bae's trough, ensuring the bear has provided grain as well as hay and water.

"Yes." Bae focuses his melancholy gaze on me. "Sad news, as I am sure you expected. Many in the village fear Master Kai has done himself an injury."

"They suspect he's killed himself?" I shake my head. "They must not know Kai well."

"Others"—the reindeer noses at the hay and carefully extracts a mouthful—"think Kai has moved to the city, gone to sea, trekked off to another country, or some such thing." Bae chews on the hay for a minute before speaking again. "Miss Gerda has disappeared as well. Left a note though, she did. Said she was off to look for Kai. Will not return until she finds him."

I lean over the trough to grab Bae by the bridle. "What do you mean? Gerda's searching for Kai?"

"As I said, Snow Queen, the little miss has taken to the road to look for her friend. Poor soul." Bae swings his head from side to side until I'm forced to release my grip.

I swallow a string of swear words as Bae calmly munches his hay.

Gerda, the shadow. Gerda, always intervening, always in my way. My logical mind tells me this simple country girl can't possibly find Kai before the mirror is complete. My fearful heart isn't convinced. Too much is at stake to take any chances.

"When did she leave?" I ask Bae. "When did Gerda depart the village?"

"Why, just yesterday, I believe." The reindeer sniffs at the trough and delicately mouths a bit of grain.

I breathe deeply. This does not touch me, I tell myself. I can't be defeated by an ordinary girl. *Let these fears fade. Let them fall away.*

Leaving the stables, I resolve to travel tomorrow, but not to the cave. That must wait. First I'll toss some stones in Gerda's path. I've an idea of how to slow her down, if I can convince Voss to grant me one favor.

He must do it. Whatever it takes, I'll force his hand. He owes me, more than he can ever repay.

CHAPTER SEVEN: FIRST THAW

IN THE MORNING I TRACK Voss to the Great Hall. He's lost in contemplation of the mirror, but glances up as I enter.

"You have made great progress, my queen." Voss taps the glass with his boney forefinger.

"No thanks to you." I pull my ivory wool cloak tight about my shoulders. "You forgot to mention that three pieces are missing."

Voss's thin lips twist into a semblance of a smile. "So that's why my chambers were disturbed? Yes, I suspected you and your human friend had been in my rooms. I have lost, it seems, one smoke bear."

"Kai isn't my friend." I stride to the table to stand face-to-face with the mage. "Merely a tool. And a useful one, you must admit."

"If he's aided you with your latest efforts in reassembling the mirror, indeed he is." Voss looks me up and down. "You want something of me, Thyra?"

"I do. I desire magic to disguise my appearance so that I can pass unnoticed among mortals. And I wish for the freedom"—I lift my chin and stare into Voss's icy eyes—"to travel to warmer realms."

"For what purpose?" The wizard's gaze pierces me. It's as if he's looking through a pane of glass.

"To find the shards whose existence has sadly slipped your mind, Master Voss."

He does not blink. "That is not all, I think."

"No." I take a deep breath. "There's a young girl searching for Kai. She must not find him."

Voss turns and glides to the tall windows, his crimson robes rippling across the floor. "You place me in a dilemma, my queen. Your request is reasonable, if you are to complete the mirror, which I dearly desire. But I fear"—he glances over his shoulder—"that granting you additional powers may not be in my best interest."

"You fear me, Master?" I fight the elation threatening to rim my words. "Surely not. You know my destiny's tied to yours. And we're both linked to the mirror. I've no intention of failing you. Such an action will only condemn me to becoming a wraith. And trust me—I've no wish to join that pack of mindless, mewling spirits."

"Yes, that would be a pity." As Voss turns his robes flicker like flames in the sunlight. "Very well, step forward. I will grant what you ask."

I cross to him with measured steps, steeling myself against what's to come. I know he must lay hands on me to give me what I desire, but I dread his touch. I recall far too well the pain—like hot coals pressed against my flesh. But I must do whatever is necessary to thwart Gerda and keep Kai focused on the mirror.

When I reach Voss he flexes his fingers before reaching out to grip my shoulders. I stand still, pressing my toes into the soles of my boots. Voss's fingers thrust daggers of fire through my body. I grit my teeth and clench my hands into fists. I won't move, or even wobble. I won't allow him that satisfaction.

After several minutes Voss drops his hands and steps back. "You may now choose to change your appearance to suit your need. You may also travel beyond our realm, but beware, my queen. There are dangers in the wider world that cannot touch you here."

"What dangers?" I rub at my shoulders with the edge of my cloak, scrubbing away the remnants of his touch.

Voss turns to gaze out the window. "There are those who will not wish you success in your quest. One in particular—a mighty enchantress who will do anything in her power to thwart my plans."

This is new. I stare at Voss's rigid back. "And why is that?"

"It is of no importance. Just watch your step. There are few who may match wits with you, but she is one who can challenge your every move."

"I'll bear that in mind, if I encounter any enchantresses." I examine Voss's face with interest. There's a shadow of actual fear in his eyes. I file this information away for future use. "Now I'll go and ready myself for my journey. I'm leaving Kai here to continue his work on the mirror. Don't interfere with him."

"I will leave him alone, as I have thus far. He is of no interest to me, at any rate." Voss's gaze rakes over my face. "I am curious, I must admit, how much he interests you."

I turn on my heel and stalk toward the exit. "As I said, he's a useful tool. A bright mind and an extra pair of hands. I value him because he may keep me from the wraiths. For that reason, I'll protect him, as long as necessary." At the door I wheel about to face the mage. "But don't think you can use him as a bargaining chip, Master Voss. I've no feelings for him. He's useful to me but I'll sacrifice him in a heartbeat if it suits my purpose."

"No doubt." Voss's cool smile conveys admiration mixed with disdain. "Good fortune on your journeys, my queen. I too will be traveling later this day. You may leave your human pet without fear."

I smile in return—a smile as slow as a glacier, and as cold. "I've no fear. Your spells and training ripped that from my heart."

He nods his head in a brief acknowledgement. "I know. And for that I am truly sorry. Not for you, Thyra Winther, but for all who oppose you."

"Something to remember, Master," I say as I turn and stride out of the room.

Kai's displeased we're not traveling to locate the lost fragments of the mirror. I watch him pace the floor of his chamber.

"I told you, Voss's set me to another task, and I dare not refuse." I lean back and rest my elbows on the pile of furs heaped on Kai's bed.

"We need those pieces," says Kai. "We can't complete our task without them."

"Obviously not. And we'll retrieve them as soon as I return. But while I'm gone, you can run a few more calculations and piece together more of the mirror. That is of equal value."

Kai pauses and spins to face me. His face, pale as a winter dawn, bears a fierce frown. "My father's life depends upon our success. Nothing's more valuable than that."

"My life hinges on our success," I say lightly. "I think that's of equal worth." I sit forward, gripping my knees. "Trust me, if there were any other way, I'd take it. But I must fulfill Voss's commands. He has the power to destroy me, whenever he wishes."

Kai stares at me, his dark eyes examining every inch of my face, before he sighs and turns away.

"Go then, and I'll see what I can do to repair the mirror while you're away. But promise me that as soon as you return we'll set out to find the missing fragments."

"I promise." I don't know if I can keep such a vow, but I'm certain I can placate this boy, whatever the situation.

Kai grabs his leather-bound notebook from a side table and crosses to the bed. "I've a question about this equation." He opens the book and thrusts it under my nose. "What do you think? Should I change this number or leave it?"

I push the notebook from my face, forcing it to my lap. "Let me think for a moment." I trace the equation with one finger as Kai leans over me. His dark hair brushes my cheek. "Sit back." I wave him off. "I can't concentrate with you breathing down my neck."

He scoots away and we discuss equations and calculations and other logical matters for more than an hour. I must confess, despite his very human failings, Kai does possess a most remarkable mind.

I saddle one of the horses Voss keeps for his sojourns into other lands. A compact bay with slender legs and a delicate black muzzle, the horse trembles at my touch. I know Voss never names his creatures, and decide to call the mare Freya. "Goddess of the spring," I say, tightening the girth, "you'll carry me to warmer climes."

Calling Bae to me, I order him to accompany us. "We travel into realms without constant snow or ice. You must follow, no matter how hot the sun." I suspect I may need the reindeer's ability to speak, if only to track Gerda.

"I will not leave you, Snow Queen, unless you command it." Bae's dark eyes remain fixed upon me as I turn away.

Luki whimpers when I tell him to remain at the palace. "Stay with Kai, and watch over him." I'm certain the wolf won't disobey me. I stroke his head before adjusting the saddlebags that hold my provisions and extra clothes. I've dressed in my chamois tunic and breeches, but packed lighter garments in anticipation of warmer weather.

When I reach the edge of my realm I'll alter my appearance to present a more human visage. For now I don't concern myself with such things, merely tying back the heavy mass of my white hair with a piece of rolled leather.

As I swing myself up into the saddle I cast one final glance at Luki. "Guard Kai," I command, digging my heels into the mare's flanks. The wolf lifts his head and howls as the horse breaks into a gallop that lifts us into the sky. We fly over the snowy valley, Bae sailing alongside.

After we cross the second range of mountains I guide Freya down to the earth. Although it's still cold, the snow is fading. Patches of bare dirt and brown grass dot the landscape like islands in a foamy white sea. I know I must now stay anchored to the ground and alter my appearance. Soon we'll be traveling past homesteads and villages.

I haven't seen anything green in so long, except for a few hardy spruces, I kneel and slide my fingers across a bit of moss that clings to a large outcropping of stone. I sniff the air, reveling in the faint scent of vegetation.

Rising to my feet, I lean against the stone and concentrate, spinning a web of magic about my form. I don't attempt major changes as I've discovered it's tiring to maintain such a transformation. No need to tax my powers now. I simply darken my hair to a pale gold and dull my icy eyes to pewter. Veiling my angular face in rounded flesh, I paint a blush of color across my cheeks and smudge my hands and wrists with dirt.

Now I can pass as an ordinary country girl. Someone who won't stop a human in their tracks. Someone like Gerda.

"Bae"—I motion for the reindeer to approach me—"run ahead and scout for any trace of Kai's young friend. You know her face, her scent. She can't have gotten far on foot."

The reindeer rattles the metal rings of his leather bridle. "I will find her. But though you may beat me or kill me, I will not harm her, Snow Queen, if that is your desire."

"It isn't. I simply want to distract her. When you locate Gerda"—I fix Bae with my fiercest glare— "return to me. If you don't, I'll hunt you down. And believe me, death will seem preferable to what I'll put you through."

Bae tosses his head. "I understand, my queen. I'll bring you any news of the young miss, as swiftly as I can." He gives me one last mournful look before disappearing into a stand of wind-whipped pines.

"Come, Freya," I say, mounting the horse. "Let's see what we can find. Surely we can track a simple country girl and send her back home where she belongs." I jab my heels into Freya's flanks and she breaks into a fast trot, carrying me farther from my icy kingdom, closer to my goal.

CHAPTER EIGHT:
THE SCENT OF ROSES

THE FARTHER FREYA CARRIES ME from my realm, the more disoriented I become. There's warmth in the breeze brushing my skin, reminding me of days spent in Inga's garden. I was often forced to weed her flower beds and the scents that now waft about me recall the feel of crumbly earth between my fingers and heat upon my neck. Such thoughts awaken other memories—of slaps, and tears, and long nights spent staring at smoke-blackened rafters. Loneliness and longing and hopes for another life. *No. This can't touch me. Release these thoughts. Let them fall away.*

Making camp beside a shallow stream, I eat a meal of bread and cheese and drink cold, fresh water from a tin cup. I rise to my feet as I hear the reindeer's approach.

"What news?" I step forward and take hold of Bae's bridle.

The reindeer presses his muzzle into my hands. He's breathing hard and his flanks are streaked with sweat. "I found the young miss," he says, raising his heavy head. "Not far from here. But I must warn you, Snow Queen, she is under the protection of a woman who possesses magical powers."

"What makes you say that?" I toss the cup into my saddlebags and wipe my hands on my breeches.

"Her garden is filled with flowers, even though it is still winter." Bae paws at the hardened ground. "All about her cottage it is chilly and gray, with only tiny kernels of buds dotting empty branches. But her garden is bright with blooms, as if she has captured summer and kept it enclosed behind stone walls."

"Gerda's there? You're sure?"

"Yes, I saw the young miss wandering about the garden. She was talking to the flowers, poor thing, and tipping her head as if she heard them answering."

I don't really care about Gerda's state of mind, though it might be easier to convince her to abandon her quest if she has gone mad. "Show the way, Bae. We'll rescue Kai's young friend from this witch. Then you may escort Gerda safely home." I step into the stirrup and swing my leg over Freya's back. The mare sidesteps nervously but I quickly bring her under control.

The reindeer leads us down a series of narrowing paths until we find ourselves on a track barely wide enough for Freya to pass. Slender pines line the way, straight as soldiers at attention. I hold back thorn bushes with one hand as we move farther into the forest, careful to duck to avoid their trajectory when I release my grip. At last we step into a clearing. A cottage rises from the middle of a leaf-strewn circle, a small building of rough stone capped with a thatched roof. A wisp of white smoke spirals up from the chimney.

I dismount at the edge of the clearing, dropping Freya's reins to the ground. She won't move as long as the leather touches the earth. Ordering Bae to stay with the mare, I stride toward the cottage. I knock decisively upon the door, which is painted the bright emerald of new grass.

The door opens slowly, disclosing a weathered, knotted hand attached to a boney arm. I lift my eyes and stare into the face of an old woman. Her wispy gray hair is pulled into a tight bun and her skin's webbed with wrinkles. Green eyes, strangely bright in her wizened face, survey me with interest.

"May I help you?" Her voice is as cracked as old porcelain. She's much shorter than I, although this is partially due to the fact she's bent almost double. She leans heavily on a thick branch polished to a smooth sheen.

"I'm looking for a friend." I modulate my voice to fit my unassuming appearance, softening my tone and adding the lilt I've heard in the speech of the villagers. "A young girl, who may be lost. She wandered away from our village a few days ago, distraught over the disappearance of a young man. Have you seen anyone who fits that description?"

"Perhaps." The old woman waves me inside.

I step into the cottage, immediately feeling heat flush my neck and cheeks. Strangely, despite the smoke, bright red geraniums fill the stone fireplace instead of flames. Still, it's warm inside the snug room. As hot as remembered summers.

"There was a girl I rescued from the river." The old woman's dressed in a faded black gown with frayed white cuffs and a tattered hem. Jet buttons march up the bodice from her waist to her neck. "She was asleep in a small boat, just drifting with the current. I pulled her to shore and kept her with me for some days. But she fled this morning. I do not know where she's gone."

I swear under my breath as I plaster a smile upon my face. "Really? Did she tell you her name, or why she was wandering?"

The old woman toddles to a table piled with fresh vegetables. "She said her name was Gerda, and she was searching for her friend Kai. I begged her to stay with me a little longer, as she was exhausted from her travels, but she was quite determined to locate her friend. Such devotion—it touched my heart, I must say."

"Indeed, that sounds like Gerda." I move closer to the woman, staring at her narrow back as she fiddles with a basket of cherries. "You've a wonderful harvest, especially for this time of year."

The old woman turns about slowly. "It's from my garden. Would you like to see?"

I nod my head, not entirely sure why I'm agreeing to this diversion. I follow the woman out the back door of the cottage and step into a garden like nothing I've ever seen.

A riot of color assails me. Flowers of every hue and description fill the enclosed space. Orange lilies waver atop spear-like stalks thrust up from tumbles of azure pansies, while fat purple hyacinths snuggle amid drifts of bell-like snowdrops. I know such flowers can't exist together, can't bloom at the same time, but somehow this garden feels perfect. I blink and examine the climbing roses blanketing the rough stone walls. The roses range in shade from moon white to deepest crimson. Their velvet petals open as I watch, disclosing the golden stamens at the heart of their delicate layers.

"This isn't possible." I breathe in the scents lacing the air. The hum of bees wraps me in a cloak of peace. I slide to the ground, my back pressed against the stone wall of the cottage. I'd like to stay here forever.

"Anything is possible, Thyra Winther." The old woman moves with unexpected grace to stand before me. She straightens into the figure of a tall, slender woman. The black gown splits and falls away, revealing a sparkling white gown pulled in tightly by a bright green bodice embroidered with an intricate pattern of vines and flowers. She raises her walking stick into the air and it bursts into bloom, the surface covered in apple blossoms.

I gaze into the woman's face. Gone are the wrinkles and sunken cheeks—her skin's as smooth as the petals of a lily. Her lips are plump and red as cherries. The gray hair is now a tumble of auburn curls. Only her emerald eyes remain the same—bright and implacable as faceted gems.

"How do you know my name?" I press my back against the rough stones behind me.

"I am well acquainted with you, Snow Queen. I have watched you for some time. Ever since Mael Voss chose you, and carried you off to his palace of ice. I have followed your progress in reconstructing Voss's magic mirror. You have accomplished much—more than any girl before you. I have seen this, and despaired. You, my dear, have the capacity to give Voss what he desires. And that cannot happen, Thyra Winther. I cannot allow that."

"Who are you to direct my actions?" I claw my way to my feet, my fingers digging into the cracks between the stones.

The woman's smile lights her face like sun glittering off an expanse of snow. "I am Sephia, enchantress and guardian of all growing things. I am Voss's teacher, and adversary. I am the one who will prevent him from achieving immortality, with all the power I possess, with the last breath in my body."

"Immortality?" I force myself to meet the woman's brilliant gaze. "What do you mean?"

"You do not know?" Sephia's eyes shine like emeralds. "So—you have not been told why Mael Voss wishes the mirror made whole? Interesting."

"No." I lift my chin. "He has not disclosed its purpose to me."

"I see." Sephia turns her head to stare at the pink blossoms festooning a cherry tree. "Well, perhaps you should be told his history, Snow Queen. At least as it involves the mirror."

"You know it?"

"I do. As I said, I was his mentor, long ago. But he abandoned me to pursue other interests." Sephia turns her gaze back on me, a shadow dimming those bright eyes. I wonder just how close she and Voss grew before he left her side.

"Did Voss find the mirror on his own?"

Sephia studies me, her expression grave. "No, and for that I suffer terrible regret. I was the one who told him of its existence. A mere mention of a fabled glass, buried deep in a cave, the cast-off plaything of some ancient god." Sephia toys with one of the cherry blossoms until she pulls it from the branch and tosses it to the ground. "I hoped to impress him with my great knowledge of arcane lore. But he was not focused on me, only on the things I could give him. He left me and found the mirror—and shattered it."

"He broke it? So all this time … "

"He's been seeking its restoration. Yes." The enchantress taps her full lips with one finger.

"But how?" So Voss shattered the mirror, then sacrificed young women to repair what he had destroyed. I dig my fingernails into my palms. Despite my own desperate fate, if he were standing before me I would slaughter him and throw his carcass to the bears.

Sephia's gaze pierces me, as if she can read the fury in my mind. "You should know, Thyra Winther, burdened with the mirror's curse as you are, that Mael Voss can conjure eternal life for others but not for himself. He possesses powerful spells to prolong his life, but only one object can grant him immortality—the magic mirror he discovered as a young man, so many decades ago. But he was young, and proud, and rash. He attempted to command the mirror before he fully mastered his powers. Chanting the spell that would allow him to cheat death, he cracked the looking glass, shattering it into thousands of glittering fragments."

"Why not repair it himself? Are his powers so lacking?" Anger crackles through my voice.

Sephia shakes her head. "He cannot reassemble it. The mirror resists him, still wielding its primal magic. So Voss found other hands to piece together his portal to eternity."

"Innocent, unsuspecting, girls."

"Yes." Sephia's gaze softens, the green eyes now velvety as new leaves. "I am sorry to tell you this, Thyra. I thought you already knew the truth, but I see Mael has deceived you, just as he kept his true counsel from me."

"He spoke of you." I observe a tightening of Sephia's lips at these words. "He said you'd try to stop me."

"Yes, indeed I will." Sephia moves closer to me. She smells of earth and rain and lilac blossoms. "Do you not wish to break away from Voss? To live in a green and growing world again? To feel, to love?"

"I know nothing of such things." I straighten until I can look her in the eyes. "I only understand what's required for my survival."

"Mael Voss cannot be allowed to gain immortality." Sephia's eyes flash like lightning. "His evil cannot be given free rein. He will blight the world with cold and frost, if only to kill that which he cannot control."

"This means nothing to me." I call upon the snow that drifts about my heart, the icy stream flowing through my veins. "I only know that I must reassemble the mirror before my eighteenth birthday or suffer a living death. I won't accept such a fate, no matter what harm befalls the world."

Sephia gazes at me, her bright face dimmed. "I am sorry for your fate, but I cannot permit you to complete the mirror, Snow Queen. It was I who took in Mael as my apprentice, who taught him all I knew. I thought he would be my companion, my helpmate. Together we would ensure the world would always blossom, that the green earth would never be blighted by either mage or human. But Mael was not satisfied with such gentle magic. He desired power and control. Not content with shared power, or even the joys of love, he fled my halls and found the mirror. Ever after he's sought to twist magic to serve his evil desires. I should have seen the fault in him, but I was dazzled by his youth, his charm. Yes, once he was fair. Bright as a crocus rising from the snow." Sephia turns her head so I can no longer see her eyes. "I foolishly equated beauty and brilliance with goodness. He is my creation, my responsibility. And I will not allow him to live forever, to gather the power such immortality will bestow. I am truly sorry, Thyra Winther, but I must stop you."

Sephia steps forward and lays hands on me. Her touch is soft as milkweed down, but as her fingers close about my wrists I know I can't break her hold. Not with any strength in my bones. I close my eyes and call upon the power I possess—bringing forth snow and glaze of ice and blast of wind. I direct them not at the enchantress, who's likely to be immune to such spells, but at her verdant garden. I call down withering cold and a blighting frost. I wish death upon everything green and growing.

A sweep of freezing wind whips about us. Sephia gasps and releases her hold on me. She spins about, watching as petals curl and drop, as leaves turn brown and crumple to dust. She dashes into the heart of the garden, spreading out her hands as if to gather all the blossoms to her bosom. But they shatter at her touch, frozen under a veil of frost.

"You!" She turns on me, but her slippered feet slide out from under her on the icy ground. She falls, allowing me time to race back through the cottage and out into the clearing. I run to Freya and leap upon her back as I command Bae to stand between me and the furious enchantress. He lumbers forward, lowering his head until his pronged horns prevent Sephia from moving from the front door of her cottage.

"This is not over, Snow Queen!" She shouts after me as I turn Freya in a tight circle and spur the horse into a gallop. "I will track you down and wrap you in chains of vines if you ever dare leave your icy fortress again."

I flee the clearing, my face pressed against Freya's neck, Bae following close behind. I do not slow the mare to a trot until we've put several miles between us and Sephia's cottage.

It seems I have a new obstacle. But this won't defeat me.

"Bae"—I pull Freya up, allowing the mare to stop and rest—"I now return to my realm. The missing pieces of the mirror have yet to be collected. You must track Gerda for me. Clearly she's not close to finding Kai yet, if she's set off from this direction, so we may allow her to wander for a while. When you locate her, report back to me."

The reindeer gives a gusty snort and shakes his head. "I will do as you ask, Snow Queen, if only to protect the little miss. I fear she may stumble into danger."

"She may indeed." I urge Freya into a walk, moving away from Bae. Gerda wandering alone in a dangerous world suits me well enough. If she meets with a mishap, without my intervention, I'll consider myself fortunate.

I must return to the palace and see whether Kai has completed any more of the mirror. Soon we travel to the cave that holds the last three fragments. With those shards in hand I'll finally be able to sleep again.

CHAPTER NINE:
ON THIN ICE

A S I STALK THE GLITTERING hall of the palace, a chill settles in my bones. The lack of color, of any scent except the mingled odors of animal hide and fur, makes me hallucinate. I imagine I can actually feel the cold.

This is nonsense. For a moment I recall the riotous blaze of color that filled Sephia's garden, the warmth of the sun, and the loamy smell of the earth. *Fantasies.* I throw back the doors and stride into the Great Hall.

"There you are." Kai spares a quick glance for me as I approach the table. "Ready to search for those fragments yet?"

He's bent over the mirror, his fingers sliding a small glass shard across the empty portion of the backing board. I note his extreme pallor and the lines bracketing his thinned lips.

"If you're up for the journey. Have you eaten anything at all while I've been gone? Or slept?"

Kai shrugs and his brown wool tunic slides down, exposing his boney shoulder. "Not important." He sighs and yanks up the neck of his garment. "I've placed two more pieces, but now I'm stuck."

"Very clever." I stand beside him. Our combined efforts have allowed us to complete three-quarters of Voss's enchanted looking glass. Peering into its smooth surface I catch our reflections. We stare back— fey creatures captured in the mirror's spell. Kai, with his face sculpted into sharp angles and his dark hair grown long and unruly, resembles an ancient faun. I look like what I am—part sharp-featured, gray-eyed girl, part glorious and terrifying queen of snow and ice.

I lift my head, tearing my gaze from that image. "I must tell you that I've finally discovered Voss's purpose for the mirror." I meet Kai's questioning gaze. "Apparently, once restored, it can be used to grant him eternal life."

"No wonder he's desperate to have it completed. So he found the pieces somehow, and used his magic to determine its powers?"

I examine Kai's face as I tell him the truth. His lips tighten to a straight line as I explain how Voss shattered the mirror through his own pride and recklessness.

"The bastard. I'd rather kill him than see him live forever, but I know that wouldn't help my father, or you."

"True. We can't let our anger control us, not if we wish to achieve our goals. Speaking of goals—we need those missing three pieces to progress any further. Can you ready yourself to travel with me today?"

"In an hour." Kai returns the shard to its wooden cradle and turns to face me. "Where'd you go, anyway? I thought you might be tracking the fragments without me, but it seems you had some other mission."

"None of your business." I meet Kai's intense gaze with an imperious toss of my head. "I've responsibilities as Snow Queen. Not everything involves the mirror, or you."

Kai studies my face with the expression he wears when calculating a difficult equation. "I'm sure that's true. Well, if you'll allow me, my queen"—he executes a slight bow—"I'll go and prepare for our journey. I should meet you in the stables, I suppose?"

"Yes. In one hour." I swiftly cross to the door, then pause, my hand on the latch, and glance back at him. "Don't forget to wear enough layers, along with gloves and a hat. I can keep you relatively warm within the palace, but outside it's another matter."

"I'll bundle up. I've lived in a similar environment, if you remember."

"Yes, but traveling with me … " I recall Kai was asleep when I brought him to the palace. "It's different than you might expect."

"I try not to have any expectations anymore." Kai walks toward me. His face, so pale, so haunted, reminds me of the wraiths.

"A good plan." I shake my head to clear my thoughts. "Better to stay focused on the task at hand."

"I'll see you in an hour, then." Kai pushes past me. I feel his fingers brush against my wrist as he shoves the door open.

I shiver unexpectedly. But that can't be right—I don't feel the cold. I thrust my hands deep into the pockets of my gown and hurry to my chambers.

Kai's waiting when I arrive at the stables. Wrapped in his felted wool coat and sporting the new reindeer hide boots I had a fox servant drag to his rooms, he leans against one of the stalls to watch me harness the ponies to the sleigh.

"So you think you've a good idea where we're going?" He pulls on heavy gloves and a gray wool cap.

"I've a general notion." I whistle for Luki, who bounds across the paddock and leaps into the back of the sleigh. "You've been digging again." I wipe the snow from his nose. Luki bumps my chin with his snout.

"Not a pet," observes Kai, as he hops up and settles onto the bench seat. I cast him a sharp glance as I climb into the sleigh and take up the reins.

"You'd better prepare yourself, Kai. When I travel, I do so through the sky. It's one of the gifts Voss has given me. You were asleep last time." I snap the reins and the ponies take off over the hard-packed ground.

"By your design." Kai throws a bearskin blanket across our laps.

"Yes, and I'll do so again, if necessary." I pull up the hood of my fur cloak, shielding my face against the wind and Kai's eyes.

I slap the reins against the ponies' flanks and call out "Starward"— the command that sends them, hooves still moving rhythmically, up into the silver sky. When we reach the lowest wisps of clouds I level out the sleigh, allowing the ponies to gallop effortlessly through the air.

I glance at Kai. He's leaning over the side of the sleigh, observing the glittering white ground below us. "Are you all right?"

"It's fantastic!" Kai shouts against the wind. His face is alight. He once again resembles the boy I watched calculating mathematical problems in a quiet church.

"Hang on," I call out. "Don't fall over the edge. Even I can't save you if you tumble from this sleigh."

Kai grins broadly. "It's magnificent!" He throws his hands out, curling his fingers as if to grasp the clouds. "The whole world beneath our feet!"

I smile in spite of myself. I remember my exhilaration on the day I first took to the air. "You need to spy a cliff face with a formation on the side. Shape of a bird, with wings outstretched, like a great eagle." I gesture toward a looming range of mountains. "We'll be approaching before long. Keep a lookout."

Kai nods vigorously and fixes his gaze upon the snow-capped ridge.

As we draw closer I pull up the ponies until they are gliding at a slow trot. I direct them to move parallel to the mountains.

"There!" Kai leaps to his feet, gesturing toward one rocky cliff. The faint outline of a figure is visible—a giant bird of prey in flight.

I grab the arm of Kai's coat and drag him down onto the seat. "You idiot!" I don't release my hold on his sleeve until he turns to me, his brown eyes smoldering like wood in a bonfire. "You could fall out and where does that leave me?"

"With yourself," snaps Kai. "The person you love best."

Luki, obviously hearing the anger in our voices, sits up and thrusts his head between us.

"Keep your eyes on that formation." I stroke Luki with one hand. The wolf lays his muzzle on Kai's shoulder and tips his head to stare at me, his eyes rolling until the whites show.

"Don't worry," I tell Luki. "I won't harm your boy."

Kai's face is as stony as the mountains before us. "No more a boy than you're just a girl, Snow Queen." He lifts his left hand to smooth the fur on Luki's shoulder, then reaches out and encircles my right wrist with his gloved fingers. "You need me, Thyra Winther, don't forget that."

I match his frigid stare. "And you need me, Kai Thorsen. Or don't you care anymore about your father and his second chance at life?"

"I care." Kai releases his grip and looks away, gazing back at the mountains. "Or I wouldn't travel anywhere with you. I know what you are, lady of cold and darkness."

"You know nothing of me." I toss my head and my hood falls back. My white curls spring away, crackling with static in the cold, dry air.

"We're close." Kai points toward the eagle formation without glancing my way. "I think I see a cave. There, under the bird's wing. It's more than a shadow."

I ease the ponies into a slow descent. As the deep snow piled at the base of the mountain rises to meet us, I pull the sleigh up, heading for an exposed ledge lying just beneath the cave.

"What's this?" Kai grips the edge of the sleigh with his right hand. "Trying to rattle me?"

"Attempting to land on a spot a little closer to the cave than the base of the mountain." I choke up on the reins until the ponies come to a stop, their front hooves balanced on the edge of the ledge. "Of course, if you'd like to climb the entire face, I'll allow you to slide down and scramble back up."

"No thanks." Kai stands in the sleigh, stretching his arms and legs. "We'll need all our energy to find the shards, I expect." He jumps out, landing waist-deep in a snow drift.

Luki climbs to the front of the sleigh and places his paws on the curved left side. He leans over the edge, stares at Kai, and yips twice.

"Yes, we'll pull him out." I step out of the right side, where only a slight swirl of snow blows over an outcropping of bedrock.

"You might have warned me," says Kai.

"You might have asked." I ease the ponies back from the ledge and cross in front of them. "Give me your hand."

Kai grabs my gloved fingers in a firm grip. I step back, pulling him toward me as he pushes against the heavy drift. A few strides and he tumbles into me, shedding snow like a shaken spruce branch.

"Careful, we could both fall." I motion toward the lip of the ledge.

Kai nods and places his hands about my waist as he walks me slowly backward, away from the edge. He releases me when we reach the center of the ledge. "So what now, Snow Queen?" He vigorously slaps the moisture from his breeches and boots.

"Now we locate the mirror fragments." I stroll toward the gaping maw of the cave, Luki at my heels. I hear Kai's boots behind me, ringing against the rocky surface of the ledge.

"You're sure this is the right place?" Kai steps up next to me.

"Yes, I'm sure." I march toward the entrance.

Luki runs ahead of us, disappearing into the darkness.

"Should you let him do that?" Kai matches his stride to mine. "Might be bear or lynx or anything in there."

"Luki isn't stupid. If he encounters something he can't handle he'll run."

Kai mutters something like "unlike his mistress," but when I turn to glare at him he smiles at me, all guileless innocence.

"Just follow me." I conjure a large globe of cold light in my gloved hands.

As we enter the cave the scent of standing water rises in my nostrils. I hold out the light and spy a dark pool stretching from one side of the cave to the other. Only a narrow ribbon of stone skirts around the pool, which is opaque as ink.

"Wonder how deep it is." Kai kneels and peers into the depths of the water. "Can't see a bottom. Without a light, anyone entering this cave would probably fall right in."

"And drown." I motion for Kai to rise to his feet and follow me around the pool. "I think it's a trap. We should watch for others."

There's barely room for me to place one foot in front of the other as I inch along, my fur-clad elbow brushing the damp wall of the cave. I glance ahead and catch sight of Luki's eyes. Illuminated by my globe, they shine like phosphorus in the darkness.

Luki waits patiently until Kai and I make our way to him. He's standing before two identical tunnels. Both branch off from the entrance chamber, leading in different directions. I hold up the light and move it back and forth, trying to discern our best option. But there's no difference between the two corridors, at least visually.

"Looks as though we must make a choice." Kai draws closer to my side. "Can your talents tell us which route to take, Thyra?"

I close my eyes for a moment, attempting to sense the presence of any piece of the mirror. I've handled the other fragments so long I believe I can feel the pull of their magic. "This way," I say at last, striding into the left-hand tunnel.

To Kai's credit, he follows without hesitation. Luki pads along before us, occasionally casting a glance over his back as if to urge us forward.

The tunnel narrows alarmingly the farther we walk into the mountain. Soon both Kai and I must bend our heads to continue down the rippled rock path. I balance the globe of light in one hand and slide my gloved hand along the rough wall, feeling for any crevices that might lead to chambers or passageways.

Kai swears under his breath as he bangs his head on a low-hanging outcropping of stone. "Sorry," he says, and steps on the heel of my boot. "Sorry again." He wobbles but rights himself before tumbling into me. "Why did you stop?"

I lift my palm toward the low ceiling, until the light throws a circle about us. "Hear that?"

"Sounds like wind whistling through something."

Luki stops and waits at the edge of the light. His nose twitches and the fur on his back bristles as I approach. "What is it, boy?" I thrust out the ball of light and stare into the darkness beyond the wolf. There's a different smell to the air.

"Another chamber, I think." I walk forward slowly, my hand resting on Luki's head. As we climb over a rise of stone, a breeze tickles my face. "Watch your step," I call out as Kai stumbles over the ridge and grabs my shoulders to steady himself. I shrug him off and hold the light before us.

A rounded ceiling rises above an empty chamber that's not as large as the entrance but also not as damp. The musty odor tainting the air since we entered the cave is replaced by the scent of banked fires and ash.

"Someone's been in here, and recently." Kai strides in front of me. He glances about the shadowy cavern. "No trace of anyone now, though."

"Not here." I walk to the center of the room and swing the hand cradling the light toward one wall. "See there—another passageway. I can feel air blowing. There must be a linked chamber."

We cross to the passage, Luki trotting before us. I move ahead of Kai and slide through the narrow opening, turn a sharp corner and step into a bright shaft of light.

"Thyra Winther," says a reedy voice. "Welcome, Snow Queen, to my home."

CHAPTER TEN: INTO THE DARKNESS

I DOUSE THE COLD FIRE IN my hand and stare at the bundle of rags that has spoken to me. The opening above my head cascades fresh air and light over my body. Following Luki's gaze I stare up at an azure circle of sky as a hawk shrieks and perches on the edge of the opening.

"I don't believe we've met." I step forward, allowing Kai to follow me into the second chamber.

"And Kai Thorsen. I welcome you also." The dark figure rises to its feet and stretches out one knobby arm. He's dressed in a tattered black robe, cinched about the waist with a piece of baling twine.

"How do you know my name?" asks Kai, as the hawk swoops down and lands on the ragged creature's forearm.

"I know much about you both." The speaker is a man, his face a map of wrinkles, his eyes sunk into his face like raisins in dough. Although thin as a skeleton, he stands straight as a spruce and his bald head almost touches the low edge of the arching ceiling. "I've been watching you for some time."

"Watching us? How?" I clasp my hands before me to still my restless fingers.

"Oh, through a bit of that mirror you're trying to reconstruct. It can show many things, you know. Not just reflections." The old man uses two fingers to strokes the hawk's sleek back.

The bird's piercing gaze is fixed on Luki, who stands at attention, his nose twitching.

"Your wolf is contemplating my hawk as dinner. Perhaps you should warn him not to tangle with a raptor."

"We require the fragment of the mirror you hold." I kneel and place one arm over Luki's quivering back. "It's needed to complete a task assigned to us by a powerful mage."

The man's laughter crackles throughout the cavern. "Mael Voss?" He wipes his eyes with the back of his free hand. "Is that how he styles himself these days?"

I watch the hawk loosen and clench its talons against the man's bare flesh. "He holds sway over a great realm."

"Of ice and snow and unending cold. Of nothingness." The man shakes his head. "I am Holger, by the way. I know Voss from long ago. Mention my name to him when you see him next. You may judge our relationship by his reaction."

"I have limited conversation with Master Voss." I rise to my feet and cross to stand before Holger, meeting his amused gaze with my iciest glare.

"Very wise, little queen." Holger examines my face without exhibiting a trace of the typical human reaction. "So, you seek my shard of magic glass?"

"We seek three fragments." Kai steps up beside me. "We've reason to believe they remained here in this cave when Voss shattered the mirror."

I cast Kai a swift glance of approval. Faced with the oddness of Holger's presence and the possibility of other threats lurking in the shadows, Kai's voice remains steady. I study his profile for a second, noting the tension in his jaw. Scared, but resolute. Indeed, a most unusual boy.

"Alas"—Holger flicks his wrist and the hawk sails from his arm to perch on a high ledge of stone—"I possess only the one piece. Though I do know where you might find the remaining two. They were stolen from me, you see, by other visitors to my home." Holger folds his lanky form and sits on a pile of bearskins.

"I'm surprised anyone else could find you." Kai crouches in front of the old man. "So, will you help us, Holger? It's quite important we complete the mirror."

"Ah yes, lest the Snow Queen melt into a wraith." Holger's dark eyes bore into my skull. "And how old are you now, Thyra Winther? Seventeen, if my information is correct."

"There are still a few months left before my birthday." Through the soft wool of my breeches I feel Luki's warm body press against my leg. "I'll complete the mirror before that day."

"Perhaps, though you must find the other shards as well." Holger motions for Kai to rise. "You needn't beg, young man. I will tell you, as it means nothing to me. The other two pieces reside at the university in our nearest city. Some men took them from me long ago, on a day when I was out hunting for food. Explorers, I suppose they were." Holger shrugs. "All I know is I returned to find several sets of footprints and two fewer pieces of the mirror. Thankfully, I had my largest shard with me."

Kai bows his head. "Thank you for telling us that much, Master Holger."

Holger's thin lips stretch into a smile. "But you, Kai Thorsen, what do you achieve by assisting our lady of the snows? Her love, perhaps?"

Color rises in Kai's pale cheeks. "No, that isn't my goal."

"What then?"

Before Kai can speak again I step forward and kneel at the old hermit's bare feet. "I'll beg you, Holger. Please grant us your fragment. It's all that stands between me and an eternity of suffering. It can prevent the destruction of everything I hold dear."

"You mean your mind and your free will? Yes, I know you, Thyra Winther." Holger examines me as if I'm a newly unearthed artifact. "If I do not grant you my shard, will you take it from me? Do you have that power?"

"Whatever power I possess, I'll use."

"I have no doubt of that." Holger tents his boney fingers and appraises me. "Strange, the girl who wept over nothing, whose heart was more tender than green shoots of grass, has become cold and hard as a glacier."

I stand as Kai turns his head to gaze at me. I refuse to meet his eyes. "I'm much changed. Living with Voss will do that. And I do have a rather pressing deadline."

"So you do. The question is"—Holger leans back against the rough cave wall—"what do I gain from this transaction? You have nothing to trade with me, Snow Queen. And I do not think allowing Mael Voss to achieve eternal life is really in anyone's best interest."

The old man's face hardens until it resembles the stone behind his head. His eyes gleam with the predatory glint I've seen on the faces of polar bears.

"You see, young Master Kai," says Holger, "the mirror holds more power than Voss ever guessed."

"Yes, I've heard … " Kai grunts as I stamp my boot across his instep.

"The mirror possesses wild magic." Holger closes his eyes, as if lost in thought. "It cannot easily be mastered, once made whole. I fear it may work great harm upon the world. Voss will not be able to control it, for all his boasts. He has not the strength."

I gather my magic and send it rocketing through my body until a pale blue light illuminates my skin from toes to fingertips. "If you don't give your fragment to me, I'll tell Master Voss where it resides. If I fail, and fade into a wraith, he'll simply conjure another Snow Queen to complete the mirror. She will know where to find you, unless you leave this place, which I suspect you can no longer do, and live."

Holger slumps, becoming nothing but an assortment of bones wrapped in rags. "You guess correctly, Snow Queen." His voice thins into a wheezing thread. "I can no longer leave this cavern. Fortunately I have long since shed the need for food, though my birds still bring me flagons filled with snow."

"You still require water." I walk forward until I'm looming over the old man.

"Yes, from time to time." Holger looks up at me, his eyes dull as bits of charcoal. "Very well, Lady of Snows, I will give you my fragment. But only if you promise to use your considerable powers to keep the mirror safe once it's made whole."

"Once it's complete"—I toss my head until my white hair shoots sparks in the dry air—"I don't care what happens to the mirror. If you wish, I'll promise to lock it away, never to be seen again by any mortal soul. Just give me the fragment."

"Very well." Holger reaches into the folds of his robe and pulls out a glittering shard. "But tell Master Kai the truth first." He holds out his fist, the piece of glass hidden by his clenched fingers.

"What truth?" Kai moves to my side.

"Ask her what the mirror can do." Holger stares straight at Kai.

"I know. She already told me." Kai reaches to enclose Holger's fist with his fingers.

The hermit squawks something that might be a laugh. "Ask again."

I focus my energy on Holger, ignoring Kai's attempt to catch my eye. The old man's eyelids flutter. His fingers loosen and the mirror fragment slides smoothly into Kai's palm.

"What do you mean?" demands Kai, pocketing the shard. He leans in and grips Holger's shoulder. "He's fallen asleep, Thyra. Can you wake him?"

I shake my head. "No, I'm afraid that's beyond me." Of course, it isn't, but Kai doesn't need to know. Just as he never must learn I slowed Holger's heartbeat and sent the old man into a stupor. I watch as Holger's head bobs and his sharp chin drops onto his chest.

I don't know if the hermit will wake in time to take the water he requires to survive. Images of Luki's mother and the struggling form of Kai's father flash through my mind. But I can't consider such things now, not with one more piece of the mirror in our possession.

"We should go." As I stride toward the passage, I call forth another globe of light and whistle for Luki, who waits until Kai treads slowly behind me before bounding in front of us. Passing into the outer chamber I hear the hawk's piercing cry followed by a rush of wings.

"Will he be all right?" Kai shifts awkwardly on the seat of the sleigh. He lays his gloved hand on my arm as I gather up the reins. "Holger was so still when we left, I thought perhaps … "

"Perhaps what?" I shake off his hand and yank up my hood, shadowing my face.

"Perhaps the shard was keeping him alive. He said the mirror has greater magic than even Voss knows."

"I think Master Holger likes to exaggerate." I cluck at the ponies, who take off from the ledge and gallop into the clear sky.

Kai's very quiet as we travel back to the palace. He keeps one hand in his pocket, obviously fingering Holger's shard. "You were a bit scary back there," he says as we fly over sparkling fields of snow.

"That was the idea." I press my spine into the rigid seat of the sleigh. I wonder if I slowed Holger's heart too much—crossed the border between sleep and death. I sigh, knowing I shouldn't dwell on such thoughts.

Luki stretches his neck over the seat, sniffling at my ear. I gently push his nose away. He whimpers and drops his head onto Kai's shoulder. The boy lifts his free hand and pats the wolf absently while staring blankly at the drifting clouds.

I still see Holger's bald head bent over his limp hands. I slap the reins and the ponies pick up speed. *Never mind,* I think, my eyes fixed on the white horizon. *Such thoughts hold no power. Let them fade. Let it all fall away.*

CHAPTER ELEVEN: DECEITS AND DIVERSIONS

KAI IS RESTLESS. AFTER A night spent calculating and arguing over equations, we placed Holger's fragment into the mirror this morning. Now Kai wants to travel to the university to collect the two other pieces.

"I've something I need to do first," I tell him as we stare into the looking glass.

"What's more important than recovering those fragments?" Kai's brown eyes rake over me. The color yesterday's cold and wind whipped into his face has drained away, leaving him pale and drawn.

"I told you—I've other responsibilities." The truth is Bae has returned with news of Gerda, but I can't tell Kai that.

"So I'm stuck here, I suppose?" Kai picks up another piece of glass and holds it over the dark section of the mirror.

"Yes, stay here with Luki."

Curled up in the sunlight spilling through the room's tall windows, the wolf raises his head at the mention of his name. His amber eyes regard me steadily. He has aged rapidly in the last few months and now resembles an adult wolf more than a pup. But he's still all legs and tail and head. He hasn't quite grown into his bones.

"Keep him locked in here when I leave so he won't try to follow me." A little smile curves my lips. Luki is likely to follow me anywhere, even into danger.

"Luki, it seems we have been given our orders." Kai leans over the mirror and slides a few pieces about, his eyes narrowed in concentration. He does not look up when I turn and stride to the door.

Luki rises and pads after me, but I press my hand into the dense fur of his chest and push him back as I close the door. I hear whining and scratching before Kai calls him away. There's a flutter in my stomach, and I bite the inside of my cheek to refocus my mind. It's a strange sensation, realizing any creature bears that much love for me.

I make my way down several icy corridors, careful to illuminate the walls before I step into each passageway. At the end of one hall is the chamber I seek—a simple storeroom. I step inside and head for the black trunk pressed against one wall.

Bae's news is sending me on another journey. Apparently Gerda's been located at a country estate, the same estate where gossip claims a young man also seeks refuge. A brilliant scholar, the boy is the new ward of the Stryker family, whose wealth is piled as high as the timber they cut and sell. In two days the boy returns from the university. The Stryker clan is taking the opportunity to throw a grand ball to introduce the boy to their friends and neighbors. According to Bae, Gerda's convinced this mysterious young scholar is Kai.

Of course, I know better. But I won't forgo the chance to confront Gerda and convince her to return home. She's already astonished me with her ability to track any information that might lead her to Kai. Her success causes me concern—I see another hand behind her actions. On her own, I don't believe Gerda presents a major threat to my plans, but I fear she's gained the support and protection of Sephia. Logic leads me to think the enchantress is using Gerda as a pawn in her war against Voss and, by extension, me.

So, like it or not, I must pause in my search for the missing fragments to chase down Kai's friend and get to the bottom of Sephia's plans. Bae tells me that Clara, the youngest of the Stryker children, has taken an interest in Gerda, who appeared on their doorstep, cold and hungry, a few weeks ago. I silently thank the Strykers' well-known devotion to charity and Voss's transformation of Bae. I've puzzled over the mage's decision to grant the reindeer the power of speech, but perhaps Voss's magic whispered something of the future. He obviously sensed I'd need a servant who could convey messages.

I slowly lift the domed lid of the trunk. Nestled in the black velveteen interior is a jumble of delicate garments. I sift through the velvets and satins until my fingers close about a hank of silk. Pulling the garment from the trunk, I hold it up against the soft blue light emanating from the walls. It's a pale gray silk gown, shot through with threads of silver and lavender. Tiny opalescent beads are sewn into its puffed cap sleeves and larger pearls encrust the low neckline. I lay the silk against my plain wool gown. The dress is sized perfectly for me. Just the thing to wear to a ball.

I suspect the silken gown is out of fashion, but that's of no consequence. I plan to disguise myself as a lady from a distant land, hoping my foreignness will excuse any oddness in my dress. I certainly can't attend a ball wearing one of my woolen gowns.

Rummaging through the trunk I uncover a pair of delicate satin slippers. Balancing the shoes on top of the folded gown, I close the lid and wonder again why Voss has such garments stored in the palace. When I first discovered the trunk I surmised it was the discarded clothing of a former queen, but logic soon disproved that theory. Voss chooses his Snow Queens from surrounding towns, not royalty. No ordinary village girl would own such finery. I shake off my curiosity as I step back into the hall. It's a mystery, and will remain so. I've no intention of asking Voss who owned these elegant garments. Personal questions are a sure way to evoke his wrath.

It's time to track down the young girl whose determination surprisingly seems to match my own.

Freya paws nervously at the ground as I slide the gown and slippers, carefully wrapped in a linen shift, into my saddlebags. I'm wearing my white furs over my chamois traveling clothes. Not my usual riding habit, but the furs are the only cloak I own that matches the elegance of the silk gown.

As we take to the sky I consider my options. If Gerda is protected under Clara Stryker's wing, I'll need to tread carefully. It won't do for me to be barred from the estate before I've a chance to talk to Gerda alone. I plan to use whatever magic is required to convince her that the Strykers' ward is indeed Kai, and that any interference will damage his opportunity for a first-class education and untold riches. I calculate such an argument will convince Gerda to abandon her search for Kai and return home. But I must meet with her before the young man arrives at the ball. Once she sees he isn't Kai, she'll undoubtedly resume her quest. I can't allow her to slip through my fingers again.

I urge Freya on unmercifully, stopping only for brief periods of nourishment and rest. As we cross the valley that lies between the mountains and the Stryker estate, I direct the tired mare to the ground. She's quite willing to land and slow her pace to a walk. I guide the horse to a small grove of trees bordering the Stryker stables. Sliding off her back, I walk Freya about for some time, until the sweat has dried on her arched neck and flanks.

"Now for my disguise," I whisper to the exhausted mare. Concentrating my power, I conjure the image of a high-born lady from foreign lands. I leave my angular features as they are but darken my skin to a creamy olive tone and convert my mass of white curls into an upsweep of sleek ebony locks. I turn my ice-gray eyes the color of walnut hulls. Satisfied with my transformation, I pull the linen bundle from my saddlebags and tuck it under my cloak. I hide my tunic and breeches by pulling my white furs tightly about me, and walk Freya around to the front of the stables.

A young stable boy rushes to meet me. His blue eyes widen as he takes in my appearance. His ruddy face is round as a full moon. "Take your horse, madam?" He flashes a smile that reveals a broken front tooth.

"Thank you, yes," I reply, handing him Freya's reins. "See she has sufficient feed and water, and two flakes of hay." I color my words with an odd inflection. I hope it will fool the boy into assuming I'm not a native speaker of his language.

"Your name, madam?" The boy's clearly confused by my unusual looks and accent. "So I can be sure to take good care of your mare," he adds, ducking his head.

"Lady LaNévé." I stress the last vowel of the word. "Yes, treat her well. We have traveled far."

As the stable boy bobs his head and leads Freya away, I walk toward the large timber and stucco manor house, shortening my stride to create a more ladylike impression. The gravel path leading to the house is lined with towering elms, their branches still bare of leaves. The path ends in a great cobbled courtyard filled with carriages of every size and color. I note the coat of arms painted on the door of one of the coaches and wonder if I can pull off my masquerade. These are true ladies and lords and I've no experience with their society. I tightly lap the front edges of my cloak and sneak around the side of the house, searching for a way to make a quiet entrance.

I find a door ajar near the kitchen garden. Sliding into the back hallway, I spy a large kitchen through an open archway to my right. The opposite passageway offers a more promising route, leading to a narrow stairway. At the top of the stairs I realize I'm in the servants' quarters. I hurry past a row of closed doors, finally discovering a small room, empty except for an iron bedstead and a small dresser. I slip into the room and latch the door. It's time for my transformation.

As I change into the silk gown and satin slippers I debate what to do with my discarded clothes, finally shoving them into one drawer of the empty dresser. I'll be pleased if I can retrieve them later, but if not, I won't fret over the loss of some old garments.

There's no mirror, but given that most of my appearance is an illusion, I don't concern myself with this minor inconvenience. I slump on the lumpy bed and calculate some equations to clear my mind. Staring at the narrow window, I wait patiently for darkness to flood the dusty panes.

CHAPTER TWELVE:
IN THE KINGDOM OF THE CROWS

WHEN I'M SURE IT'S TIME for the ball to begin, I leave the room and stride to the end of the hall. A simple wooden door opens with one twist of the knob and I step into a different world. Creamy plaster walls rise above dark wood wainscoting. Ivory candles set in silver sconces light the hall, and a brilliant crimson runner covers the mahogany floor. A series of paintings line the walls—darkly varnished portraits in gilded frames. I allow my cloak to fall open, exposing the exquisite silk gown, as I stroll past the paintings. I wonder how many of these glassy-eyed lords and ladies are actual ancestors of the Strykers, and how many were simply purchased to lend an air of antiquity to the family line. My limited knowledge of the family, gleaned from Inga's rhapsodies on their wealth and virtues, leads me to imagine few of these elegantly dressed puppets are any relation to the family that built an empire from a single logging camp.

The end of the passageway opens onto a balcony overlooking the manor's grand entrance hall. A double staircase, its treads wide enough for three people to walk abreast, curves away at either end of the balcony. I cross to the intricately carved railing and survey the scene below.

A swirl of vivid silk, satin, and velvet gowns is set off by the somber black of the men's clothes. The women bob and weave like songbirds among crows. I grip the railing and search the crowd for Gerda, but I don't spy her amid the flock of guests. A tall man sporting a brilliant tapestry waistcoat under his black jacket glances up and stops talking to his companion, a tiny woman lost in the ruffled excess of a sapphire gown. As the man stares directly at me his hazel eyes narrow in concentration. He leans down to whisper something in his companion's ear. She glances up at me and shakes her head.

I move to one set of stairs and descend slowly, allowing my fingertips to glide along the polished banister. Sapphire-gown whispers to her companion. She's holding up her black lace fan so I can't read her lips. They're discussing me, of course. A stranger at the party, someone whose dress and appearance is at odds with every other woman in the room. Reaching the bottom of the stairs I approach the couple.

"Lady LaNévé," I say, extending my hand. "So good of you to invite me."

The man and woman exchange a look. "Ah, yes. You are connected to one of our gentry, perhaps? Lord Lind, is that right?" The man takes hold of my fingers and gallantly kisses the back of my hand. "I am Hans Stryker, your host." He nods his head toward his companion. "My wife, Elise."

I smile and concentrate on my fantastical accent. "It is very nice to meet you both. I have heard so many wonderful things about your family. Your charity work is renowned." A young chambermaid flutters forward. I shrug my cloak off my shoulders and hand it to her.

"What an unusual gown." Elise Stryker's face is a study in confusion.

"Do you like it? It's the latest fashion in my country." I toss off the words as I watch the maid carry my furs into a small anteroom off the main hall. I'll need them if I have to make a quick exit later. Even I can't cross the mountains in a thin silk gown. "I am used to warmer climes."

"I see." Hans Stryker is staring at something over my head. "Well, Lady LaNévé, I hope you enjoy our little party. Let us know if you need anything." He smiles and absently pats my hand. "I am sure Lord Lind is around here somewhere. If I see him I will send him to you."

"Oh no, don't bother. We are not, how shall I put it? On the best of terms right now. Still, family is family." Manufacturing a gracious smile for Elise Stryker, I walk into the milling crowd before she can respond.

I thread my way past the guests, who are clustered in knots as tight as birds picking over a solitary kernel of corn. Their voices fill my ears with shrieks and squawks. Crows indeed.

"Excuse me, have we met?" asks a stylishly dressed young man with a shock of blonde hair falling into his eyes. He holds out a fluted crystal glass full of a sparkling liquid. "Champagne?"

I've never sampled anything stronger than hard cider but I smile and accept the glass, pressing it to my lips and taking a tiny sip. "Thank you, sir. I am Lady LaNévé."

"Karl Friis." The young man looks me up and down, his blue eyes finally coming to rest on my neckline. I don't believe he's admiring the pearls.

"Well, Master Friis"—I press my slippered foot over his instep until he looks up into my face—"perhaps you can help me? I would love to meet Miss Clara Stryker, as I've heard so many marvelous things about her, but I'm afraid I don't know what she looks like. Could you point her out to me?" I flick away his wandering fingers before they come to rest upon my arm.

Karl Friis steps away from me, smoothing down the lapels of his gray frock coat. "She's just coming down the stairs," he says sullenly.

I turn to gaze into the entrance hall. A young blonde woman is descending the curving staircase. She's wearing a bell-shaped gown of pink tulle from which her slender white neck rises like the stem of an inverted flower. Trailing in her wake is another blonde girl, dressed in a simple white eyelet dress with a lavender sash. "Gerda," I mutter under my breath, earning a searching look from Mr. Friis.

"Friend of mine," I say airily, thrusting the full champagne glass into his hands. "Please excuse me, Master Friis. I must give her, what do you say? Ah yes, my best wishes." I stalk off, not bothering to maintain a ladylike stride.

As I approach the hall a tall, slender woman steps in front of me. Her auburn hair is piled high upon her head, a few ringlets cascading over her neck and ears. She's wearing a gown of sea foam silk, embroidered with pastel roses and twisting green vines.

"How delightful to run into you again." The woman's emerald eyes flash. "Though not surprising, all in all."

"Sephia," I dig my fingernails into the palms of my clenched fists. "Are you following me?

"No." The enchantress smiles sweetly. "I am simply keeping an eye on Gerda. I've taken quite a fancy to her, you see. Rather like a mother watching over her only child."

I attempt to step around her. "You're in my way."

"Now, now, Snow Queen." Sephia grabs my elbow. Her grip's tight as a clamp. "Or whatever you are calling yourself." She looks me over as I twist my arm to loosen her hold. "An interesting disguise, I must say. Although I think pale coloring suits you best."

"I'm not interested in what you think." I wrench my arm free and step back. "Gerda lives in my realm. She's my subject and none of your business."

Sephia leans in, whispering in my ear. To the other guests we must appear like two close friends sharing a confidence. "You blighted my garden, Thyra Winther. And you seek to reconstruct the mirror. That makes everything you do my business."

Clara Stryker and Gerda enter the ballroom arm in arm. As they stroll past Gerda turns to stare in our direction. Sephia hides her face behind a painted silk fan. I meet Gerda's gaze and smile. The girl looks puzzled and pauses for a moment but Clara pulls her away. They head toward the small chamber orchestra set up at one end of the room.

"What do you want with Gerda?" whispers Sephia from behind her fan.

I lift my chin and meet those glittering emerald eyes. "Merely to send her home, where she'll be safe."

"To keep her from her friend. You forget, I know who she seeks, Lady of the Snows. Do you have any knowledge of a boy named Kai?"

Behind my false face it's not difficult to lie. "No. I only know Gerda's far from home and her family misses her. It's time she returned to them."

"And you expect me to believe you only have her best interests at heart?" Sephia tosses her head, her hair gleaming like the borealis.

"It doesn't matter what you believe. You have no power here." I turn on my heel and stride away from the enchantress, daring her to follow.

I approach Clara Stryker and Gerda, glancing over my shoulder just once to watch Sephia watching me. Smiling as brightly as I can, I introduce myself to the two young girls.

"LaNévé?" Clara's pronunciation of the words is more accurate than mine and her soft brown eyes are brimming with intelligence. I'm instantly aware I shouldn't underestimate her. "That means snow, doesn't it?"

"Why yes," I say, silently cursing her expensive education. "An old family name. We live in the mountains, you see."

"So do I." Gerda's blue eyes are dimmed, like a summer sky filled with storm clouds. "Where's your country, Lady LaNévé?"

"Far from here." I examine the girl with interest. Sorrow has dulled the color in her cheeks but her face is still round as the curve of an apple. Her lower lip is fuller than the upper, making it appear she is pouting. She hasn't grown tall, but her figure has blossomed. It fills out the white dress in a way that's sure to capture the attention of young Master Friis.

"Lady LaNévé, your gown is quite beautiful," says Clara. "I don't believe I've ever seen anything like it."

"I imagine not." I toss my head and attempt a trill of laughter to match the chirping of the ladies surrounding me. "It's all the rage in my country but not quite the fashion here, as you see." I fix my gaze on Gerda and call up a bit of my magic to focus her attention on my words. "But you, Miss Gerda, why are you not at home? You seem so young to be traveling on your own."

"I'm fifteen." Gerda squirms under my intense gaze. "I'm searching for a friend. He's gone missing and I … " The girl blushes. "Well, I must find him and bring him home."

"That's very commendable. But just suppose your friend has found a great opportunity." I glance at Clara, who doesn't flinch under my scrutiny. "Would you deny him that?"

"No, no." Gerda shares a look with Clara. "That's the thing, you see. A young man recently appeared at the university, penniless but desperate for knowledge. Mr. Stryker met him there, when he was visiting Clara's brother, and agreed to sponsor his studies. The young man's coming here tonight and I think … " She turns to Clara and lays her hand on the other girl's arm.

"Gerda thinks the young man might be her friend, Kai," Clara says. "Traveling under another name, of course. We are anxious to see if her guess is correct. It would be quite wonderful, don't you think? If my father were to help her friend, I mean."

I spy Sephia advancing on us. "An amazing coincidence. Now, if you'll excuse me, I must speak with some of the other guests." I turn away, calculating how to simultaneously get Gerda alone and prevent Sephia from speaking to her. As I move to waylay the enchantress the small orchestra launches into a rousing medley of opera tunes. Someone shouts "Quadrille!" and a wave of couples pours into the center of the room. The rest of the guests fall back against the walls like a receding tide.

Master Friis is instantly at my side, asking me to dance. I brush him aside and cross to the entrance hall, following the floating hem of Sephia's gown. At that moment the great wooden doors are thrown open to the cobbled courtyard. A tall young man sweeps into the hall, followed by another boy. The young man whips off his maroon riding cloak and tosses it to a waiting footman. "We're here at last," he calls out in a clear tenor voice.

Hans and Elise Stryker hurry forward. The young man engulfs Elise in an embrace, lifting her off the parquet floor and spinning her about. "Mother! How well you look."

"Put me down, Matthias," scolds the older woman fondly.

Her son lowers her to her feet and kisses both her cheeks before turning to hug his father. "Mother, I'd like you to meet my friend, Jan. You've heard Father speak of him."

Mathias draws the other young man forward. He's short and rather plump, and wears wire-rimmed spectacles balanced precariously on his wide nose.

In observing this welcome I've lost sight of Sephia. I turn to see her shepherding Clara and Gerda into the front hall. I swear silently and move toward them, but Sephia's too quick for me.

"Look, Clara, your brother and his friend have finally arrived." Sephia's words ring out above the din of other voices. She pushes the two girls forward. Clara skips into her brother's waiting arms while Gerda hangs back, staring at Jan.

"It's not Kai," she says, her lips quivering. She uses the back of one hand to dash away the tears welling in her eyes.

Clara turns and glances from Jan to Gerda. "Oh, I am sorry, Gerda." She bustles forward to clasp the younger girl's trembling hands. "But we can keep looking, you know. And we'll ask Matthias and Jan to help. You will assist us, won't you?" Clara gives the two young men a meaningful look.

"Of course," says Matthias. Jan just smiles and nods his head.

"It doesn't matter." Gerda yanks her hands free. "Thank you, Clara, for everything, but I can't stay. Not now."

"Don't be foolish, child," says Elise Stryker. "We can't allow you to wander off alone again. Remain with us until you feel strong enough to travel home."

Gerda shakes her head, loosening one of her golden braids. It snaps against her bare shoulder like a whip. She dashes up the staircase, weeping.

"I'll go and see if she's all right, if you wish." Sephia smiles sweetly at the bemused Strykers, who are staring at Sephia and me as if wracking their brains to remember how we're acquainted with them. "I know Gerda. Perhaps I can calm her."

Hans Stryker nods brusquely as Clara retreats into her mother's arms.

"I'll go with you." I stride to Sephia's side. "I've some experience dealing with distraught young girls."

With our backs to the others, only I catch the flash of concern in Sephia's emerald eyes. I meet her intent gaze with my cold stare. "I hope you don't think that presumptuous of me, Madame … ?"

Sephia lifts her auburn head and stares down her nose at me. "Come then, Lady LaNévé," she says, stressing the name. "Let us see if we can assist Miss Gerda."

We pace each other up the stairs. Marching side by side past the row of portraits, we reach the end of the corridor as sounds of weeping seep around the corner.

I stride ahead of Sephia to the half-open door. "Miss Gerda," I call, modulating my voice into something resembling concern. "Can we offer any assistance?"

"Go away, please." Gerda's voice is choked with tears.

I lay my hand on the knob just as the door is slammed in my face. The lock clicks but I still rattle the handle.

"Perhaps we should leave her alone." Sephia's words drip into my ear, sweet as honey from the comb. "I'm sure she'll come out, sooner or later."

"Too late now." I step away from the door. "For me."

"Yes, I daresay Gerda will resume her search for Kai Thorsen as soon as possible."

I turn to face the enchantress. "And you'll assist her?"

"I?" Sephia raises one delicate eyebrow. "No, I will simply stay out of her way. I've no wish to interfere directly, now she knows Kai is still missing."

Staring into those green eyes, I realize I can't tell if she's lying. "It would be better for Gerda if she just went home."

"No doubt. But then you and Kai Thorsen—yes, I know he is helping you, though perhaps not by choice—might finish the mirror and I can't allow that."

"But you," I speak slowly, the answer to a thorny equation finally apparent, "can't travel to my realm, as I can to yours. You need Gerda to make the trip for you."

Sephia's eyes darken like the sea before a storm. "Such a clever girl. Mael did well to select you."

"It's good for him, at least." I hear the echo of screams in my mind. "Now, shall we go back to the party? I'd like to collect my furs. I'm feeling a bit chilly."

"You're an accomplished liar, Snow Queen." Sephia spins on one slippered heel. Her sea foam gown ripples like a wave about her slender form. "Come then, let us descend together. I warn you though—I intend to keep my eye on you."

"How flattering," I say, following her down the hall. "Perhaps I should introduce you to Master Friis. He likes to keep his eye on me as well."

When we rejoin the party I watch the dancing for a while, using my concentration and a little magic to absorb the basics of the movement. I then seek out Karl Friis and dance with him and several other young men for hours. It's a gambit that successfully prevents Sephia from leaving the ballroom.

The ball winds down with no further appearance from Gerda. She's obviously chosen to lock herself away for the evening. As I gather up my furs and say goodbye to the Strykers, I calculate my next move. It should be easy enough to wander back to that empty room and change both my clothes and appearance. If I can slip outside without being seen I can make my way to the stables and saddle Freya. The woods behind the stables provide enough cover for me to watch for any sign of Gerda. I suspect she will set off early in the morning to resume her search for Kai.

My plan works perfectly, but as I guide Freya toward the grove of trees I hear voices and pause to listen.

"The young miss took off in the middle of the night," says the stable boy, shaking beneath Sephia's imperious gaze. "Miss Clara ordered a pony and trap. I dare not refuse."

"So Miss Gerda left with Miss Clara's help?" Sephia pulls a spring green cloak about her shoulders as she confronts the trembling young man.

"Yes." The stable boy licks his lips and glances about, as if seeking rescue. "Miss Clara said to give the girl any assistance she needed." He twists his tweed cap in his hands. "I saw her, Miss Clara that is, press several pieces of jewelry into Miss Gerda's hands. They argued, but Miss Clara insisted the other miss take the jewels. Then they embraced and Miss Gerda took off in the pony trap. I didn't do wrong, did I? I mean, Miss Clara gave the orders. I'm supposed to obey commands from any of the Strykers."

"No, no." Sephia pats the stable boy's arm. "You did well."

I curse Clara and the Strykers along with the stable boy. Gerda has fled before I can thwart her quest. There's nothing more to be done here. I mount Freya and fasten my furs about me, preparing for my journey back to the ice palace. I have failed once again, but I can't focus on that. There are the two remaining pieces of the mirror to obtain. Little time remains, yet I still have hope. Kai will travel with me to the university and we will collect the missing shards before Gerda can track her childhood friend. *It must be so.*

Freya and I take to the skies before any of the Strykers' guests are awake to observe our departure. Only Sephia watches as we disappear into the clouds. I urge the mare on, confident where I'm going, the enchantress can't follow.

CHAPTER THIRTEEN:
A SCIENTIFIC CURIOSITY

I MUST ADMIT KAI'S A USEFUL traveling companion. He's making a fire as I walk the horses to cool them down before allowing them water. The last thing we need is for our mounts to founder, especially so far from the palace.

"Tomorrow's the day then." Kai glances up at me as he feeds kindling into the growing blaze. His face is flushed with warmth by the firelight, but his dark eyes are cool. "Have you any idea where we should start our search at the university?"

"Well, Holger said the men were explorers. I imagine we should focus on buildings that house the scientific faculty." I pull a cloth-wrapped hunk of cheese from my saddlebag and toss it to Kai. "Here—find a stick and melt a bit of this. We can eat it on the bread."

Kai rocks back on his heels and surveys me as I unsaddle the horses. "Do you always tell people what to do in that peremptory fashion?"

I drape the saddles over a low hanging branch. "No, because—if you recall—I haven't had anyone to tell anything for some time."

"Right." Kai rises to his feet and crosses to the tree where he hung his pack. "I suppose that explains a lot."

"A lot of what?" I tether the horses to a tree, allowing them room to wander. There's a small stream where they can drink, and enough vegetation on the bank to provide them with supper.

"Your less than polite behavior sometimes." Kai spears the cheese on a stick he's just sharpened with his pocket knife.

I grab the linen bundle that holds a loaf of bread. "I don't have time for such niceties. I'm not like your friend Gerda—cosseted and kept safe by family and friends."

"Don't bring Gerda into it." Kai waves the stick at me. "She's a sweet girl who works very hard. Her life isn't all roses, you know. It's not like our families are wealthy."

"So"—I sit on a rock near the fire and hold out the loaf—"are you and Gerda betrothed or something?"

Kai yanks off a hunk of bread. "No. What makes you ask that?" He avoids my eyes, busying himself with smearing the softened cheese on the bread.

"Well, your families are so entwined. I just thought you might be expected to marry. And you seem close, you and Gerda."

"We are close." Kai hands me half of the cheese and bread. "But I can't imagine marrying anyone any time soon. I want to go to the university. To study, not just steal pieces of glass." He finally meets my questioning gaze. "I plan to learn all I can about mathematics and science and anything else that interests me. That could take years. It'll be some time before I can consider marriage."

"And Gerda's aware of this?" I blow on my bread to cool the hot cheese, then stretch out my legs until the tips of my boots rest near the glowing embers.

"Of course. We don't have secrets." Kai chews for a moment, staring into the dense glade of trees surrounding us. "You're right, though. Our families do expect us to marry. But I don't know. I'm not sure it's fair to ask Gerda to wait for me to finish my studies."

"Wouldn't she? Wait, I mean?" I nibble at my bread and cheese.

Kai shrugs. "Maybe. Probably. But that isn't really the point. The truth is"—he turns and stares into my face—"I'm not really sure I want to marry anyone. Ever."

"Oh. Well, that I understand."

"I thought you might." Kai looks away again. "I'm going to get some water. Want some?"

"Sure." I watch him make his way to our saddlebags and pull out our goatskin flasks. He fills them from the stream, pausing to pat the horses before returning with the full skins.

Kai hands me my flask before he sits down. "I just have this burning desire to know more, to learn, to travel. I can't stay in my village forever. I think I'd go mad."

"I can see why you'd feel that way." I tear off another small hunk of bread and chew on it moodily. "Sometimes I wish I could go to a university, but that's impossible. And not just because I'm the Snow Queen."

"Because you're a girl." Kai takes the piece of bread I offer him. He spears another slab of cheese and holds it near the flames for a moment. "It isn't fair for someone with your mind, but that's the way of things, I'm afraid."

"So it is." I contemplate this fact. Perhaps it's just as well Voss chose me as Snow Queen. At least I've power now, and the opportunity to use his library to teach myself. I wouldn't have a chance at more than a basic education if I were just another village girl. Even less than Gerda if I'd remained what I was—a penniless orphan. "So, tomorrow we enter the university grounds. I think it's best if you pose as a student and I pretend to be your sister."

Kai raises his eyebrows. "We scarcely look like family."

"Oh, no one will question it. I'll change my appearance a bit, just so I look less … "

"Distinctive?" Kai smiles before taking a long swallow of water.

"I was going to say peculiar, but distinctive will do." I hide my own smile by taking another bite of bread.

"Here's to success." Kai holds up his water skin. "May we swiftly locate the shards and just as quickly return them safely to your palace."

"We will." I tap his flask with my own. "Between the two of us we should be able to accomplish this task. Those people at the university— they won't be expecting us."

"I doubt anyone expects a girl like you, Thyra." Kai rises to his feet and tosses the sharpened stick on the fire. "I'm going to grab my blankets and try to get some sleep. I don't want to be too tired to think tomorrow."

"Good idea." I stand and stride over to my saddlebags to retrieve my own blanket. "Shouldn't we douse the fire first, though?"

"It'll die down on its own." Kai leans back against a broad tree trunk and drapes the wool blanket over him. "Just don't sit too close. Sparks might fly."

I settle against a tree on the opposite side of the fire. "I'll keep watch. We probably shouldn't leave the horses unguarded. We don't know what might be out there, in the dark."

"I told you we should've brought Luki," says Kai, his voice laced with exhaustion. "But you're right, we need to stay alert. You watch now, but wake me in a few hours so I can keep a lookout and you can get some sleep."

"All right," I reply, though I've no intention of waking him. I can manage without sleep, and my magic can keep any wild creatures at bay. Kai doesn't possess such gifts.

I stare into the dying flames, working through as many equations as are required to keep me awake all night.

The morning dawns cool but clear. Kai and I eat a quick breakfast and saddle the horses before the sun rises above the distant mountains.

"You were supposed to wake me," says Kai as we set off toward the walls of the city.

"Well, you were sleeping so soundly, and I don't require as much rest as mortals do."

Kai shifts his reins from hand to hand and shoots me a sharp glance. "You're still human."

"Mostly." I stare straight ahead. "But I can call on my magic if I grow weary. You can't."

Kai falls silent. We ride without speaking until we reach the city gates and mingle with a throng of other riders. Following tarp-covered wagons bulging with mysterious goods, we move slowly into the main square. A utilitarian fountain, ringed by numerous people clutching buckets and pails, sits in the middle of the square. Looming over the cobbled courtyard is a slender brick clock-tower. As Kai and I ride into the square the clock strikes the hour and a bevy of mechanical figures spit out of the clock, performing a pantomime that involves a hunter chasing a fox that chases a dog chasing a cat that chases a mouse. They spin in and out several times before the chimes die away and the doors on the clock face slam shut.

"Thyra," says Kai, "we need to ride on."

I realize I've been staring at the clock without moving for several minutes. Shaking my head, I dig my heels into Freya's flanks and head toward the main avenue leading from the square.

"You've never been in the city before, have you?" Kai pulls his horse alongside Freya.

"No." I keep my gaze focused straight ahead, where I spy two tall towers.

"Well, stick close to me. It's easy to lose your way."

I toss my head. "I won't get lost." I point toward the towers. "I assume that's the university?"

"Yes, that's it."

I hear something in Kai's voice that spurs me to look at him. He's staring at the towers with such longing I catch my breath. I know the emotion lying behind that look. It's the wish for something more, something just beyond one's fingertips.

It's the mirror completed and my mind and body preserved, safe from harm forever.

"Come on," I say, "let's find those shards."

We ride to the edge of the university, dismounting at one of the ancient oak trees that flank the entrance. Tying the horses to two of the metal rings studding the brick outer wall, Kai and I walk onto the university grounds. Unlike the rest of the city, trees shade all the buildings except for the two stone towers springing from either end of a two-story brick structure.

"Time to locate the science building," whispers Kai, taking my arm.

I glance at him in surprise, but he just smiles. "You're my sister, remember? I can't let you roam about unescorted. It simply isn't done."

"Very well, but when we find the shards you follow my lead." I wiggle my arm until Kai loosens his grip slightly.

"Whatever you say, Thyra."

We stroll the grounds, the perfect picture of a student and his young lady, be that sister or sweetheart. My plain cape and my wool gown—the skirt pulled down to hide the tight breeches I wear while riding—don't look out of place here, where everyone's dressed in muted, unadorned clothes. I've also spun some magic to alter my appearance so I draw no special attention. After wandering for a while we stumble upon a timber and stucco building bearing a plaque proclaiming that it's the Hall of Mathematics and Science.

Kai's fingers dig into my arm. "Here we are. Time to work your magic." He leans in to whisper in my ear. "Can you sense the fragments of the mirror?"

"Not yet." I pull away from him. As we enter the hall Kai releases my arm and I stride forward to the center of the black-and-white tiled floor, where a mosaic seal depicts a night sky filled with figures formed of stars.

"It's the constellations." Kai steps up beside me, gazing at the seal. "And look, the phases of the moon." He points to the painted dome above our heads.

"Can I help you?" asks a voice behind us.

I turn to face an older man. Shorter than either Kai or me, he's as round as the full moon painted on the ceiling. His pink face is fringed with wisps of pale hair and his nose and cheeks are flushed red as ripe berries. But his arctic blue eyes examine us with an intensity that belies his jovial appearance.

"Oh, hello." Kai extends his hand. "We're just looking about. I'm attending university next year and I wanted to show my sister where I'll be studying."

The man takes hold of Kai's hand. "I'm Professor Daman, Head of Mathematics. And you are?"

"Kai Thorsen."

I wonder why Kai's using his real name but immediately realize he must, if he ever intends to enroll here. He can't pretend to be someone else now and appear as Kai Thorsen in another year, not with the primary professor in his field standing before him.

I, of course, have no such problem. "My brother is so looking forward to studying with you." I dip a little curtsey, not certain what's appropriate in this situation.

"Oh, sorry, sir. Where are my manners? This is my sister … Caris."

"Nice to meet you, Miss Thorsen." Professor Daman looks me over with those piercing eyes before turning his gaze on Kai. "So, young man, you are joining us next year? Studying what, may I ask?"

"Mathematics, I hope, sir." For the first time since I've known him, Kai appears flustered in another person's presence. "And some sciences too, if possible."

"Really?" Daman surveys Kai as if estimating his mental capacity. "Well, I suppose we shall see how that turns out. Now, perhaps Miss Thorsen would like a proper tour of our facilities?"

"Oh yes," I say, a little too fast.

Kai bangs his elbow into my arm. "Very gracious of you, sir."

Daman waves aside Kai's continued thanks. "Not at all. Come along, then. I haven't much time." He glances at his gold pocket watch. "Have a lecture in half an hour."

We follow the professor on a swift tour of the building, making the appropriate approving noises as he guides us in and out of various classrooms and labs. Watching Daman waddle before us, leading us toward one more lecture hall, I feel a tingling in my fingers. I glance to my right and see a door standing ajar. It opens into a small storeroom.

"What's in there?" I fight to keep my voice light, displaying none of the excitement I feel.

"Oh that? Just a closet where we store some artifacts. Things collected over the years. Scientific curiosities and the like." Daman glances at me. "Would you like to see, Miss Thorsen?"

"If it's not a bother." I give him my best imitation of a proper young lady's smile.

"Not at all. But I'll have to leave you after this, I'm afraid. Need to make that lecture, you know. I dock the students' grades if they are late so I must set a good example." Daman pushes open the door and leads us into the storeroom. A mullioned window allows in enough midday light to illuminate the laden shelves.

Sensing the mirror's beckoning magic, my fingers are twitching. I clasp my hands demurely before me. *The shards are here,* I mouth at Kai when Daman's back is turned.

Kai doesn't falter. "Well, Professor Daman," he says smoothly, "thank you so much for showing us about, but we don't want to keep you any longer. We'll just find our own way out."

The professor turns to face us. "Yes, I must go. Perhaps, Master Thorsen, you'd like to sit in on my lecture? Just to get a taste of what you can expect next year."

I can tell by Kai's rapid blinking that he's attempting to solve this problem. "Uh, very nice of you, Professor. I'm not sure, though, if I should leave my sister …"

"Nonsense," I say firmly. "You should go. I'll simply wait for you in the main hall. I believe I saw some benches there, along one wall."

Kai shoots me a glance but I refuse to acknowledge his glare.

"You are very observant, Miss Thorsen," says Daman. "Indeed, there is some seating in the entrance hall." He smiles encouragingly at

Kai. "Your sister will be quite safe there, I assure you."

"Oh, I'm sure she will be, sir." Kai waits to grip my arm until Daman steps out of the room. "What are you thinking?"

"I'm thinking," I reply, under my breath, "that the good professor will be occupied with his lecture and you'll possess a wonderful alibi when you're seated right in front of him. And no one will suspect"—I allow a cold smile to flicker over my face—"your sweet sister of stealing anything from a dusty old storeroom."

Kai releases my arm and steps away. "You can be quite terrifying, you know."

"It's a gift." I rub my arm. Somehow the sensation of Kai's touch always seems to linger longer than it should.

Daman insists on escorting me to one of the benches in the front hall before he leads Kai into an adjoining lecture hall. I watch as other students run in from outside and pile into the room. Many dash inside just before the heavy oak doors are closed. A few stragglers find the door shut in their face and turn away, their expressions ranging from dismay to elation. I wait until the hall clears before I rise and make my way back to the storeroom.

The tingling returns to my fingers as I enter the small room. I move to the center of the wood plank floor and drop my hands to my sides. Clearing my mind of everything except thoughts of the shards I allow my feet to carry me to the shelving lining one wall. I hold one hand over each shelf, until my fingers flutter. Dropping my hand onto the surface of a glass curio box I feel the magic of the mirror radiate into my body.

I gently lift the glass box with both hands. Blowing off a layer of dust, I glimpse a jagged, glittering object. I clutch the box to my bosom. The lost pieces of the mirror are in my possession.

The box is locked, but that's of no consequence. I rub my fingers over the lock, willing it to release, and the lid springs open. Peering into the velvet-lined interior, I spy only one shard.

"So where's the other one?" I mutter, glancing about the room. Carefully lifting the shard out of the box, I wrap it in my silken handkerchief and tuck the small bundle into the bodice of my gown.

With the first shard secured, I attempt to sense the second piece, to no avail. There's no other pull of magic in the room. I move back to the shelf where I found the box and search again. My fingers, scrabbling over the wood, fall upon a piece of heavy paper the size of a calling card. I lift the paper and carry it to the window to read the faded writing. It's a label detailing where and when the mirror shard was found. "Nothing is known of its powers," the note reads, "except it appears to exert a strange hold over anyone who keeps it in their possession." At the very bottom of the card is a notation in another hand—"Another piece was found but lost on the journey home, when we encountered the wanderers who haunt the forests outside the city."

This does not touch me. It won't defeat me. Let it fall away.

After several deep breaths I brush the dust from my gown and make my way back to the entrance hall, where my cloak's draped over the back of the bench. I grab the wrap and pull it about me, tight as a comforting embrace. Staring at the wooden doors of the lecture hall, I decide to slip inside to hear at least a portion of Professor Daman's class. It might be the only opportunity I'll ever have to attend a university lecture.

Fortunately the heavy doors are not locked. I pull one slightly ajar and shimmy through the narrow opening. Keeping my back pressed against the wall, I slide to a point where I can see the front of the lecture hall.

Professor Daman is illustrating a point by writing on a large slate board. I watch his plump hand move across the dark surface, creating an equation that takes my breath away. It's simple, yet elegant. As he speaks I realize I can follow his explanation of this mathematical theory without difficulty. It's perfectly logical, and I wonder why I never envisioned this particular calculation before.

I glance about the room until I spy Kai's dark head. He's sitting to one side, his gaze focused on Daman. Kai's expression is one I've only seen before at Inga's church, illuminating the faces of the most devout believers.

As I listen to the professor's brilliant explication of another theorem I sneak glances at Kai, knowing my face must reflect the same wonder and delight. To sit in classes like this, and learn, and be able to reach beyond what my own mind can conjure is a dream—one I know I can't entertain for longer than this lecture. But Kai can obtain this goal, if he can leave his village.

My lie rolls up the back of my throat like a ball of acid. Of course, Kai loves his father, and wants him returned to health and vigor. There's guilt, too. But more than that, much more, I realize, is Kai's need for his father to be well enough to manage the mill. Because without that, Kai may have to sacrifice his university dream so he can support his family.

I slip back through the doors and walk slowly across the hall. Settling on the bench with great deliberation, I stare at the dome above my head. Phases of the moon. The passage of time caught in a never-ending cycle. I close my eyes for a moment, allowing my mind to entertain the thought I've held at bay for some time now—only two months remain before my eighteenth birthday.

The doors fly open and a whirlwind of young men pours into the hall. They're gesticulating wildly and talking over one another as their eyes glow with the light of new ideas. Amid the beaming faces, Kai's shines the brightest. He strides to me and grabs both my hands, pulling me to my feet.

"It was amazing, inspiring, brilliant! You should've been there, Thyra." He blanches as he realizes what he's said.

I lean forward to whisper in his ear. "It's all right. No one can hear you amid this din." I pat the neckline of my gown. "I found it. One of the shards. I have it."

"One?" Kai releases my hands and steps back. "I thought …"

"The other was lost in the forest." I slip my hand through the crook of his arm. "Now escort me out like a good brother. We can talk more later."

We walk in silence until we reach the edge of the university grounds. I hitch up my skirt, exposing my breeches and earning shocked glances from a cluster of students. Staring them down as I untie Freya, I toss my head before I look away. I stroke the mare's velvety neck for a moment and lay out my plan.

"You must return," I tell Kai. "Take the mirror fragment we found today and carry it safely to the palace. Then you can continue our work of reconstructing the mirror while I track down the final shard."

Kai swings up into his saddle and sits facing away from me. His dappled-gray gelding side-steps nervously as Kai fiddles with the reins. "I suppose that's the most rational plan, considering our deadline." He wheels the horse around to face me. The glow from the lecture has faded from his face. "But how do you intend to locate this lost fragment?"

I mount Freya in one swift movement and turn her toward the city gates. "The card said the other shard was lost to the wanderers who haunt the forest beyond this city. I've heard of these people—a band of folk who roam far and wide. I don't know if I'll find them in the forest, but I may be able to glean information on their current whereabouts."

Kai's brown eyes survey me solemnly. "And you think they still have the mirror piece after all this time?"

I shrug. "I don't know, but it's our only lead. I must pursue it."

"Very well, give me the shard and I'll make for the palace. I only hope"—Kai takes the small silken bundle from my hand—"I can find my way back."

"I can help with that." I pull Freya up close beside Kai's mount. Leaning forward, I whisper magic words into the gelding's twitching ear. Backing Freya off, I meet Kai's bemused gaze. "There. He knows what to do now. Let him carry you home."

"So I just hang on?" Kai tucks the wrapped shard into an inner pocket of his tunic. "Well, I suppose it's better than getting lost."

Outside the gates of the city Kai turns to me again. "Are you sure you'll be all right? I don't know anything about these wanderers, but they don't sound like they'd welcome strangers."

"I'll be fine." I shake off my altered appearance until I'm once again the Snow Queen. "Don't forget what I really am."

"I never forget that." Kai bends forward, granting me the ghost of a bow.

I straighten in my saddle and cast Kai a frosty smile. "I'll meet you at the palace soon. With the final shard."

Kai kicks his horse into a trot. "Safe travels, Thyra," he calls over his shoulder, "and happy hunting."

I watch him ride away before turning Freya about and urging her into a fast walk. We follow a narrow path leading into the forest. I don't know what lies within that gloomy green cathedral, but I'll brave any danger to find the final shard. Nothing can scare me more than what waits for me if I fail in my mission. The wraiths' words never leave my mind, their hollow voices howling my doom. "Soon you will be one of us. Soon."

No. Never. I urge Freya into a gallop and we plunge into the woods.

CHAPTER FOURTEEN: TRUTH IN THE SHADOWS

SPRUCE TREES TOWER OVER MY head, their heavy branches bobbing and swaying in the light breeze, infusing the air with the sharp scent of pine. The forest's sunk in a hush and Freya's hooves ring against the rocks studding the path. I listen in vain for the sound of birds or small animals rustling amid the leaves and undergrowth.

Something urges me on, despite the folly of my quest. Kai's right—it's unlikely the lost fragment's still in the possession of those who stole it. There's also no guarantee the wanderers currently roam these woods. But a gentle force tugs me forward. It's as if a thin, silken line's attached to my breastbone—a thread of magic unreeling off an unseen spool.

The pull grows stronger as Freya and I move deeper into the forest. As I guide the mare down a side path the reins flutter in my trembling hands, and I know the shard is here, somewhere close.

The path ends in a large clearing ringed by a motley assortment of wagons and carts. A clump of shaggy horses and ponies mill about under one stand of trees. In the center of the clearing a fire pit's piled high with ashy logs, their dark hearts glowing red. A dozen people turn and stare at me. They have strong-jawed faces weathered brown by the sun, their noses and cheeks chapped pink by the wind. Their eyes and hair are dark as newly turned soil, save for one or two whose fiery locks blaze in the gloom. I cast a bit of magic, taming my appearance until I'm simply a gray-eyed girl with dull blonde hair pulled back into a single plait.

"What have we here?" asks one of the dark-haired men as he strides toward me. "A creature pale as a ghost. Are we to be haunted?" He's short, but his well-muscled arms bulge beneath his white linen shirt. He's wearing a brightly embroidered black vest and brushed leather breeches tucked into knee-high boots.

"I am no spirit." I swiftly dismount and tug down my skirt with a flourish as I stand face-to face with the man. "My name is Thyra Winther and I'm searching for something that belongs to me."

"And why would we"—the man's black eyes flash—"hold anything of yours?"

"I can feel it." There's no point in denying magic. I suspect these people believe in its existence and respect its power. "It calls to me."

The man looks me up and down before thrusting out his hand. "Nicu Ravn. Leader of this group of wanderers." He clasps my fingers tightly and pulls me close. "You are more than a young woman trespassing in our woods, aren't you, Thyra Winther?"

I lift my chin and counter his bold stare with my iciest glare. "As I said, I'm a seeker. Tracking something lost for many years. I've reason to believe it's here, and I've no intention of leaving until I obtain what's rightfully mine."

"Really?" Ravn's bushy eyebrows rise to the ragged edge of his thick bangs. He releases my hand and his gaze flickers over the faces of the people who've formed a circle about us. "The young lady wishes to reclaim her property. But I don't think we've anything of hers, do we, my friends?"

The crowd shouts out a chorus of "no" liberally laced with jeers and laughter.

I slide my hand down Freya's neck, soothing her. "You may not recognize this object. It was lost long ago."

"If it disappeared so far in the past, how can it be anything of yours?" Ravn's dark eyes bore into me. "You're quite young to have lost anything for many years."

"I'm older than I look." I draw up to my full height, which is several inches taller than Nicu Ravn.

The other wanderers take several steps forward, tightening their circle. I watch them out of the corner of my eye, noting the distrust on their faces. One blast of my magic could disperse them but I don't wish to disclose my identity yet. I must first uncover the location of the shard.

"Another girl stumbled into our camp about a week ago." Ravn draws a knife from a leather sheath fastened to his belt. He examines its gleaming blade, turning it over and over against the palm of his hand. "She claims to be looking for something as well. But her lost object is some boy. You wouldn't happen to be seeking the same thing, now would you?"

"No." So Gerda's here. I bite the inside of my cheek to prevent a swear word from flying off my tongue. "I'm seeking a simple piece of glass—a fragment of a mirror."

Ravn's eyes narrow. "Broken glass? This is your treasure?" He throws the knife up in the air and catches it by the handle. With one sweep of his arm he thrusts the weapon forward until the point of the blade is tickling my chin. "Why do you need a scrap of mirror, Thyra Winther?"

I press one finger against the blade and push the knife toward Ravn's chest. "That's my business."

"Perhaps, but I'm making it mine." Ravn whistles and two men step out of the circle and stride to his side. "You've ridden into my camp, demanding some object that you cannot prove is yours." Ravn gives me a broad smile and taps the knife lightly against his front teeth. "There's something not quite right about you. Not sure what it is, but I can tell you're not being entirely honest with me. I think until you're willing to tell us the truth you should cool your heels with our other little friend."

I consider my options. I could unleash an icy blast or simply freeze anyone who attempts to touch me. But I've no desire to display my true powers at this point. Logic tells me these wanderers are adept at disappearing if threatened. A storm could scatter them and leave me no closer to finding the shard than when I entered the forest.

"You needn't put hands on me." I hand Freya's reins to Ravn. "Just promise to take good care of my mare, and I'll come with you quietly."

Ravn's eyes rake over my face. "We always treat animals with respect. As well as girls who don't lie or try to steal from us." He gives a jerk of his head and the two brawny men move to flank me. "We'll talk again later, Thyra Winther. I've a feeling you'll have more to tell me once you've time to think things over."

The men march me to the edge of the clearing, where I spy a small stone shed hidden beneath the drooping limbs of a pine tree. One of the wanderers pulls an ornate metal key from his pocket and opens the padlock holding the wooden door fast. Without a word the other man shoves me through the half-open portal. I stumble and fall onto the hard-packed dirt floor, catching myself with my hands. The door slams behind me, and I hear the rattle of the padlock as the key is turned, sealing me inside a small, windowless room. It's dark and musty—the only air seeps in through the bundles of thatch that cover the wooden rafters. I slump back onto my heels and glance about me, but can't see anything except the vague outlines of lumpy sacks and wooden boxes.

One of the sacks shifts and I realize it's a person, curled against a stack of boxes. "Who's there?" asks my fellow prisoner.

I recognize that voice. "Just another traveler," I tell Gerda. "Caught by the wanderers while searching for something I've lost."

"You're a woman?" Gerda's voice radiates relief. Of course it's only natural she'd fear some strange man thrown into a locked room with her.

"Yes. And you, it seems."

"I'm just a girl." Gerda shifts again and I hear the rustle of her gown and petticoats. "I wish I could see you, or move closer, but they've chained my ankle to a ring in the wall."

"Oh," I think quickly. There's no advantage in Gerda getting a good look at me. I've abandoned my illusionary appearance to give my mind a respite. "Me too."

"Really?" There's a tinge of suspicion coloring Gerda's voice. "But no one came in with you, did they?"

I don't reply and Gerda sighs deeply. "Or maybe they did." Desperation sharpens her tone. "I don't know anymore. It seems I've lost all sense of time."

"What's your name?" I settle back against the rough stone wall.

"Gerda. Gerda Lund. What's yours?"

"Clara," I reply, using the first name that comes to mind. "Clara Hess."

"I know a Clara." A wistful note creeps into Gerda's voice. "She's my friend. She helped me, gave me her own jewels to aid me on my journey. But the wanderers took them. They stole everything, and threw me in here. I'd be dead, I think, except their leader's daughter took pity on me and begged her father to spare my life."

"Well, that's one blessing." I calculate the odds that Gerda, once freed, will simply return home. "Excuse my curiosity, but why are you traveling on your own, a young girl like you?"

Gerda's shadowy form straightens. "I'm looking for someone. A friend who's disappeared. I'm trying to find him so I can convince him to come home."

"Him? A boy, then?"

"A young man. He's seventeen. Almost eighteen."

"Surely old enough to travel then. Why do you feel such a need to track him down?"

"His father's gravely ill. He was caught in a great blizzard and now lies like one dead, seeing and hearing nothing." Gerda's words are spoken simply, but with great firmness. "Kai was upset over this, and felt guilty, though it wasn't his fault. Not at all. It was just some freak winter storm. No one's fault."

Oh, Gerda, there is fault, but none that can ever receive your forgiveness. Or Kai's. Because I could have saved that poor soul, if I'd been willing to risk my own life. *No, these thoughts can't touch me. Make them fade. Let them fall away.*

I press against the wall until the sharp edges of the stones bite into my back. "So, Kai. That's your friend's name?"

"Yes, Kai Thorsen. He's needed at home, you see. His family's quite frantic with worry. My family too. We've been friends forever and are very close."

"And you? You're upset he's gone, obviously. Is he … " I lighten my tone. "Is Kai more than a friend to you? Your sweetheart, perhaps?"

Gerda's silent for a moment. "Not exactly," she says at last, her voice very soft. "I mean, he wouldn't say so."

"And you? What would you say?" There is no real advantage in pursuing this line of questioning, but my curiosity overwhelms my logic.

"I hope to be, one day. I do love him. I guess I always have. But Kai's very clever. He's the smartest boy in our village." Admiration shines through Gerda's words. "So of course he wants to go to the university to study."

"I see." I sit forward, lacing my fingers together in my lap. "You'll wait for him, I suppose. And when he returns to the village after his schooling you can marry."

"Yes, well … " Gerda's voice falters. "I'd rather marry sooner than that. I'm almost sixteen, you know, and many girls in my village marry at that age. But Kai won't hear of it. He says he can't think of such things until he's finished with his studies."

"He sounds very wise."

"That's what my family says. They like that he wants to provide for me, but … "

"But?" I fight to keep any hint of irritation out of my tone.

Gerda's silent for a few minutes. When she speaks again, her voice trembles slightly. "Well, you're a woman. What do you think? I can't help but wonder, if someone loves you—really loves you—wouldn't they want to spend as much time with you as possible? I mean, as soon as they could? I'd be willing to marry Kai even without money, even if he's in school for years and years and we have to scrimp and make do or go hungry some days. Just so we're together. That's all that matters."

"You love him that much?" I contemplate Gerda's shadowy form. She's very young, of course, and ignorant of anything except her secluded corner of the world. I suppose her life holds few options other than marriage and children. I shift my position on the hard ground, concentrating on several equations to calm a strange wave of anxiety.

"Yes. I haven't told him all this, you understand. He knows I love him as a friend, but nothing more. I've never felt"—Gerda's voice cracks—"I've never been sure he feels the same, so I've been afraid to be so bold. Although this past year I've tried to do more to share my feelings, to show him how much I care."

"As you are now, by trailing him to the ends of the world?"

Gerda's head drops to her chest. "I suppose so."

"So you end up here, imprisoned, with no one to help you. I doubt your Kai would be happy to hear that."

"No, he wouldn't."

"I imagine"—I allow a tiny vine of magic to coil about my words— "Kai would prefer you safe at home, waiting patiently for his return."

"But what if he doesn't return?" Gerda's voice shakes. "What if he finds some other place, some other life he likes better? What then?"

"Then you must make a different life for yourself as well," I reply firmly. "Listen, Gerda. I may be able to get us out of here, but if I do, will you promise to go home and abandon this foolish quest?"

Gerda claps her hands. "Oh, Clara, really? I must get away from here and if you can help, I'd be so grateful." She sighs deeply. "But of course, I can't promise you I'll give up searching for Kai. I'd never promise that, even if my life depended on it."

"It might," I say, and grind my teeth.

"So be it. My life isn't worth much if I lose Kai."

I hear Gerda's sharp intake of breath as a swear word flies out of my mouth. "Honestly, your life's still valuable, Gerda, with or without some young man." I rise to my feet. "Love's not worth losing your life."

"I'm sorry you feel that way," Gerda says softly as the padlock rattles against the wooden door.

Light floods the room and I remember in that moment to alter my visage to match my first appearance in the clearing. One of the wanderers' bulky figures fills the doorway. "You." He points at me. "Follow me. Ravn wants to speak with you."

I move swiftly to the door, feeling Gerda's eyes on me. She obviously realizes I lied before, when I claimed to be chained to the wall, but I shrug off that minor complication. If my plan works she'll not see me again.

"Stay strong, Clara," Gerda calls out as I'm grabbed by the elbow and shoved out the door. "I'll pray for you."

Outside the small building the wanderer locks the door behind us. "So it's Clara now, is it?" He bares his teeth in a grimace that reminds me of a cornered wolf. "Well, well, Ravn will be interested to hear that." He grips my arm and pulls me toward a wagon enclosed in a wooden frame. It resembles a small house on wheels.

I climb meekly into the caravan, imagining the ice and snow I'll conjure when I flee this place, the shard safely tucked into my saddlebags. A storm the likes of which these people have never seen. A tale of devastation to tell for many years, around innumerable campfires.

CHAPTER FIFTEEN:
THE LURE OF FARAWAY LANDS

STEPPING INTO THE CARAVAN TRANSPORTS me to another world. The wood interior's painted gleaming white, a perfect backdrop for the riot of brilliant fabrics draping the walls. Lanterns hung on wrought iron brackets cast an amber glow.

Ravn is standing at the far end of the wagon, his back to the entrance. My escort crosses swiftly to the shorter man and whispers something in his ear before brushing roughly past me and taking up a position just outside the door.

Seated cross-legged on one of the upholstered benches lining the two longer walls is a young girl. She's wearing a voluminous white blouse over crimson breeches. Her dark eyes shine like enamel against her olive skin.

She runs one hand through her lustrous black hair. "What's your name? Are you a friend of Gerda?" The girl shoots a glance at Ravn's back. "Who is she, Papa?"

"That's the problem, Mirela. We don't really know." Ravn turns to face me. "Apparently she possesses more than one name."

I lift my chin and level my most imperious gaze on the dark-haired man. "I am Thyra Winther. I told you that before."

"So who's this Clara our other prisoner mentioned?"

"It's an alias, of course." I shrug. "The girl's *your* prisoner. I assume you've good reason to keep her captive. Why would I give some thief or vandal my real name?"

Mirela leaps to her feet. "Gerda's not a thief! She's just a girl searching for her lover."

Ravn shifts from foot to foot under his daughter's fierce gaze. "She was trespassing, like you, Thyra Winther. And as for her excuse"—Ravn casts a warning look at Mirela—"I'm not convinced by her story. She's far too young to be tracking a missing sweetheart."

Mirela tosses her head. "She's not. She's only a little younger than me."

"My point," says Ravn firmly.

I examine the two faces before me. Mirela's mouth is pursed in a pout, while Ravn's lips are pressed tightly together. I suspect there's a story behind their words. Perhaps something I can turn to my advantage.

"I can't imagine such a girl's any threat to you." I smile coolly as Ravn unsheathes his knife. "And I certainly pose no danger." I watch Ravn toy with the weapon and consider freezing those long, tapering fingers until they blacken and fall from his hands.

Ravn slices the air with the knife. "That remains to be seen. Now, take a seat and tell me, why do you seek a piece of a broken looking-glass?" He points the tip of the blade toward the side of the caravan.

I stride to the padded bench and sit, keeping my eyes on Ravn and his knife. Mirela settles into the cushions next to me. "It's part of a mirror that belongs to my master, the mage Mael Voss. Perhaps you've encountered him during your travels?"

Ravn's eyes narrow. "I've heard the name."

I lean into the embroidered pillows behind my back. "If you know of Voss, then you're also aware of his power. While he may not be able to track you everywhere, his reach is long. Do you wish to anger him? You may find your travel restricted to lands that lie far from Voss's realm."

Ravn's smile tightens. "No man controls our movements."

"Voss might, if you refuse to give me the mirror fragment."

Mirela glances from me to her father, fingering her gold necklace. "This?" Surprise colors her voice. She frees the long chain from the folds of her linen blouse and holds it out before her breast. A small object dangles from the chain. It winks in the flickering lantern light.

It's the final shard, encased in an oval frame of gold.

"Yes, that's what I seek." I struggle to keep my hands in my lap.

Mirela closes her fingers over the pendant. "But this was my mother's. And her mother's before her. It's been passed down in our family for generations."

Ravn doesn't meet his daughter's pleading gaze. He keeps his eyes on me. "So—you're Mael Voss's emissary? Why didn't you say so when we met?"

"I was assessing the situation."

"I see. Being thrown into a shed with another prisoner was part of this survey?" Ravn sheathes the knife and takes a seat on the other bench.

I order my thoughts. It won't do for Ravn or his daughter to suspect my real connection to Gerda. "It was. I wanted to see if your prisoner was also seeking the shard."

"She isn't," insists Mirela. "I told you—she's looking for her lover, Kai. Papa wanted to kill her because she was grabbing one of our ponies, but I stopped him." Mirela matches her father's scowl. "I know stealing's wrong, but she was just desperate. Love can drive you to do almost anything, you know."

"I'm afraid I don't," I reply as the girl turns to me, her dark eyes filled with emotion.

"That's enough, Mirela." Ravn leans back and crosses his arms over his chest. "Our guest isn't interested in your notions of love."

So I'm now a guest. I stretch out my legs and relax my clenched hands.

Mirela sighs gustily. "I know what love is." She slumps into the corner where the bench abuts a brightly painted cabinet.

"You think you do." Ravn smiles at me. "Please forgive my daughter. She believes love trumps wisdom."

"Gerda will do anything to find her Kai," mutters Mirela. "She loves him and lovers can't be kept apart. Just like Paavo and me." Mirela's dark eyes flash as she casts a glance toward her father.

"Yes, yes, you and that foolish boy." Ravn raises his hands in a dismissive gesture. "A discussion for another time. Now we must consider our guest's request."

Mirela straightens, clutching the pendant. "You're not going to give her my necklace, are you?"

"I haven't decided." Ravn eyes me. "Voss's power can't be easily dismissed. If she's telling the truth I'm afraid we must relinquish the mirror fragment."

"No!" Mirela leaps to her feet. "I won't have it!" She stamps her booted foot.

Ravn's expression changes to something that would freeze anyone's blood but mine. "You have nothing to say about it." Ravn holds out his hand. "Give me the necklace, Mirela, or join your friend Gerda in the darkness."

Mirela chews on her lower lip. Her face is a stony mask but her hands are trembling. She inhales deeply before whipping the chain over her head and stepping forward to drop it in her father's open palm.

"Thank you, my daughter. Now, please leave us." Ravn motions toward the door.

Mirela's boots shake the floor as she stomps out of the wagon.

"Forgive my daughter." Ravn's expression softens. "She believes herself to be in love, you see. With the most unsuitable boy. Of course, it's all nonsense, but it leads her to do foolish things."

"Love often does, I'm told." I watch Ravn's hands as he rolls the golden chain between his fingers.

Ravn raises his eyebrows. "Don't you know? Ah well, I suppose you may be too young for such things. As is my daughter, though she claims otherwise."

"I know nothing of love." I shift on the bench, my gaze fastened on the pendant. It's time for a new subject. "I suppose you've traveled your whole life?"

"Yes, quite far and wide." Ravn balls up the chain and pendant in his palm and makes a fist, hiding the shard from my view. "As Voss's proxy surely you've traveled as well?"

"No, not really." I sink deeper into the cushions. My bones feel like melting ice. It's been some time since I've had any real rest.

"There's nothing like it." Ravn glances about the interior of the caravan. "This has been my place to sleep, never my home. My home is the road. Every place I travel becomes a part of me."

"Tell me," I say, not entirely sure why I'm encouraging his reminisces. I allow my head to drop back against the down-filled pillows.

Ravn smiles and speaks of mountains without snow and wide plains of golden grass, of cities whose spires pierce the sky and lakes whose depths have never been plumbed. Lands where great drifts of sand replace mounds of snow. Countries where men guide tall ships by the stars and women waltz about ballrooms with tiny replicas of those ships sailing through towering wigs. Ravn's words wrap about me like a blanket of soft wool as he talks of strange creatures and even odder human habits.

"Birds that talk?" I ask, wondering what sorcerers live in such realms.

Ravn shakes his head, as if guessing my thoughts. "It's not magic. They merely mimic what they hear."

"Have you ever seen"—I gaze at him from under my half-closed eyelids—"women attending any universities in these other lands?"

Ravn wrinkles his brow. "Few," he admits. "But I did see that, yes. Far from here, in warmer climes."

"Ah, far." I close my eyes. "So far away."

Ravn speaks again but after a few moments his words lose all meaning and I drift into a dreamless sleep.

I wake to sounds of shouting and metal hitting metal. Springing from the padded bench, I glance about and realize I'm alone. The noise is coming from outside.

As I stride to the door of the caravan, something moves against my neck. I raise my hands to my throat and touch the links of a chain. Sliding my fingers along its length I encounter a smooth oval object and pull it away from my body. It's the pendant containing the shard. Ravn must have slipped the necklace over my head while I was asleep. I stare at the mirror fragment for a moment, then tuck the pendant into the bodice of my gown, pleased my gamble's paid off. Ravn's obviously willing to trade the fragment for the freedom to travel through Voss's realms.

I make my way to the door and open it slowly, trying to determine the source of the commotion before I step outside. I poke my head out and a metal ladle flies past my ear.

Pots and pans and other cooking utensils are caught up in a whirlwind that swirls about the clearing. Standing near the fire, seemingly unaffected by the gale, is a tall, slender woman. Her auburn hair gleams like flame in the firelight. I pull my head back and crouch behind the door, peering out into the darkened clearing.

Sephia. I wonder if she's protecting Gerda or tracking me.

Ravn battles the gusts to reach the fire pit. The wind obliterates his words but I can imagine his rage as I watch him gesticulating wildly.

Sephia reaches out and covers his hands with hers. Instantly the wind dies down and the suspended objects fall to the ground with a clatter.

"Simply give me the girl," says Sephia. "I have no wish to cause you any more trouble."

Ravn faces the enchantress without flinching. "The girl, as you call her, tried to steal one of my ponies. She's a horse thief. I'm within my rights to kill her."

"But you haven't yet." Sephia's clear voice is filled with amusement. "I suspect you're not one to kill indiscriminately, Nicu Ravn."

"My daughter saved her." Ravn pulls his hands from Sephia's grasp. "She has a weakness for thwarted love."

Sephia's smile is clearly visible, even from a distance. "Ah, yes. Young girls often do."

I take a deep breath and push open the caravan door. As I step to the ground, I relinquish my illusionary form. Ravn's face reflects the shock most mortals display when they view my actual appearance, especially when I'm calling forth my power.

"Sephia, how surprising to find you here." I stride into the center of the clearing.

"Who are you?" Ravn moves away as I draw closer. He's glancing about and his hands are clenched. When his gaze falls on a dark-haired girl standing at the edge of the clearing he visibly relaxes. Of course, he's making certain his daughter's safe.

"I am Thyra Winther." I say to Ravn. "And I am the Snow Queen."

"Here to stop Gerda, are you?" Sephia smiles sweetly. "Perhaps you should have spoken with her instead of sleeping." Sephia's eyes are as green as spring leaves.

"I have spoken with her." I pace slowly, circling the enchantress. "I know she's determined to locate her friend, Kai Thorsen."

"The boy she loves."

"Yes. But I think, if you care, you'd encourage her to go home. Especially after this incident. She's fortunate to still be alive."

"That would suit you, wouldn't it, Snow Queen?" Sephia lays her hand on Ravn's arm, preventing him from moving away from us. "Then you'd be free to complete the mirror with no interference."

"What mirror?" Ravn's dark eyes sweep over me, his gaze coming to rest on the golden chain about my neck. "You lied to me."

I touch the chain with two fingers. "I didn't lie. I simply didn't tell you the whole truth."

"You didn't reveal your true form."

"No, I did not. But you see, I am that other girl too. Just Thyra Winther."

Ravn's eyes darken. "You're not *just* anything. I gave you the mirror fragment, thinking you an emissary from Mael Voss. Now I find you're the Snow Queen, with magic of your own. How do I know you won't keep the shard for yourself, and my people will still suffer Voss's wrath?"

"I've no interest in the mirror once it's completed." I shove my unruly white curls away from my face. "And I've no desire to see you or your people punished. The shard's in my possession—that's enough. Now, if Sephia will allow me to depart without further incident, I'll trouble you no more."

Sephia moves toward me. "I cannot permit you leave with that necklace."

I throw up my hand, palm facing out. A blast of cold air knocks Ravn off his feet. Sephia plants her legs apart, bending but not crumpling under the force of the freezing gusts. Her fingers trace a figure-eight in the air and a warm breeze swirls through my icy whirlwind.

A column of mist forms as our winds collide, filling the clearing with clouds. There is nothing but whiteness, punctuated in the next instant by Sephia's hand thrusting toward me. I grab her fingers and allow blighting cold to seep through my skin.

The acid touch of frost forces Sephia to rip her fingers from my hand. She cries out in pain as the mist clears, disclosing a tableau of Ravn and several of his men flanking the enchantress. Sephia stares at me, her emerald eyes glittering. She's cradling her injured hand against her breast.

"This one"—Sephia jabs toward me with her other hand—"brings nothing but death. Ice and snow and the blight of winter. Will you not cast your lot with me? Give me Gerda and I will protect you from this frozen queen."

"Can you do so?" Ravn stares pointedly at Sephia's hand. He shakes his head. "This is not my fight. I want no more dealings with either one of you." He motions for the burly man who acted as my guard earlier. "Go—bring the girl from the shed. I'll release her." He glances from Sephia to me. "But not into either one of your hands."

"What will you do with her?" Sephia straightens and tosses her head. A faint scent of roses wafts through the clearing.

"Give her a pony and send her on her way." Ravn smiles as Mirela runs to him from the edge of the clearing. "As my daughter wishes." He wraps his arms around Mirela, who presses her dark head against his shoulder.

The enchantress levels her stare on me. "Very well. I will not interfere. But you may wish to detain this one. She wants to harm the girl."

"I don't." I shake the remnants of icy power from my hands. "I'll do nothing, if you allow me to leave with the shard." I meet Sephia's gaze and hold it. "But if you attempt to take the fragment of the mirror, I promise you"—I clasp my hands about the golden chain—"I'll track down Gerda and slow her heart as she sleeps. She'll fall into a state no spring warmth can thaw."

Sephia looks down her nose at me. "I'll protect her."

"You forget, Sephia—you can't travel to my realm. While Gerda must, if she's to find Kai." I turn as Sephia's eyes darken. I stride over to the milling horses and grab Freya's halter. "If someone will provide my tack, I'll take my leave."

Ravn barks out orders and Freya's soon saddled and bridled. Swinging up on the mare's back, I cast a final, icy glare about the clearing. I kick Freya into a trot as a guard leads Gerda, blinking and shaking, from the stone shed. Mirela rushes to her side as Sephia nods at Ravn and stalks out of the clearing.

"Do not follow me, if you value your life," I call over my shoulder as I guide Freya into the woods. Gerda's clear voice is carried on the wind, asking who I am, but I'm too far away to hear if she receives any answer.

CHAPTER SIXTEEN:
THE FROZEN PRINCE

BAE'S STANDING IN THE PADDOCK when I ride into the yard outside the stables. His liquid brown eyes follow my every move as I dismount and hand Freya's reins to a waiting groom, a polar bear whose fur-backed hands tremble slightly. I read pain and confusion in the bear's black eyes. It's the expression all our animal servants wear—the look that asks why they've been ripped from their natural state and transformed into creatures neither fully human nor truly animal. I turn away.

"So, you've returned, Snow Queen."

I turn to face Bae. "I have the final missing shard. The mirror will be completed."

"And Voss will have eternal life, and you will have, what?" The reindeer lifts its shaggy head and stares at me.

"My own immortality, as the Snow Queen."

Bae snorts. "Are you certain of this, Thyra Winther? You only have Voss's word, and what is that worth?"

I yank off my gloves and stuff them in my pockets. "He wouldn't lie to me about such a thing."

"Truly? You know his other lies. What proof do you have that he will keep any promises?" The reindeer rubs his muzzle against a fencepost, as if scratching an itch.

"He can't control that aspect of the enchantment. His own magic constrains him. If I complete the mirror before my eighteenth birthday I'm freed from the curse of the wraiths and will reign as Snow Queen forever."

Bae shakes his head, jangling the metal on his halter. The sunlight reflecting off his dark eyes lends them a blue hue. "And that's what you desire?"

"It's better than the alternative."

"To remain in some strange, hybrid form forever? I am not so sure, Snow Queen."

A series of excited yips makes me turn as Luki races through the kitchen door. The wolf barrels across the yard, his tail waving like a flag. When he reaches me he leaps up and places his paws upon my waist.

"Come to greet me, have you?" I rub Luki's shoulders before gently taking hold of his front legs and lowering him to the ground. He leans heavily against me, his amber eyes shining. His tongue slides over his sharp white teeth as he pants with excitement.

"The wolf has missed you," observes Bae. "He did not take his daily runs, simply lay at the kitchen door or in the stables, waiting for your return."

"Foolish creature." I pat Luki's head. "I hope you at least ate something while I was gone."

Bae's eyes glisten. "He did, but the other one did not."

"Who, Kai?" Luki bumps his muzzle into my leg. I reach down and scratch behind his twitching ears.

"Yes, Gerda's friend. I don't think he's ever left the room that holds the mirror, or at least not to eat or rest. I could look up and see his shadow moving behind the windows at all hours of the day or night." Bae expels a gusty sigh. "Tell me, in your travels, did you receive any news of the little miss?"

"You mean Gerda?" I eye the reindeer, attempting to read the thoughts that spark behind his placid visage. "She's safe, though only through others' interventions. If she possesses any wisdom she's on way back home. But I doubt that's the case. She's unusually determined for someone so young and inexperienced."

"She has a big heart." Bae drops his head and paws at the frozen ground. "Do not underestimate her, Snow Queen. Her love grants her great power."

"Well, love will scarcely keep her warm if she attempts to cross into my lands." I toss back my heavy hair. "If her heart magically guides her to our realm she'll surely freeze before reaching this palace."

"You do not understand love." Bae's gaze fastens on me.

I swear I read pity in his dark eyes. I spin and stride away from him, Luki at my heels.

The palace is dark. I can't call forth illumination in the ice-block walls fast enough to prevent a cluster of wraiths from swarming my path. Luki growls but their desperation drives them forward.

"You have it," they whine. "The final piece. Give it to me."

I swat at their amorphous limbs. "Back to the shadows, you foolish wretches." Luki howls as I spit out the words.

"Soon," they shriek as they fall back into a darkened corridor.

This does not touch me ...

I stride off, wiping my hands on my tunic. Luki follows, still growling softly.

Drawing in a deep breath, I throw back the doors to the Hall.

Kai's bent over the mirror, moving shards around with one hand. He glances up as Luki and I enter the room. "Do you have it?" There's a rasp in his voice. His thin face is blanched white as fine linen.

"I do." I direct Luki to wait at the door while I cross to the table. "You've accomplished much in the short time I've been gone." The mirror reflects my pale face. Only one corner of the surface is missing.

Kai straightens with a grimace. "Has it been only a little time? I've lost all sense of day and night."

I examine him critically. Dark shadows encircle his reddened eyes and sharp lines bracket his mouth. "Have you slept at all? Or eaten anything?"

"No. Not since I returned. I was able to place the fragment from the university, but the rest"—he waves his hand toward the box of shards—"elude me."

"Well, I do have the final missing piece." I pull the necklace from the inner pocket of my cloak. As I toss it onto the table Kai's tired eyes narrow.

"Grab that bin of tools." His fingers tremble as he lifts the necklace.

"I'm not your lackey." I reach for the golden chain.

Kai takes two steps back, clutching the necklace to his chest. "I need those tools to extract the shard."

"No one's debating that. I was merely offering to hold the pendant while you collected the tools." I stare at Kai, evaluating the odd look in his eyes. There's something empty about his stare. Something that reminds me of the mindless focus of the wraiths.

"Never mind." Kai pockets the necklace and scuttles over to the bin holding a selection of tools. He rummages through the box, tossing out several items. They bounce off the stone floor with a *clang*. One mallet skids toward me, skittering to a stop at the toe of my boot.

"Careful," I say, leaning over to pick up the object. A pair of metal pinchers flies over my bent form. It would have hit my head had I remained standing. "No need for such a rush." I straighten and fix my stare on Kai's back.

"So you say." Kai hurries back to the table, clutching a fistful of tools. He drops them on the table and gently lays the necklace beside them. "But it isn't your father."

"No, only my life."

Kai turns his gaze on me. "Thyra," he says, as if he's just recognized me. "Thank you."

"For what?" I frown as his eyes dim again, shadowed like the sun sliding behind clouds.

"Obtaining the shard, of course." Kai bends over the pendant, his hands carefully manipulating the delicate tools. After several minutes he lifts the fragment from its golden frame. "Not damaged in the slightest." He holds the glass to the light.

"You should take a break." I move closer to Kai. "I can work on the mirror for a while. Perhaps I may be able to position those shards that have defeated you."

Kai lowers his arm, his fingers curling about the jagged glass. "Nothing's defeating me. I'm the one who's fit together most of the pieces of your precious looking-glass over these last months, or have you forgotten?" His eyes are flat and reflective as the mirror. "You'd never have gotten anywhere close to completing it without me."

I stare at him. His face is all angles—sharp cheekbones and a razor slice of jaw. If his hair was white, he'd resemble a young Mael Voss.

A trickle of red slides from under his fingers. "Your hand's bleeding." My gaze follows the trail of blood as it drips to the floor.

He lowers his arm and uncurls his fingers. Crimson blossoms in his palm. He plucks the shard from the blood and blindly wipes it on his tunic before depositing it on the table.

"Here," I lean closer and press my silk handkerchief into his palm.

Kai roughly shoves me aside. I hear a deep rumbling and spin about to see Luki crouched low, his belly dragging the ground, his snout thrust out straight before him. His lips are pulled back, displaying the knife-points of his incisors. His ears are pinned flat against his skull as he advances on us. No, not us. On Kai.

"No, Luki." I step between the wolf and the boy. "He's not hurting me. He can't harm me." I kneel and put my arms about Luki, burying my fingers in his thick fur. Luki relaxes under my touch, then whimpers and lifts his head. I sit back on my heels, dropping my hands in my lap. "Never attack Kai, you understand?" I stare into the golden eyes of the wolf, who finally blinks and thrusts his muzzle into my hands, licking at my fingers.

"Perhaps it's time he lived outside," says Kai.

I give Luki's head a final pat before rising to my feet. "That's rich, since you're the one who pushed him on me in the first place."

Kai's huddled over the mirror. My handkerchief's tied about the hand he's using to shift fragments about. "He's almost grown. Time he was returned to the wild or at least left outdoors." Kai appears oblivious to the blood still trickling onto the mirror.

I reach over and grab Kai's wrist. "You're dripping. I think you'd better go and wash up and wrap a decent bandage about that cut before you've anything more to do with this."

Kai turns on me, his eyes flashing in his pale face. "You'd like that, wouldn't you? Get me out of the way so you can finish the mirror and take all its power for yourself."

I release his wrist and step back. "Not my intention, as you know. I think you need some sleep, Kai."

Our stares lock for a long moment before Kai sighs deeply. "You're right." He rubs at his eyes with his uninjured hand. "I can't think straight anymore. All I see before me are mirror shards and equations." He slumps against the table. "And I hear those horrible wraiths constantly, like a whistling in my ears."

"You need food and sleep. In that order. Go to the kitchens and then to bed. You're no use to me like this."

Kai straightens and steps around me. "I don't do this for you."

"I know. But what benefits me aids you as well. Don't forget that," I warn him as he crosses the room.

"How can I?" he calls back, striding into the hall. "When you won't let me?"

I work on the mirror for several hours, finally placing two more pieces. It's more difficult as we reach the end of the reconstruction, and I mentally acknowledge the validity of Kai's frustration. As the light wanes I turn to stare out the tall windows. Luki lies curled in the last patch of sun with his nose touching the tip of his tail. He lifts his head as I stretch and shake the tension from my arms and fingers.

"I think that's all for today," I tell the wolf. "Tomorrow Kai and I can work together. We're so close … " I glance back at the table.

Luki rises to his feet and pads over to me. I pat him absently as I stare out across the winter landscape. Two eagles spiral one another in the darkening sky. I cross to the windows to follow their soaring flight.

Something catches my eye on the ground and I glance down into the snow-covered yard. Bae circles the paddock, dashing from corner to corner as if chased by some predator. But that's impossible—our transformed bears keep any such creatures at bay. There's something dark pressed against the fence, though. A human form.

It's Kai. I watch as he throws out one arm, hurling something into the paddock. I don't understand the logic of this. It makes no sense, but Kai's tossing some type of missile at the frightened reindeer.

"Come, Luki." I stride out of the Great Hall and swiftly make my way down to the kitchens, the wolf trotting at my heels. The doors to the yard are standing open, allowing snow to drift across the kitchen floor. Luki leaps in front of me and leads the way outside.

"What are you doing?" I shout as I approach the paddock.

Kai's entered the enclosure and stands at the reindeer's head, gripping its halter with both hands. The bandage that wraps his injured hand matches the whites of Bae's rolling eyes.

"Trying to get this abomination to give me news of home." Kai's voice cuts the cold air like a blade. "I know it can speak, but it tells me nothing."

"I thought you were going to bed." I hold out my palm, forcing Luki to sit as I climb over the fence.

Kai's face resembles a relief carved in ice. Only his eyes show any signs of life and they burn coldly, like banked coals. "I did. But then I dreamed—a nightmare about Gerda, lost in a blizzard, frozen like my father, but truly dead. She lay buried in a snow drift, her skin as blue as her eyes. Then I saw my mother and our friends, prostrate with grief as Gerda's sisters wept and drowned in a lake of their own tears."

"It was only a dream." I approach with measured steps, holding out my hand. "Come now, leave Bae be." I eye the whip dangling from Kai's fingers.

"He will speak to me first." Kai releases the grip of one hand, then swings his arm and cracks the whip hard across the reindeer's muzzle.

I jump aside as the reindeer rears back and slashes out with his front hooves. Kai's hit on the shoulder by the edge of one hoof. He falls into me, knocking both of us to the stone-hard ground. The scent of damp hair and hide fills my nostrils as Bae leaps across our bodies and flies over the wall of the paddock. I struggle to my feet, attempting to gather enough magic to stop the reindeer in his tracks. But it's too late—Bae has already sailed into the sky and disappeared into a bank of violet-tinged clouds.

"How's that possible?" Kai sits, rubbing his shoulder and wincing. "I thought he was under an enchantment. How is it possible for him to escape?"

I stare into the sky. "I don't know. Perhaps his fear and anger gave him the power to break away. Magic can be occasionally mastered by will alone." Turning my gaze on Kai, I adopt my frostiest tone. "What were you thinking, hitting him like that? What logical purpose could that ever serve?"

"None, none," mutters Kai, burying his face in his hands and rocking back and forth. When he lifts his head there are tears streaking his pale cheeks. "I hit him. I never hit animals, never. But I wanted to hurt him, to make him feel pain. Because I'm in pain, Thyra. I'm here in a frozen wasteland, lost in a palace haunted by specters, living in a world devoid of love and laughter, trying to accomplish the impossible, and I'm feeling so much pain … "

I extend my hand and Kai silently grips it, staring into my eyes as I help him to his feet. "You need more rest." I infuse a touch of magic into my words.

Kai's eyelids flutter and he nods. He follows me meekly into the palace, Luki padding in front of us. I deposit Kai in his chambers, weaving more magic so he passes out the moment he falls across the bed. I stay just long enough to cover him with a bearskin throw and ensure he experiences a long, dreamless, sleep.

In my own chambers, with Luki resting at my feet, I slump in a chair and stare moodily into the fire. It's only natural for Kai to buckle under the pressure of our painstaking task, and to feel alienated and altered in this strange, cold, palace. A frozen wasteland, haunted by specters, where one must accomplish the impossible. Yes, he was correct in that assessment.

Luki lays his head across my feet and sighs. I lean forward to stroke his silver-tipped fur before I sit back and draw a blanket about my shoulders. Of course I don't feel the cold, not really, but the weight of the throw is comforting.

A world devoid of love and laughter. Enough to make anyone lose all sense of right, of self.

Kai's been in the palace for a few months.

I've lived here for years.

I wish I had the magic to provide myself a peaceful rest, but such power is beyond me.

CHAPTER SEVENTEEN: COLD CALCULATIONS

I WAKE TO A STAND-OFF. A rabbit huddles at the small opening cut in the door, clutching a folded piece of paper in its hand-like paws. Its eyes dart from me to Luki, who's crouched down, nose twitching, as he stares at the hare.

"Luki, leave it alone." I straighten in the chair, rubbing at the crick in my neck. Obviously I never made it to my bed last night.

The rabbit's trembling so hard it drops the paper. With one terrified glance at me it scoots through the opening and disappears.

"Now look at what you've done." I shake my finger at Luki as I rise stiffly to my feet. "You really must stop stalking our servants."

The wolf's ears perk up at the sound of my indulgent chiding. He pads over to me, tail swishing back and forth.

"So, what do you think this is all about, boy?" Luki thrusts his muzzle into my palm and I pat him before I retrieve the paper abandoned by the frightened rabbit.

It's a summons from Voss. I'm to meet with him in the Great Hall as soon as I'm dressed.

So the mage has returned. I briefly speculate what he might want with me this time.

"You'd better have your breakfast and then take a run," I tell Luki as I change into a clean gown. "You know how Voss feels about wolves."

Luki yips twice. His amber eyes shine with such intelligence I almost believe he comprehends my meaning. I motion for him to follow me out of the room and lead him to the kitchens.

As I cut up some rabbit from a previous supper, it occurs to me many of our animal servants must live in constant terror. Their natural instincts are subsumed but not eradicated by Voss's enchantments. A rabbit is still a rabbit, after all, even if it has hands. The bear and lynx and other predators roaming our halls are conjured into creatures that can't attack their fellow servants, but the lust of the hunter still gleams in their eyes.

I toss the rabbit onto a pewter platter and set the food in front of Luki. "I suppose I shouldn't be too hard on you for chasing our servants," I tell the wolf. "You can't know the difference between the creatures we eat and those that serve us." I wait until he's absorbed in his meal before I depart, closing the door behind me so Luki will have no alternative but to stay in the kitchens or run outside. I've no desire to remind Voss of the wolf's existence.

When I reach the Great Hall I'm shocked to see Kai. "What are you doing here?"

"I was summoned." Kai holds up a folded piece of paper.

"It seems we both were." I stare at the double doors for a moment, tapping my foot. "Listen, Kai, you must be careful. Voss is dangerous. He may look human, but he isn't, not really."

"So I assumed." Kai shrugs. "Don't concern yourself with me. I can take care of myself."

I lift my chin and fix him with my most imperious glare. "Don't assume too much, Kai Thorsen. You've never encountered a wizard before."

"I've dealt with you."

"Not the same thing. I've magic, but I only use it when necessary. For logical purposes. Voss"—I bite the inside of my cheek, remembering certain previous encounters with the mage—"delights in wielding power for its own sake. He's been known to take pleasure in the pain of others."

I meet Kai's intense stare. It's as if he's trying to extract a clue from my carefully composed expression

"How long have you lived here, Thyra?" he asks in a subdued tone.

"Long enough." I toss off the words before throwing open the doors and striding into the Great Hall.

Voss is standing by the table, his fingers stroking the completed surface of the mirror. "Ah, Thyra, how nice of you to finally answer my invitation."

"I had some other business to attend to this morning." I cross the room and take a stand at the foot of the table.

Voss's ice-clear eyes survey me with barely disguised displeasure. "You are quite haughty for one who faces a rather unpleasant future, my queen." He shifts his gaze over my shoulder. "And what have we here? Kai Thorsen, the village boy who's mastered a few mathematical concepts." Voss bends forward in a mocking semblance of a bow. "So pleased to meet you, Master Kai. Your work with the mirror has been exemplary. I am, frankly, amazed."

Kai steps up beside me. I glimpse his scowl out of the corner of my eye and clench my fists.

"I'm only here because you summoned me, Master Voss." Kai's voice drips with indignation. "What is it you want with me?"

Voss plucks at the jewel-encrusted edge of his indigo robe. "My, my, you two are well-matched in pride as well as intellect. Be careful, my boy." The expression on Voss's face shifts to something that makes my fingernails dig into my palms. "You only remain alive at the Snow Queen's pleasure. She apparently values you, or at least your mental abilities. I, however"— Voss whirls around, turning his back to us—"do not."

"You did ask us to meet with you, Master." I do my best to modulate my tone to something resembling deference.

"Yes, well, I thought you should know about a certain problem. One that you, Thyra, have already been dealing with, I believe."

I feel Kai's hand brush mine as he turns to me. I ignore his questioning stare. "Oh, what problem is that? We've faced several, as you know. Such as finding the three missing shards—the ones you never bothered to mention to me."

Voss turns around slowly. His face gleams, pale as a skull. "The young woman trailing your assistant, Snow Queen. A most determined girl."

"What girl?" Kai's voice cracks on the word. "Gerda?" Kai steps away and stares at me accusingly.

I take a deep breath before replying. "Yes, your shadow. She's been trying to find you ever since you left home."

"You've seen her?" Kai's dark brows draw together. He slams his fist into his bandaged palm and winces.

"A few times, yes. Don't worry. She's safe, or at least she was the last time I saw her."

"Perhaps not at this moment, though," interjects Voss. The good humor in his voice doesn't bode well for Gerda.

I cross to the mage, standing toe to toe with him. "What do you mean? Don't toy with me, where is she?"

Voss looks me up and down. "Do you actually care? How extraordinary."

"I care because she could disrupt our work." I give a jerk of my head toward Kai.

"A problem you must solve, my queen. And the reason I wished to speak with you." Voss lifts his hands and spreads his fingers wide. "It has come to my attention one of our conjured creatures has escaped."

"Bae? What's he got to do with anything?" I feel a flush of heat rise in my face.

Kai frowns and pulls at the collar of his tunic. "Yes, what's the reindeer have to do with Gerda?"

Molten metal runs through my veins. I stare into Voss's bone-white face. "Bae's found Gerda, hasn't he?"

Kai gasps and grabs for my arm to steady his shaking limbs. "What's going on?"

"Stop it!" I cover Kai's hand, locking it onto my wrist. "No need to torture the boy."

"He's responsible for the loss of a valuable resource." Voss's eyes shine as clear and hard as diamonds.

"And he's the reason your mirror will soon be completed." I spit the words at the mage from between clenched teeth. "Harm him, or me, and what will you do? Raise up yet another Snow Queen from among the foolish village maidens? That hasn't worked so well for you in the past."

"Or for them." Voss curls his fingers into his palms and drops his hands to his side.

The heat searing my body drains away. I look to Kai as he straightens, still gasping for air. "All right now?"

Kai nods, and his dark eyes search my face for a moment. *Thank you*, he mouths at me as Voss turns from us.

"At any rate," the mage says, "I have received word that one of my enchanted creatures—yes, the reindeer Master Kai allowed to escape—has met up with this girl Gerda. She could never cross the mountains or journey through our realm on her own, but with a flying reindeer's assistance … "

"She's headed here?" I release my grip on Kai's hand and step around to face Voss.

"So I am told." Voss dips his fingers into the bin holding the few remaining shards. "It would be a pity for your excellent work to be interfered with in any way. That is why I tell you this, Snow Queen, and why I am conjuring a storm that will remove this distraction once and for all." He pivots, almost catching me with his razor-sharp elbow. "I tell you this so you can cease your excursions to waylay this girl and concentrate on your work here."

Kai's instantly by my side. "You'd better not do anything to harm Gerda."

The mage smiles. It is not a pleasant expression.

Kai's moving too close to Voss. I put out my arm to bar his forward motion.

Kai grabs my hand and whips me around to face him, pulling us so close our noses bump. "And you," he says, holding me fast. "What does he mean about your waylaying Gerda? What have you done?" His breathing is shallow.

"Nothing but attempt to convince her to return home." I concentrate cold into the wrist he holds until he drops it and steps away, shaking out his fingers. "I'd think that would meet with your approval."

"Now children," the pleasure in Voss's voice puts me on guard, "no need to fight with one another. I would like to see you both back to work on my mirror, as soon as possible. Thyra really has little time left, you know, and I must confess she's right—I doubt any other village girl possesses her particular abilities. Even with my training, they always fall short. So if you wish the mirror completed, Master Kai, you had best follow her lead."

I've never told Voss of the lie I used to capture Kai, but when I meet his gaze I realize he knows. He continues to smile, but all I see is a grinning death mask.

"What do you mean about a storm?" I ask, shaking my head at Kai when he opens his mouth to speak.

Voss shrugs. "Just a minor blizzard. Nothing you couldn't conjure yourself, Snow Queen, if your mind was on your duties."

"Blizzard?" Kai's dark eyes blaze with anger. "Now, just a minute ..."

I should have frozen Kai's mouth shut. I step in front of him, blocking his path to Voss. "I doubt a blizzard's required. Send enough snow and clouds to make Bae lose his way and perhaps they'll simply turn back."

"*Perhaps* does not suit my plans." Voss whips his robes about his skeletal form. "I am afraid you have no influence in this matter, Thyra Winther. I must punish my rogue reindeer before all our enchanted animals consider fleeing. The girl is collateral damage, but it's probably best if she is eliminated, all things considered."

I step on Kai's foot as he shouts, "Eliminated!" Turning to face him, I stare into his eyes, conveying a need for silence.

"It really is your fault." Voss glides toward the doors. "Both of you. Now concentrate on the mirror. Time is running out. I would hate for Thyra to become a wraith." Before entering the hall he turns to cast a final threatening glance in our direction. "And, Master Kai, just so we are clear—if you fail, your father will not be the only tragedy to affect your family."

Kai's in my face as soon as Voss disappears. "He's going to kill Gerda and Bae!"

"He's going to try." I capture Kai's flailing hands in my own and lower them to his sides. "It's never any use going up against Voss on his own terms. But he's fickle. He'll conjure the storm and assume all is well, especially if I can arrange for a distraction. That will give us time to act."

"Distraction? Whatever are you talking about?" Kai paces to the windows. "And what can we do?" He slumps against the sill and slides to the floor, his back pressed against the wall. "It's all my fault." He drops his head into his hands. "Gerda and Bae. My fault. Just like my father … "

"Stop it." I march over and kneel in front of him. "Stop sniveling and use that brilliant mind of yours, Kai Thorsen. Or would you rather just give up and turn into a useless whiner, no better than the wraiths?"

He throws up his head, banging it back into the stones. "You really are cold, aren't you?"

I rise to my feet, brushing furiously at my gown, refusing to meet his eyes. His words sting more than I expect. Why should I care what Kai thinks of me? "I'm smart, inventive, and willing to save your little friend. Are you coming with me, or do you prefer to cower in the palace?"

Kai grabs the window sill and pulls himself up to face me. "I'm in." He takes hold of my hand in a tight clasp. "Whatever it takes to save Gerda and Bae."

"Well, dress for a snowstorm and meet me in the stables as soon as possible." I pat his hand awkwardly.

His eyes widen as Kai glances from his hand to my face. I can read surprise in his expression, and something else. Something that makes me bite the inside of my cheek to keep from exhaling the breath I'm holding.

Kai lifts our hands and kisses my knuckles. "Whatever you say, my queen." He flashes me a ghost of a smile. His expression sobers as he releases my hand. "If you help me save Gerda I'll be forever grateful."

I nod, unable to speak. For some reason the touch of his lips on my hand sparked like a static charge. I watch him stride out of the Great Hall before I lean against the windowsill and stare out at the desolate landscape.

Voss can conjure a blizzard as fierce as mine, and as deadly as the natural one that injured Kai's father. I sigh and turn from the vista to head for my chambers. I too must prepare myself for this rescue and, unlike Kai, I know just how dangerous it might be.

CHAPTER EIGHTEEN: A BLIGHTING FROST

K AI'S SEATED IN THE SLEIGH, clutching the reins too tight. The ponies side-step and paw at the ground. "Aren't you getting in? We've no time to waste."

I hold out my hand and whistle. A dark object hurtles from the threatening sky. It shrieks once before landing on my wrist. Swiveling its head it stares at me, unblinking. Its pupils are as dark and dead as beetles caught in amber.

"What do you want with a falcon?" Kai visibly relaxes as he releases one hand to pat Luki, who's leapt up into the sleigh beside him.

"He's one of our messengers." I use two fingers to smooth the speckled feathers on the bird's breast. He shrieks again and sinks his talons into the leather of my gauntlet-length gloves. I extract a rolled slip of paper from my pocket and insert it into the metal cylinder attached to the falcon's leg. Bending my head to his, I whisper an incantation to direct the bird to the intended recipient of my message. I throw my arm high to send the bird soaring back into the sky.

"Exactly who are you contacting?" Kai eyes me as I climb into the sleigh. "I didn't think you had any friends … " His face, framed by the fur-lined hood of his cloak, reddens.

"Not a friend." I take the reins from his hands. "But in this instance, possibly an ally."

We take off, sailing into the heavy banks of clouds. I can't see anything but the whiteness enveloping us. I concentrate and conjure a wind that swirls about the sleigh, breaking up the clouds just enough for me to guide the ponies toward the mountains.

"Kai, I must warn you—this storm won't be easy to navigate, even for me." I glance at the boy, who's peering into the heavy clouds.

He turns to gaze at me. "But you can control the snow and wind."

"I can, but this is no natural storm. And not one of my making. It's Voss's creation, and that makes it more difficult for me to master." I urge the ponies forward as the winds buffet the sleigh, swinging us to and fro. "Stay down, Luki," I command. The wolf's gray head disappears as he drops to the floor.

Kai's gloved hands grip the edge of the sleigh. "His power's greater than yours? Even over wintery weather?"

"Yes. He gave me my magic, remember. And taught me to use it. He knows how to create a blizzard that will challenge my powers." A gust whips my hood back, exposing my head. I blink as tiny ice crystals sting my face like a spray of needles.

Kai leans over and pulls my hood back over my hair. As I shoot him a grateful, look, I'm surprised by the searching gaze he's leveled on me. "You'd better hold onto something." I turn until my profile is hidden behind the edge of my hood. "We're in for a rough ride."

I focus on keeping the sleigh, and us, aloft. The ponies push bravely against the headwinds as snow swirls about their straining bodies. I concentrate all my magic to keep the worst of the blizzard at a distance, but all I can achieve is a bubble of lighter snow and wind. There's no glimpse of Gerda or Bae. Of course, we can't possibly see them, but even my attempts to sense their whereabouts are futile.

After some time I glance at Kai and notice the blue sheen veiling his face. He's huddled down in the seat, one hand gripping the side of the sleigh. The other hand clutches at the blanket that covers our laps and legs. His gloved fingers twitch, digging into the heavy fur. I redouble my efforts to warm his body with the shield I've cast over him, but logic tells me I can't provide enough protection, whatever the enchantment. Voss's unnatural storm is too powerful.

"We must find shelter," I say, but my words are lost to the roaring wind.

Kai turns to me with a questioning look. There's a violet tinge to his trembling lips.

"Shelter!" I shout and point toward a cave that's a barely discernible blot on the face of the looming mountain.

Kai shakes his head violently, but I hold the reins. I direct the ponies to land on the wide ledge skirting the cave. As they pull up before the dark opening, Kai leans in to me, gesticulating wildly.

"What are you doing?" His voice is rough as new-cut timber, and oozes anger like sap. "We can't stop. We haven't found them yet."

"You're freezing." I jump from the sleigh, throwing Kai the reins. He fumbles and drops them into his lap. "Your fingers will soon be blighted with frostbite, even in your gloves. We must seek shelter and wait for this storm to die down."

"We've no promise it will dissipate anytime soon." Kai crawls out of the sleigh, his whole body shaking. He stumbles and falls back against one of the ponies.

"Look, the ponies are also trembling with cold. We must wait this out. If my ally fulfills my request"—I unhitch the sleigh and grab hold of the lead pony's harness—"the storm will die down soon, and we can resume our search." I wait for Luki to leap out of the back of the sleigh before leading the ponies toward the mouth to the cave. "Come on. You're no use to Gerda, or me, or anyone, dead."

"But they could be freezing right now." Kai takes hold of the other bridle and aids me in guiding the ponies into the cave. Luki trots behind us, his nose twitching and his eyes alight.

"Bae knows how to survive a blizzard," I reply, as we move deeper into the darkness. The cave is shallow, merely an indentation in the cliff, but it offers protection from the worst of the storm. "I'm sure he's found shelter, as we have. And he can use his body to keep Gerda warm." I release the ponies, who wander over to one side of our stony shelter and huddle together.

Kai trails me to the back of the cave, the fur blanket draped over his arm. "I thought we might need this," he says, as he sinks to the hard stone floor. He presses his back against the cave wall and pulls the blanket over his trembling limbs.

Luki pads up to Kai and drops to the ground, curling his body into a tight ball as he nestles against Kai's right side.

"Good thinking." I sit on the other side of Kai. My skills allow me to avoid some of the biting cold but even I'm chilled. Voss's magic is too powerful to ignore completely.

Kai shifts and throws a portion of the blanket over me. "I wish I had your confidence in Bae. He's just a beast, after all, even if an enchanted one."

"Beasts can survive better in the wild than humans." I rest my back against the stone wall of the cave. "Gerda's safer with Bae than she'd be with you."

"Yes, I'm certainly not the safest person, as far as Gerda's concerned." There's a bitter edge to Kai's voice. "If it weren't for me, she'd be home."

"That was her choice." I lean in to Kai. "It might help if we're touching," I say, as Kai turns to look at me. "My magic might warm you better."

"Oh." Kai's dark eyes survey me with interest. "Well, that sounds logical." He places his arm about my shoulders and draws me close to his side.

My decision to rest was the correct choice. Kai's no longer shivering. I glance at his profile, relieved to see the blue tint fading from his face.

It's strange, feeling another human body close to mine. I close my eyes for a moment and recall the last time I was physically close to a mortal for any length of time. In the sleigh, pressed between my mother and father … I jerk upright.

"Something wrong?" Kai adjusts his arm until the back of my head is resting against his chest. Luki examines us for a moment before dropping his head across Kai's right leg.

"No. Just a memory." I hear his heart thudding through the thick layers of clothing separating our bodies. "Nothing significant." My own heart's fluttering like a moth mesmerized by a candle flame. I've never wanted so much to stay and to flee at the same time.

"This ally of yours," says Kai after a moment. "Who might that be?"

"Her name's Sephia. She's an enchantress and was once Voss's mentor. No friend of mine, I can assure you, but she does care for Gerda." I plunge ahead, telling Kai of my encounters with Sephia and the assistance she's provided his friend. "So you see, she wouldn't help us if it meant aiding me alone, but I suspect she might do as I ask to help Gerda, and to thwart Voss."

Kai tightens his grip on my shoulder. "What can she do, though? You say she can't travel into realms of ice and snow."

"No, but she can draw Voss to her, away from here. If his attention's diverted he won't be able to perpetuate this blizzard."

"Sounds like a gamble."

"But a calculated one."

Kai glances at me. "Logical Thyra Winther, always calculating."

I raise my head and adjust my position so I'm leaning against Kai's arm instead of his chest. "And what's wrong with that?"

"Nothing, nothing at all." A faint smile flits over Kai's face. "It's just unusual, in my experience."

"Oh, and you have such vast experience?" I lift my chin and meet his steady gaze.

Kai looks away, staring moodily at the storm raging just beyond our shelter. "No, not really."

We sit in silence for several minutes before Kai speaks again. "I want that experience very badly." His voice is so low I must lean in close to hear him. "To learn, to discover, to really understand … "

"Yes, I could tell at the university how much you want that." I allow my head to rest upon Kai's shoulder.

He sighs deeply. "It's that obvious?"

"For anyone with eyes." I reach out and lay my right hand on Luki's head. The wolf opens his eyes and gazes up at me.

"It is my dream to study at the university." Kai uses his free hand to stroke Luki's back.

Luki's tail beats rhythmically against the stone floor of the cave.

"And then what? Aren't you supposed to run the mill someday?"

Kai's shoulder twitches beneath my head. "Well, yes. But if I can learn enough during my schooling I plan to continue my studies on my own once I return home. Sure, I can run the business, but I can also conduct research and work on mathematical theories in my spare time. It won't be perfect, but it'll be better than just staying in the village with nothing but the mill to occupy my thoughts."

I close my eyes for a moment, enjoying the sensation of being held close. Despite my power to temper the cold, I've never felt so warm.

"You should be a professor. Like Dr. Daman. Let someone else run the mill."

"There is no one else." Luki stops wagging his tail in reaction to the tone of Kai's voice. "I'm the only boy, you see. Between the two families, I'm the only boy."

"And you're an only child." I remember this from my observations.

"Yes, and Gerda has only sisters."

"But one of them might marry someone who could eventually run the business. I mean, if we're being perfectly rational, that could be your way out."

Kai's laugh holds no humor. "I'm the one who's marked for that task. You see, if I marry Gerda it will please our families and protect our business interests. Oh, don't get me wrong"—Kai covers the hand I'm resting on Luki's head with his own gloved fingers—"Gerda's a truly sweet and loving girl. And pretty, too. I could do a lot worse."

"And you love her." I fight to keep this observation from turning into a question. It's none of my business, of course. But I must know.

"I do, actually. I love Gerda as much as I love anyone I've ever known, up to now." Kai glances at me, his brown eyes unreadable. "But I wonder if that's enough. I feel like there's something more. Something I'd be missing if I just follow the path laid out for me."

"You have a great hunger to learn, I understand that." I gaze down at Luki, who's fallen asleep. His muzzle twitches and he whimpers, obviously chasing some creature in his dreams.

"Yes. Sometimes I think if I don't get that chance, if I have to stay in the village, with no real education, with nothing but the mill and work and family and all that—wonderful as it can be—I'll go mad. I'll wake up one day and just walk off into the wild and let the winter take me."

"I've been given to the winter. It's not what you want, I can assure you." My tone is as acrid as the scent of pine needles.

Kai looks at me with curiosity. "So, what about you, Thyra? Once we complete the mirror and you're free from the curse, what will you do?"

I shift, attempting to pull away, but Kai's hold on my shoulder keeps me pressed to his side. "I'll be the Snow Queen. Forever and ever."

"I know that. I mean, what will you do with your forever?"

I look away from his penetrating stare. "I will learn as well. Gather all the knowledge I can. Study about every land, every language. Fill the palace with books and read them all. Work out my own mathematical formulas, solve unsolvable equations." I look back at Kai. "I won't be able to leave the realms of snow and ice, you understand. Voss granted me that ability only for a limited time. But I can still learn, and study, and discover the answers to so many questions … "

"And when I'm a famous mathematician"—Kai's eyes are brighter than I've ever seen them—"I'll send you my theories and you can proof them. Then you can wing your calculations and ideas my way. Just imagine the sensation it'll cause on campus when a falcon delivers messages to me." Kai slides his arm out from behind me and points from my head to his. "We'll be mysterious geniuses, collaborating to provide answers to equations others can't solve. No one will ever guess my partner is an immortal queen."

"No, I don't suppose they will." I focus on Luki's sleeping form. "A very nice dream, but we must finish the mirror first."

"We will. Of course we will. Then my father can be brought back to health and I'll be able to take my place at the university. We must succeed, and we will." Kai places his hands on either side of my face and tilts my head so I'm forced to stare into his eyes. "Thyra Winther can't become a wraith. That would be such a foolish, terrible, waste."

I'm aware of the sound of breathing, but can't distinguish Kai's from mine. Kai strokes my nose with one gloved finger before dropping his hands and turning to gaze outside. "The storm seems to be subsiding," he says, in a strangely hoarse voice.

"Is it?" I rise to my feet and stride to the cave opening, acutely aware Kai's following right at my heels. "You're right. I can see farther now, and the snow's much lighter. Perhaps Sephia has fulfilled my request, after all."

"We should resume our search for Gerda and Bae." Kai turns and heads toward the ponies. "I'll hitch them up, if you want."

I nod, absently patting Luki, who's trotted up beside me. "That's a good idea. It'll give me a moment to concentrate and see if I can pick up anything."

I close my eyes, chasing an image of Kai's face from my mind before focusing on Gerda and Bae. A flicker composed of their combined essences touches my thoughts and I concentrate all my power to evoke an image of their location.

"I see it!" I shout, startling the ponies.

Kai swears and yanks down the animals' tossing heads. I run to the sleigh and help him tighten the straps of the harness as Luki dances about us, yipping in delight. "Yes, we're headed out again," I tell the rambunctious wolf. "Hop in the sleigh and cease that racket."

Luki bounces over to me and gives my hand a lick before leaping into the back of the sleigh. He perches on the bench seat, panting with excitement, his mouth slightly open and his tongue sliding over his sharp white teeth.

"You know he adores you, right?" Kai tests the last buckle of the harness before climbing into the sleigh.

"He sees me as his pack leader." I settle onto the front seat and take up the reins. "No more, no less. Don't go assigning emotions to creatures that don't have them."

Kai makes a strange, strangled noise as I call "Starward" and slap the reins against the ponies' flanks, sending them sailing into the swiftly clearing sky. As Kai throws the fur blanket over our legs I turn to give him a quick smile. "We'll find them now. I know exactly where they are. Clever, clever, Bae."

"And clever, clever, Thyra." Kai gazes into my eyes, as if searching for the answer to an equation. "Sometimes." He turns and stares down at the snow-drifted landscape.

My vision leads us to another cave, on the other side of the mountain. Deep in the recesses of the cave we discover Gerda and Bae. The reindeer's lying on the ground in a jumble of long legs and shaggy fur. Of course he's chosen this awkward position to allow Gerda to nestle next to his warm torso. As Kai and I make our way to his side, Bae looks up at us with a pleading expression.

"Please, Snow Queen, do not harm the little miss. She has suffered much already."

Kai kneels before the sleeping girl. He lightly brushes back the dark gold hair springing free from her braids. Her plump, cheery beauty has been transmuted into the pale perfection of a marble statue. Shadows lurk beneath her lower lashes and hollows sculpt her cheekbones.

"Gerda," he says softly as Bae nuzzles the back of the girl's neck.

She wakes to Kai's concerned face. I shift from foot to foot, glimpsing an expression in those blue eyes that reminds me of Luki. A look that speaks of adoration. Perhaps Kai was right about the wolf. Gerda's gazing at Kai with an identical expression and there's no question what it means.

"Kai!" Gerda throws her arms about his neck and buries her face in his shoulder.

He takes her in a close embrace, rocking her gently back and forth for a moment before holding her at arm's length. "You're much too thin."

Gerda brushes the tears from her face. "Where have you been, Kai? Our families have been so worried."

"And now they're equally worried about you," Kai chides, before releasing her and sitting back on his heels.

"I had to find you, Kai. I couldn't go on, not knowing." Gerda rubs at her eyes.

"Very well, it's done." Kai rises and holds out his hands. "Come, let's get you somewhere safe."

Gerda takes his hands and allows him to pull her to her feet. Behind them, Bae lumbers to his full height, shaking his shaggy body as if dispelling any stiffness.

"I found the little miss wandering on her own, about to cross into your realms of ice and snow." Bae's liquid eyes are fixed on me. "I could not convince her to turn around so I offered to escort her."

Gerda's face lights up and she claps her hands. "Kai, he flies! Can you imagine?"

"Yes, I can." Kai places one arm around Gerda's shoulders and turns her to face me. "Gerda, this is Thyra Winther. You met her once before, long ago. In the church, remember?"

Gerda examines me carefully. "Yes, but …" Her bright blue eyes narrow. "She looks quite different."

"Yes, she's changed." Kai keeps his arm about Gerda as he walks her closer to me. "She's the Snow Queen now, Gerda." His fingers tighten on her shoulder as she instinctively stiffens. "Don't worry, she'll not harm you. We're working together, reassembling a magic mirror that can save Father."

Gerda gazes up into Kai's face. "What do you mean, Kai? How can a mirror help your father?"

The absolute trust in her eyes makes my fingers curl into my palms. Luki's nose bumps at one of my fists and I release my clenched fingers to stroke his head.

"It's complicated." Kai pats the girl's shoulder. "I'll explain later. Now, don't panic over the wolf. He's quite tame."

Gerda's face has gone white as a sheet of paper. She clutches at Kai's free hand, drawing him closer to her. "You must come home with me, Kai. You can't stay here, in this wilderness of ice and snow."

"I'm sorry, Gerda, I can't return yet. We must complete the mirror. I'll explain as we travel to the palace."

I stare at the young couple. Kai's arm is still about Gerda's shoulders, but his eyes are fixed on me. "What are you thinking, Kai?"

"I'm thinking we can't waste any more time. The mirror must be completed, for your sake and for mine."

I meet Kai's implacable stare with a glare of my own. "Gerda should return home."

"No, Gerda can travel with us to the palace. Both she and Bae will be safe there, despite Voss, if you'll offer them your protection." Kai drops his arm from Gerda's shoulder and steps forward until he's toe to toe with me. "You know it's the only way."

"Bae can take Gerda home." I poke Kai's chest with my finger. "It isn't your call, Master Thorsen."

"If they are out of our sight, can you guarantee their safety, Snow Queen?" Kai takes hold of my finger and wraps his own fingers about my hand. "Can you, Thyra?" he asks, more softly.

I shake my head. "No. Very well, we all travel back to the palace."

"What palace is this?" Gerda moves to Kai's side, laying her hand on his elbow.

He looks down at her. The tenderness he displayed in his first moments with Gerda is slipping away. Now irritation appears to wrinkle his brow. "It's the Snow Queen's castle, Gerda. Thyra's home. You'll be perfectly safe there."

I think about the wraiths and our strange servants. "If we are going, let's go before Voss realizes he's been fooled. He's likely to conjure another blizzard out of spite." Kai's still clasping my hand. I wiggle my fingers until he releases his hold, then turn on my heel and stride out of the cave. Luki leaps about, circling Kai, Gerda, and Bae as they make their way outside.

Kai insists Gerda sit in the front of the sleigh, while he settles in the back with Luki. He leans against the front seat, one hand gripping the top edge. Gerda casts furtive glances at me as I snap the reins and urge the ponies forward.

"Hang on," I tell her. "We fly as well."

Gerda's blue eyes widen and she whips her head around to look at Kai. She fumbles for his hand, but he pulls it back before she can take hold. "You'll be fine, Gerda," he says. "Just hold on and don't lean over the edge."

"I'm not likely to do that." Gerda grabs for the right edge of the sleigh. She keeps her eyes fixed on the horizon as we head into the sky. Bae sails along beside us, his legs moving in rhythm with the pace set by the ponies.

"Do not fear, little miss," he calls out to Gerda. "I won't allow you to fall."

I glance at Kai before I focus on urging the ponies toward home. It's strange how pensive he appears. Gerda's presence hasn't lifted his spirits like I thought it would.

"We should make much better time," I call back to him, "now we're not fighting the weather. You and Gerda can share a real reunion soon."

My hood is pulled back. Kai leans forward and whispers in my ear. "We can continue reassembling the mirror soon. That's what truly matters. Trust me, I won't allow Gerda to interfere with our work."

My hood is gently pushed forward to cover my springing curls. I don't turn around, but cast a glance at Gerda. Tight-lipped and wide-eyed, she's staring straight ahead. I know she's scared but as if she senses my interest she turns and give me a tremulous smile.

A brave child, if nothing else.

CHAPTER NINETEEN: CRACKS IN THE ICE

I KNOW GERDA'S TERRIFIED.

She cowers on the bed shoved in one corner of the small bedchamber. The room is clean and furnished with the necessities, but the very fact it remains locked at all times is enough to rattle anyone, much less a young, inexperienced girl.

Gerda shrank into her heavy cloak when we arrived at the palace. She gasped when she caught her first glimpse of our transfigured animals. Thank goodness the wraiths made no appearance when I marched her to her room. She'd probably have fainted, and I would've had to command a bear to carry her, Kai having vanished the moment we entered the palace.

"Where's Kai?" Gerda huddles on the bed, buried under a pile of furs.

I lean against the door. "Working on the mirror, I suppose. At least that's where he was when I last saw him."

"He hasn't come to talk to me. I thought he would." Gerda's voice breaks on the last word.

"Well, he wants to complete the mirror as much as I do. To save his father, you know."

"I know." Gerda straightens and throws off the blankets. She looks very fragile, cocooned in a pile of brown and white fur like a butterfly just breaking out of its chrysalis.

Butterflies. I rub my forehead. I haven't seen a butterfly in years. "He's quite determined when he puts his mind to something."

"Yes, I'm aware of that." Gerda's blue eyes are clear as a summer sky. "It worries me."

I walk toward her. "Why?"

Gerda slides over so I can perch on the edge of the bed. "I wonder if he'll ever be happy, ever be satisfied."

"In the village, you mean." I lift one foot and survey the well-worn tip of my soft leather boot.

"Yes. I know he wants to attend the university, and I hope he can. But I worry that when he's there, he'll become so absorbed in his studies he'll forget to eat and sleep. That's why"— Gerda meets my gaze without flinching—"I think we should be married before he leaves for school. I can keep house, and cook meals, and make sure he stays well. I can take care of him."

"Very commendable, but what about your own life?" I absently bounce my foot in the air as I twirl one strand of my white hair about one finger.

"Kai is my life. I mean, my love for him is what really matters to me."

"You're entirely too young to decide that."

"I'm not." Gerda stares at her clasped hands. "Lots of girls in the village marry at my age. And this would be next year anyway, when I'm sixteen."

"Oh, sixteen." I drop my foot and tap it against the stones. "Really Gerda, don't you think it's best if Kai goes off to the university by himself? You can wait a few years, surely, before you two get married."

"I can wait forever, but ... " Gerda glances up at me. Tears glisten on her lashes. "It's just—sometimes I think Kai will never come home, not once he breaks away."

"You'll have your answer then." I rise and pace the room. "If Kai loves you, he'll return for you. Otherwise, why would you want him?"

Gerda sighs deeply. "You really don't know much about love, do you, Thyra? I suppose that makes sense, though."

Of all the impertinence. I wheel about and fix her with a fierce glare. "Why?"

Gerda eyes me speculatively. "Well, you were orphaned, and raised by that horrible woman ..."

"Inga? I thought everyone considered her a saint."

"Not everyone," Gerda replies mildly. "And of course, you were stolen away by some wizard and brought here, to this horrible place."

She shivers. "Living all alone, I'm guessing, for many years, with a terrible curse hanging over your head."

I stride to the bed and loom over her. "What do you know about my situation?"

"You must reconstruct some enchanted mirror before your eighteenth birthday or you'll be turned into a wraith. Bae told me." Gerda's eyes are brimming with something that looks like pity.

"It's no concern of yours." I head for the door. Pressing my forehead against the silky wood, I close my eyes for a moment.

"Do you really think this wizard, whatever his name is, will let Kai go when the mirror's complete?" Gerda's voice pierces my concentration.

"His name is Mael Voss and why wouldn't he?" I turn slowly, resting my back against the door.

"I don't know. I just imagined he'd kill Kai, and me, when all was said and done." There isn't even a trace of self-pity lacing Gerda's voice.

"And you came anyway."

"That's what love is." Gerda pulls up one of the blankets and arranges it about her shoulders.

"No, that's foolishness." I examine the girl's drawn face. "Anyway, I won't allow Voss to harm Kai, or you, for that matter. What useful purpose would that serve?"

Gerda smiles. "Is everything sensible in your world, Thyra?"

"I try to make it so." Laying my hand on the doorknob, I reach in my pocket for the key. "Anyway, I've a very logical proposition for you, if you'll agree to listen."

"I'll listen."

I point toward her with the hand gripping the key. "You can leave now. Travel home today. I'll even send Bae with you to make sure you arrive safely. All you have to do … "

"Is give up Kai?" Gerda tilts her head and continues to gaze steadily at me.

"Yes. Well, for now. He'll return to you eventually, after the mirror is complete. Simply go home and wait for him."

"No." Gerda sits cross-legged on the bed, her golden head poking out of the brown fur wrap. She looks as delicate as some small bird peeking out of its nest. But, like a bird, her eyes are bright and unblinking.

"Otherwise"—I sharpen my tone—"you may actually find yourself in danger."

"No," repeats Gerda. "I'm not leaving. Not without Kai."

We stare at each other for a minute before I turn and thrust the key into the lock. "Suit yourself," I snap, opening the door. "I can't promise anything, you understand. If you left now, I could guarantee your safety. If you stay, I don't know what might happen." I pause in the hall to cast one final glance at the girl.

"Please tell Kai to come and see me," Gerda calls out before I shut and lock the door.

Kai, always Kai. Silently confessing he haunts my mind as much as Gerda's, I pocket the key and stalk the corridors, headed toward the infernal mirror.

As I approach Voss's chambers I'm surprised to see the doors standing open. I stride past but Voss's words draw me back.

"Thyra, come here." The cold command in his voice is impossible to ignore.

I turn and walk into his chambers. The clutter I remember from my foray with Kai is still present. Indeed, it seems the center table is littered with even more mysterious objects.

"I thought it was time I showed you where I keep my shard." Voss holds up a small pewter box. "In case I happen to be called away when you are about to complete the mirror."

"In that, I assume?" I step forward until I am facing Voss across the table. "And where do you keep the box?"

"On this table, now. It was hidden before, but I think we've come far enough that I can trust you to retrieve the fragment for its proper purpose." Voss is wearing an emerald green robe of brushed wool, with a tracery of brilliant vines and flowers embroidered about the neck and hem.

I narrow my eyes as I examine the robe. The needlework looks familiar.

"Ah, I see you are admiring my garment." Voss carefully places the pewter box on the table and flashes me one of his humorless smiles. "I haven't yet changed from my recent journey, one I believe you may have had a hand in arranging, my queen. It was worn in honor of an old …

friendship, but alas, it appears I was duped by my former acquaintance. She really had no intention of making amends."

I bite the inside of my cheek, seeking a jolt of pain to prevent sinking to the floor under the force of that crystalline glare. "I'm sorry, I'm afraid I don't know what you're talking about, Master Voss."

His thin lips roll back, exposing his white teeth. "Now, now, Thyra. You can drop the innocent act. It doesn't suit you." He turns his back on me and glides over to the row of windows. "I received a most unusual message, from someone I haven't seen for decades. It seemed as if she wished to make peace with me. After all these years." His voice drops to a whisper on the last word.

"So you went to see her?" I press my palms against the edge of the table, steadying my legs.

"I did. But apparently it was all a ruse." Voss turns and fixes me with a penetrating stare. "It did cause me to break off my blizzard a bit earlier than I planned. I don't suppose you know anything about that, do you, Snow Queen?"

At the sound of my title I draw myself up to my full height. "No."

"Or about the enchanted reindeer who is now eating his head off in my stables? The creature who escaped only to meekly return?" Voss lifts his hands and examines his fingers. "Perhaps I should conjure him into something else entirely, just to ensure he never attempts to escape again."

"Don't harm Bae." Rage vibrates my voice. "He's not at fault."

"No, I daresay he is not." Voss lowers his hands. "You play a dangerous game, Thyra Winther. If you were not so close to completing the mirror … "

"You'd kill me. Yes, no doubt." I force the fear from my mind. It isn't logical for Voss to harm me, despite his anger.

"And then there is this other mortal you've hauled into the palace. Really, it might be best if you limited your collection of strays to wolf pups."

I toss back my heavy mass of hair. "She was with the reindeer. I saw no value in leaving her to freeze. It's Kai's little friend, of course. Gerda. It occurred to me"—I think furiously—"Kai might work harder if he knew his friend was safe."

Voss laughs coldly. "I cannot imagine anyone working more industriously than Master Kai already does. But let that pass." He eyes me with great interest. "So, about this young woman named Gerda Lund. Yes, I know her name. I too have observed the village in the past."

"She's only fifteen." I match Voss's glare.

"Yes, an innocent young miss. Very sweet, very loving. Very much out of place in this palace."

"I'll agree with that."

"I wonder"—Voss taps his pointed chin with one boney finger—"how long it would take to twist her trusting soul into something a bit more dark and desperate? It would be an interesting test, don't you think? I'm intrigued to find out just how much time it takes for a loving heart to wither when faced with the darkest depths of the human soul. Will such a person cling to their notions of love and loyalty in spite of the truth?"

I remain silent. I know if I speak I will say things that will only endanger Gerda further.

"Yes, a most intriguing experiment." Voss turns to gaze out the windows at the storm clouds gathering in the dove gray sky. "You may go now, my queen. Go back to work on the mirror. You have only a few weeks left to finish your work, or off to join the wraiths you go."

"That won't happen." I somehow manage to speak without my voice shaking, although my fingers aren't so accommodating. I thrust my hands deep into the pockets of my gown and stride out of Voss's chambers.

I make it all the way to the Great Hall before I collapse against one of the icy walls. After several moments of concentrated relaxation I'm finally able to throw back the doors and walk in to join Kai.

CHAPTER TWENTY: NEW VISIONS

KAI PACES BACK AND FORTH in front of the windows of the Great Hall. "There are only a few pieces left. Why is this so difficult?" His voice is raspy with exhaustion.

"The mirror appears to be resisting us." I give a shard a miniscule turn to fit it to the finished edge of the glass, but the fragment vibrates in my hand. When I release my grip it skitters to the opposite side of the frame. "Damn it." I allow my forearms to drop to the surface of the table and lay my head on my clasped hands. Pain throbs in my right temple. Neither Kai nor I have slept much in the last few days.

Luki's sharp yips pierce the quiet. Raising my head I watch the wolf stand amid the pile of furs that form his bed. As I follow his gaze a bird wings its way into the chamber. It's the falcon I sent to Sephia. Somehow it has entered the palace and navigated the corridors to locate this room. That can only mean one thing—Sephia's sent a reply.

Straightening, I step away from the mirror and hold out my arm. The bird ignores me, spiraling up to the rafters.

"Is that your messenger falcon?" Kai crosses to me and gazes up at the bird.

"Yes. I suppose my acquaintance ordered it to return home." I lift my arm a little higher and whistle. The falcon tips its head to the side and stares at me with its brilliant, unblinking eyes.

"How did it get inside?" Kai moves closer to me.

As his arm brushes mine I feel that strange, fluttering sensation I felt while huddled with him in the cave. I take a few steps away. "I don't know. It must have been put under enough of an enchantment to seek me out."

The falcon eyes both of us for a moment before diving straight toward Kai. The boy flings one arm over his face as the bird circles him once and lands on his shoulder.

I approach Kai with one arm crooked in front of me. Staring at the falcon I send it a silent command, urging it to fly to my arm. It ignores me.

"I think it might be carrying a message." Kai tentatively touches the cylinder on the bird's leg. "See, there's a bit of paper poking out."

I fume inwardly. Having Kai see Sephia's message, whatever it is, does not appeal to my sense of control. "You stand still. I'll retrieve the message."

"No, I can get it." Kai's fingers work the lid off the cylinder. After he pulls out a rolled piece of paper and replaces the lid the falcon soars from his shoulder and perches on a rafter.

Kai unrolls the small scroll. I notice the paper is bordered in black. As Kai reads the message his face blanches white as the snowy landscape framed by the windows.

"What is it?" I cross to him, holding out my hand. "Whatever does it say?"

Kai crumples to the floor as fluidly as water. He drops the paper and buries his face in his hands.

"What's the matter?" I kneel in front of him. Luki whimpers and pads over to us.

"My fault." Kai speaks in a broken whisper. "All my fault."

Luki nuzzles at the back of Kai's neck while I pick up the piece of rolled paper and read its contents.

It's a death notice. Kai's father has finally succumbed to his injuries.

Staring at the notice, I focus my thoughts on the effort required for Sephia to obtain a copy to send to Kai. Because, of course, she did not whisper enchanted words to wing the falcon to me. Still fighting to prevent Voss from obtaining immortality, she meant this message for the boy helping me reconstruct the mirror.

"I'm so sorry, Kai," I say, placing my hands on his hunched shoulders.

Kai makes a choking sound and leans forward until his head's resting on my breast. I stay very still as he weeps in earnest. The sobs shake his whole body. I slide my hands around to his back, until I'm holding him in a close embrace. After a few moments I lift one hand to smooth down the strands of his silky dark hair tickling my nose.

"It isn't your fault, Kai. It was a freak storm. You couldn't predict it, or that your father would search for you. You can't blame yourself." The warmth of Kai's body pressed into mine is affecting me in a way I find alarming. A strange heat rises up the back of my neck. I worry Kai will sense how wildly my heart is beating.

"If I'd followed his instructions, Gerda and I wouldn't have been anywhere near the mill, much less lost in that storm." Kai lifts his head and sits back without dislodging my hands. "I disobeyed him because I wanted more. That's me—always wanting more, no matter who it hurts." He wipes his wet face on his sleeve before looking at me. "I'm sorry, Thyra. Didn't mean to fall all over you."

"It's all right." I drop my arms to my sides.

Kai stares intently into my eyes. "Rather childish of me, I know. Weeping like a baby." He raises one hand and traces the line of my jaw from my ear to my chin. "Thank you for not pulling away."

"It seemed you needed something to lean on," I say lightly, my skin tingling under his caress. I fight the urge to take him back in my arms, to conjure away the misery I see in his dark eyes.

"All that work for nothing." Kai waves his hand in the direction of the mirror.

"It does help me," I say, but Kai's not really listening.

He rises stiffly to his feet and wanders to the windows. "Maybe if I'd worked a little faster, with more concentration … "

"No one could've worked harder than you." I cross to him, Luki at my heels.

Kai's back is to me as he stares out at the frozen landscape. "I failed him. I had the power to save his life, and I couldn't do it." He grips the window frame with both hands and presses his forehead against the center pane. "I wish these windows would open."

I move closer and lightly place my fingers on his shoulder. "You don't mean that. Life isn't something to toss aside so carelessly."

Kai bangs his head against the thick glass. "I do. I do mean it." Desperation cracks his voice but our windows can't be shattered by human hands.

Luki presses his head against Kai but is thrust away by one swing of Kai's leg. The wolf whimpers and slinks off a few paces.

This is serious. Kai wouldn't kick an animal unless his mind was clouded with despair. I tighten my fingers on his shoulder blade and lay my head against the curve of his back. "It's not your fault, it isn't."

"If only we could've completed the mirror sooner."

It feels natural to stand like this, so close together. I can almost believe I'm entirely human, a girl with a future. I treasure the sensation—the rapid rise and fall of Kai's breathing beneath my temple. "It wouldn't have mattered," I say, foolishly allowing my mouth to frame my racing thoughts.

Kai wheels about, knocking me backward. I fall onto the stone floor with a thud. Luki rushes to my side and crouches before me, growling ominously. I touch his bent neck and lean in to whisper a command in his folded-back ear. The wolf turns his head to gaze at me. I know his instinct to protect me is vying with my order. I lay my hand on his head and Luki expels a gusty sigh before rising and loping out of the room.

After Luki disappears into the hall Kai strides forward and looms over me, his hands tightened into fists. "What do you mean, it wouldn't have mattered?"

I straighten, rubbing my hip. "There was no guarantee the mirror would save your father." Thinking furiously, I wonder if my face is betraying my lie.

"I don't think that's what you meant." Kai's eyes are as fathomless as crevices in a glacier.

So it's true. I can no longer school my expressions around Kai. I rise stiffly to my feet. Kai makes no move to aid me. "Of course that's what I meant." I face him, planting my feet slightly apart to aid my balance.

"It isn't. I can see the lie in your eyes." Kai grabs one of my wrists and yanks me forward. "Tell me the truth. Tell me now." His fingers squeeze my bones.

I lift my chin. I won't look away, no matter how fierce his gaze. I can face down Kai Thorsen. I won't be intimidated by him, or anyone. I've been trained by masters. "Very well, I'll tell you." Even though I could hurl Kai across the room, I refuse to call upon my magic.

Kai pulls me so close his face is inches from mine. "Speak the truth," he commands.

I take a deep breath and toss back the weighty mass of my curls. "The mirror may do many things, but all I know for certain is that it can grant Voss eternal life. Its other powers are hidden from me. So when I told you it could restore your father to health … ”

“You lied.” Kai sounds as inhuman as the wraiths.

“Yes, I lied to you. It’s unlikely the mirror could’ve done anything to aid your father. I told you a lie, and continued lying, because I so desperately needed your help.”

“And that’s all that mattered to you, isn’t it? Yourself.” He stares at me, his eyes filling with tears.

It’s strange. I expect anger, not sorrow, from him. “I must take care of myself. If I don’t, who will? You don’t understand.”

Kai releases my wrist and steps back several paces, his gaze still fixed on my face. “No, I don’t. I don’t understand how we could work together so long, share so much, and you had no problem lying to me the entire time.”

“Kai, I was brought to this frozen prison against my will. Turned into the Snow Queen without my permission. Placed under a dreadful curse to satisfy the needs of an ancient, evil, mage who cares no more for me than for the ice lining the palace walls. I had no choice, no options. If I wanted to live, I had to take care of myself. There was no one else here, ever, except for Voss.” Taking a breath to steady my voice, I fix Kai with my iciest glare. “I’ve done whatever was necessary, whatever it took to survive. And I’d do it all again, to avoid becoming a wraith. I’d rather die than live forever as one of those mindless things.”

Kai examines me as if contemplating an unsolvable riddle. “You could’ve asked me for help. Told me the truth and asked for my aid.”

“You would have refused.”

“How do you know? You never asked.” Kai turns away and strides to the table. “I could smash it.” He glances at me, his brown eyes unreadable. “Take the mallet and shatter it again. Why not? It’s no good to me anymore.”

“Don’t!” I conjure a cold wind that blasts Kai against the window wall.

Kai stays seated, his back pressed against the wall. “I know you can kill me whenever you wish, Snow Queen. Go ahead. But you needn’t worry. I’ll not touch your precious mirror. My father’s dead and you’ve betrayed me.” He buries his face in his hands. “What does it matter now? What does anything matter?”

I watch him for some time as he weeps soundlessly, his shoulders shaking. He doesn’t look up when I walk out of the room.

Luki's waiting for me in the hall, just outside the doors. I give him a pat before I head for my chambers, flaring the light in the walls until a cluster of wraiths falls back, shrieking, into a darkened side-corridor. As my soft boots slap against the stone floor I wonder if Sephia has bested me. Logic tells me Kai will flee the palace as soon as possible, abandoning me to my fate. Even if I imprison him, I can't force him to work on the mirror. I shake my head. *These thoughts are foolish. They don't touch me. Let them fall away.*

Pausing before the door to my rooms I clear my mind and evaluate the situation. I suspect Kai's slipping into the despair that afflicted him in the village. If by some miracle he agrees to continue his work on the mirror, he'll need love and support to retain the full use of his mind.

After several minutes of cold, hard consideration I conclude I can't be the one to comfort him. He no longer trusts me, and anyway, what do I know about such things? Luki thrusts his head under my hand and I stroke him absently as I consider my options. There's only one person who may be able to help Kai and, by extension, me. His shadow, his friend—Gerda.

I lift my chin and set off toward the girl's chamber.

Gerda cries silently as I lead her to the Great Hall. Given the closeness of the two families I suppose she's as heartbroken as Kai. But I can't dwell on such thoughts. I need Gerda to comfort Kai, to prevent him from sinking into mind-numbing despair.

"Please keep up," I tell her. Luki trots in front of us, his tail swinging from side to side.

"Sorry," Gerda snivels. "My legs aren't as long as yours."

I gaze down at her. She was sleeping when I pulled her from her room. Her loose hair still bears the crimp from tight braids. "You do want to help Kai, don't you?"

Gerda casts me a furtive glance. "Of course." Her face is streaked with tears and the whites of her eyes are tinged pink. She isn't too lovely at this moment but I know Kai won't care.

Lost in thought, I forget to illuminate the hall far enough ahead. A wave of wraiths rolls forward, washing over us. Gerda screams and beats wildly at the amorphous figures.

"The last piece," they wail. "I will place it. Give it to me." They descend upon Gerda, pressing their hideous faces against her body and threading their smoke-like fingers through her golden hair.

"Get out of our way!" I shout, calling forth a flood of light as Luki crouches and growls, snapping at the air.

Gerda drops to the floor and curls up in a ball, her arms covering her head. She rocks back and forth, whimpering softly.

"To the darkness with you!" I draw a circle of cold fire with my hands, enclosing the spot where I stand and Gerda cowers. The wraiths shriek and groan as they drift away, leaving only curling trails of mist.

The sounds pouring from Gerda's throat I've only heard before from injured animals. I bend down and place my hands under the girl's armpits and yank her to her feet. She falls against me, trembling like a cornered rabbit.

I hold her upright and let her sob for a moment before I give her a firm shake. "It's all right now. They're gone."

Gerda gazes up at me, her blue eyes wide. Tears tremble on the tips of her lashes. "What are those things?"

"Those are the wraiths. They have no power to harm you, despite their fearful appearance." I rummage in my pocket and pull out a handkerchief. "Now, wipe your face. You don't want Kai to see you looking like this."

"Wraiths?" Gerda hiccups a few times before she stills her shaking hands and dries her eyes. "That's what you'll become, if the mirror isn't completed by your birthday?"

"Yes," I reply shortly. I lean in and brush Gerda's tangled hair away from her face. "Pull yourself together. We'll see Kai soon."

Gerda doesn't take her eyes off me as she adjusts her laced bodice and tugs down her woolen skirt. "No wonder," she says softly. "No wonder you'd do anything to avoid that fate."

There's something in those gentle eyes that makes me clench my hands. Something I remember from long ago, from a time before my parents died. I whirl about and stride down the corridor. "Come along," I call over my shoulder. "Keep pace with me if you don't wish to encounter those creatures again."

Gerda trots to keep up with me, her heavy boots clattering on the stone floor. Luki views this as a game and runs about in circles, just managing to keep enough distance to avoid tripping us. When we reach the doors to the Great Hall I hold up my hand to stop Gerda in her tracks. The exertion has brought some color back into her pale cheeks, making her resemble more closely the girl I remember from the village.

"Kai's inside." As I open the doors Luki scoots under my arm to dash into the cavernous chamber. I motion for Gerda to walk into the room ahead of me.

She's hesitant until she spies Kai sitting under the windows, his back pressed against the wall. Running to his side, she sinks to the floor next to him and immediately clasps his hands in hers.

"Gerda." He stares blankly at her, his eyes dull as charcoal.

I linger at the doors. Luki approaches Kai, wagging his tail slowly. Kai frees one of his hands from Gerda's grasp. "Sorry, old boy," I hear Kai say as he pets the wolf.

Luki drops his head onto one of Kai's legs. His tail thumps against the floor. I marvel at the speed at which the animal has forgiven Kai. If only humans possessed that ability.

Kai obviously does not. He glares at me over Gerda's golden head. "Don't you have a storm to conjure somewhere, Snow Queen?" His tone's sharp and cold as an icicle.

"Kai, I know you're hurting, but please be kind." Gerda places her arm about his shoulders and snuggles into his side. "Thyra has a lot to deal with, you know." The girl casts me an encouraging glance. "Those terrible wraiths."

"She belongs with them," replies Kai roughly. His dark eyes rake over my face. "She lied to me, Gerda. To keep me here, away from my family. Away from you." He cups Gerda's chin in his free hand and lifts her head until she's gazing into his eyes. "She lied about the mirror. It can't restore health to anyone, or at least she doesn't know if it can. She only told me that to trap me here as her slave."

"You were never a slave." I stride forward until I'm standing a few feet away from the young couple. "You weren't locked up. You were never forced into anything. You said yourself that you did what you did of your own free will."

"Based on a lie." Kai strokes Gerda's cheek before gazing up at me. "You manipulated me. Used me."

"As you used me, to achieve your ends." I clasp my hands before me to halt their shaking. "Did it matter to you at all that I was fighting for my sanity, my soul? Or was it only thoughts of your father keeping you working day and night? You aided me for his sake, and your own."

"A noble goal, at least." Kai straightens, dislodging Gerda's arm. She prevents herself from tumbling over by pressing her hand against the wall.

"Is it?" Something tugs at my thoughts, telling me to abandon this thread of conversation, but I ignore the warning. "I believe you're lying to me, Kai Thorsen. Of course you wanted to restore your father to health, but I suspect that wasn't the only thing driving you."

"What do you mean?" Kai pulls his other hand free of Gerda's fingers.

I match Kai's furious glare. "With your father incapacitated or dead you may not be able to attend the university, isn't that right?"

Kai's eyes narrow. "Gerda, go and prepare your things. We're leaving."

"Oh, and how far do you think you'll get?" I flick open one hand, hurling a spear of ice against the far wall.

"We'll make it, despite your tricks." Kai brushes aside Gerda's protestations and rises to his feet to face me. Luki scrambles out of his way and pads to my side. "You've little time left, Snow Queen. Shouldn't you spend it on the mirror, rather than tracking two mortals who are likely to die in your bleak mountains, with or without your interference?"

"I've no desire for either of you to die." Thoughts of Luki's mother and Holger well up in my mind. I beat them back, focusing on Kai's pale, resolute face. I sigh as the anger drains from my body. It's all over. I can read my future in Kai's implacable glare. I spread out my hands. "You needn't worry. I'll let you go, as long as you do nothing to sabotage my work. Go—take Bae and a sledge if you wish. Just allow me to complete the mirror in peace."

Kai pulls Gerda to her feet, but keeps his gaze focused on me. "You see, Gerda, we can leave. Nothing's holding us here."

"Nothing at all," I reply, laying my hand on Luki's head.

"No, no." Gerda grips Kai's arm and shakes it until he looks down at her. "You must stay and help Thyra complete the mirror."

"What are you talking about?" Kai shoots the girl a questioning glance.

"It's only a week before Thyra's birthday. Perhaps she can finish the mirror in time or perhaps not. But it's much more likely she'll succeed with your help. We must stay." Gerda's blue eyes plead with Kai as she squeezes his arm.

"My sweet friend." A faint smile flickers over Kai's face as he pats Gerda's hand. "I know you've a big heart, but you needn't waste your pity on Thyra Winther. She only cares for herself—why should you care for her?" The pain in Kai's voice belies his harsh words.

I meet his gaze as he stares over Gerda's shoulder. His thinking is so like mine, I'm certain his mind commands him to hate me. But I read another emotion in his dark eyes. Love and desire wage war against his logic. As they do in my heart.

"Because I've encountered the wraiths." Gerda sneaks a glance at me before looking back at Kai. "You must have seen them, Kai. Such terrible, pitiful, creatures. Bae told me Thyra's condemned to become one of them if she fails at her task. I can't bear the thought of that. No one deserves such a fate. No one."

I stand very still. Never in any of my calculations did I anticipate this act of kindness.

Kai takes Gerda's face in his hands and leans down to kiss her gently on the forehead. "You're far too good for me." He embraces her, turning her slightly so he can stare at me over her head. "Very well. For your sake, Gerda, I'll stay and assist Thyra with the mirror. But as soon as that task is done we leave." He pushes the girl back, still holding onto her shoulders. "We go home. Back to our village. Back where we belong, where we should stay."

Gerda nods and lays her head on his chest. "Oh, I am glad, Kai. I doubted you for a little while, I admit, but deep down I was sure you were still the person I've always known and loved."

"Of course," replies Kai in a tone inspiring nothing but trust.

Gerda, hugging him, can only hear his words. I can see his face. Defeat is stamped upon his thinned lips and despair haunts his eyes. I meet his gaze and hold it.

I understand, I tell him without speaking any words. You stand in that moment when all your hopes and aspirations melt to nothingness. The second when every dream dies.

I haven't reached that moment yet, but it's rushing toward me. It lies in wait, ready to pounce—at midnight on my eighteenth birthday.

Kai lifts Gerda's hands and presses a kiss into each of her palms. "Go now, my friend. Thyra and I must resume our work." He glances over at me. "Would you send Luki with her, to keep the wraiths at bay?"

I nod and kneel down to whisper my instructions in the wolf's ear. Luki licks my hand once before trotting to Gerda's side. "Watch over her," I remind him as he leads the girl from the Great Hall.

Kai crosses to the table. "Time to put everything aside and focus on our task, Snow Queen." He slides one hand over the polished surface of the looking glass, his fingers tracing figures like skaters gliding over a frozen lake.

"It's Thyra," I say, joining him in contemplation of the mirror. I lay my hand over his restless fingers. "Thank you."

"I did it to please Gerda." He doesn't look at me but his fingers curl about my hand.

Staring at our clasped hands, I catch a glimpse of our faces reflected by the mirror. Mine is strangely fragile, my clear gray eyes appearing far too large for my face. As for Kai—warring emotions twist his reflection into a puzzle I can't decipher. "Yes, we've wasted enough time today." I pull my hand from Kai's grasp and thrust it into my pocket.

"I don't want you to become a wraith." Kai's voice is very soft. "But you should never have lied to me."

"I won't do it again." I cross behind him and grab the box holding the remaining shards. Walking around the table, I examine the final corner. "Will you bring the notebooks, please? I think we need to study our equations once more. Perhaps we've missed a vital clue."

Kai leans over, his hands pressed against the surface of the table. As he lifts his head I meet his despairing gaze. I shake my head. "It doesn't have to mean the end of your dreams. There must be some way to solve your problem. If we can reconstruct this mirror, we can surely figure out a way for you to attend the university."

"A new set of equations?" His smile's as resigned as it is fleeting.

"Why not? If we put our minds to it, what problem is unsolvable?"

Kai gathers up our notebooks and two pencils. "I can think of one."

"Nonsense," I reply as he joins me on the other side of the table. "Our minds, together, are quite formidable. What problem stands a chance?" I turn my head and catch him staring at me with an expression in which longing and pain vie for dominance.

"The problem of us," says Kai.

We work in silence for the rest of the day.

CHAPTER TWENTY-ONE: HEARTS BREAK LIKE GLASS

FOR SEVERAL DAYS AND NIGHTS Kai and I work side by side, taking turns sleeping for a few hours at a time. Instead of walking back to our respective rooms we simply curl into furs piled on the stone floor of the Great Hall, Luki pressed up against our backs. Other than these brief respites we toil constantly, pausing only when Gerda brings the food she's prepared. We must stop at that point, as she won't leave the room until we've eaten something. She also orders us out once a day to clean up and change clothes. She claims we need to be sensitive to the odors assailing her nostrils, even if we're oblivious to the smell ourselves.

Fortunately Voss has stayed away from the palace, traveling on one of his mysterious journeys. This suits me well enough. I don't trust him around Gerda, or Kai. I pray his fascination with testing Gerda's good nature was just a passing fancy.

It's difficult to see the days fly by, knowing what waits for me, but I fight my fears and focus on my task. I allow nothing else enter my mind, although I must confess I catch myself carefully observing every interaction between Kai and Gerda. I know once the mirror is complete they will both disappear from my life. That's to be expected. The joys of friendship or family are not for me. I am doomed to live alone, whatever happens. So for now I shove my terror into the recesses of my mind and take pleasure in sharing a little time with human companions.

In truth, I find Kai's behavior around Gerda baffling. He's very sweet, but in an off-hand manner that reminds me of the way he treats Luki. I see her desire for something more—she's always finding reasons to touch him—but Kai seems oblivious to her adoration. I know nothing of family, yet even I recognize his attitude as one an older brother might adopt toward an admiring younger sister. Glimpsing the hurt in Gerda's blue eyes twists something in my breast. I understand that yearning for a dream one can't quite grasp. I felt it so keenly that day in the university lecture hall.

"There was a commotion in the kitchen just now." Gerda hands Kai a bowl of stew. "Luki dashed off for a run as if the devil was behind him, and the other animals were all darting about, scurrying to make everything just so."

"Oh." I look at Kai. "Voss must have returned. That always throws them into a panic." I swirl my spoon in my bowl of stew. "Try to avoid Voss, if you can, Gerda. He's not the most pleasant individual."

"I don't plan to seek him out." Gerda perches on a stool dragged in from the kitchens. "Don't just play with your food, Thyra. Eat."

I lick the spoon and wave it at her. "One thing's for sure, you have that mother talk down pat."

Gerda blushes and casts a glance at Kai. "I'd love to have a lot of children."

Kai pauses in his effort to shovel stew into his mouth. "What's a lot?"

"Oh, at least four or five."

Choking on a bit of stew, Kai doesn't answer. I lean over to slap him on his back as water fills his eyes. "Sounds charming. So you don't plan to have anything to do with the mill? After all, you're the eldest in your family, so you're equal to Kai in my opinion. In terms of inheritance, I mean." I smile at Gerda, who's eyeing me inquisitively.

"I could, I suppose," says the girl. This sends Kai into another paroxysm of coughing. Gerda stares at him suspiciously. "I'm not stupid. My mother kept the books after my father died. She's taught me quite a bit. I think I could contribute to the business, if need be."

I turn my gaze on Kai who shakes his head.

"I'll let you get back to work." Gerda hops off the stool and collects my bowl, frowning at the food I've left. As she takes the bowl from Kai she allows her fingers to linger on his hand. "Did you like it?" She looks up at him from under lowered lashes.

"It was good," Kai replies absently. "Thanks, little one."

Gerda cradles the bowl to her breast and stares at his averted profile. He's already examining one of the remaining shards. Her lower lip trembles, but she straightens and offers me a quick smile before leaving the Hall.

Not only brave, but tougher than she first appears. Kai could do worse, indeed.

"So, what do you think?" I ask as I join him in studying the mirror fragments.

"About what?" Kai glances from the empty section of the looking glass to the shard he's holding.

"Marrying Gerda. She's not half-bad, you know, for a village girl."

"What?" Kai leans in and adjusts the fragment with great precision. It clicks instantly into place against the finished edge of the glass. "Yes!" He turns and grins at me. "Another piece placed."

"That means we only have four left, including mine and Voss's."

"And a good thing too." Kai's expression sobers. "There are only three days before your birthday."

I look away, toying with the shard I'm holding. "I know."

"Don't worry. We'll do it. I swear." Kai plucks the shard from my fingers and lays it on the table. "We still have time." He takes hold of my crooked elbows and turns me slightly, so I face him. "I won't allow you to become a wraith."

"It's not necessarily in your power to prevent it." I meet his intense gaze, wondering if I'm blushing as much as Gerda was earlier.

"You said you'd rather die." Kai leans in and presses his forehead against mine. "It would destroy me to do it, but if you wished … "

I place my hands against his chest. "No, Kai. I appreciate the offer, but it wouldn't help. If I die before the deadline I still become a wraith. It's part of the enchantment of the mirror, a magic even Voss can't overrule."

"Damn him to hell," says Kai with sudden fury. He slips his arms about me, pulling me close. "I don't suppose killing Voss would do any good either?"

"Not that we could accomplish it, but no—the enchantment would still hold." I shift in his arms until my head's resting on his chest. Kai's heart beats rapidly beneath my ear but I'm strangely calm. A wave of pleasure washes over me. It's a sensation I haven't felt in so long I can barely name it.

"You should consider teaching Gerda how to manage the mill." My words are muffled in the folds of Kai's woolen tunic.

"Gerda? Why are you talking about Gerda all the sudden?" Kai pushes me back and holds me at arm's length, examining my face.

"Because you must attend the university. You'll be miserable if you give it up and stay in the village to run the family business. Even if you are happily married to Gerda and have a large, lovely family."

Kai frowns. "How many times do I have to tell you I'm not marrying anyone? And what's that smile for?"

I lift my chin and wrinkle my nose at him. "Picturing you with a cottage full of children racing about and screaming as you attempt to solve a sticky equation."

The corners of his mouth twitch. "I see. You don't think I could handle that?"

I shrug. "Well, you've snapped at me often enough when I've disturbed your train of thought."

"Oh, and you haven't laid into me for the same thing?" Kai taps my lips with his fingers. "Face it, we're very much alike in that regard."

I catch his fingers as they fall away from my face. "We're alike in many ways, Kai Thorsen." I raise our clasped hands and press them against his chest. "Equal in intellect and determination."

"And pride, as Voss observed."

"That too." I feel Kai's heartbeat drumming under my fingers. "I haven't spent a lot of time with people these last few years, but even before, in the village, I always felt alone. It never seemed as if I could connect with other humans, not really. They all stared at me as if I was something foreign or strange. Not just because I was an orphan but also because the things I wanted to know, to talk about, were of no interest to them." I look into Kai's eyes and read understanding there. "When I met you, as a child, it was like a window was opened to another world. I saw there were other people like me, that I wasn't the only one who found mathematics as fascinating as the cut of a pair of shoes."

Kai lowers our hands, loosening his grip to caress my fingers. "And I saw a girl who could challenge any boy, at anything, and win."

"And that didn't bother you?" I lift my free hand and stroke the side of his face.

"No." Kai captures my hand and presses a kiss into my palm.

"Most boys don't care to be challenged by a girl." I shiver as Kai gently pushes back my sleeve and trails kisses up my arm to the curve of my elbow.

Kai lifts his head and pulls me closer. "Most boys—and sadly, men—don't appreciate a woman who's as intelligent as you. But I can't imagine spending my time with anyone who doesn't keep pace with me. How boring that would be."

"You like spending time with me, then?" I allow his arms to fold about me.

"Usually. When you aren't driving me to distraction." Kai's expression changes to an intent stare that makes me inhale sharply. "Thyra Winther, the only girl who can calculate almost as well as me."

"As well," I reply, tilting back my head.

Kai smiles. "As well." He lifts one hand from my back and uses his fingers to trace the contours of my lips. Trailing the fingers along my jaw, he slides his hand around to cradle the back of my head. "The only girl." He kisses me.

He kisses me. I know nothing of love or lust, but it doesn't matter. Nothing matters except the touch of his lips on mine. I savor the taste of him for a moment before I return the kiss, allowing my instincts to guide me.

Kai lifts his head and gazes into my eyes. His fingers caress my neck, sliding down to the hollow of my throat. "This is impossible, you know."

"I know." The look in his dark eyes is heating my blood faster than Voss's magic ever could.

"Once the mirror's complete you'll come into your full power as the Snow Queen." Kai strokes my shoulder before sliding his fingers down my arm. "Your immortality puts you out of my reach." He entwines my fingers in his.

I shake my head. "I'm not interested in immortality. I simply want to live, in my own body, with my mind intact. That's all that matters to me."

Kai kisses me again before whispering in my ear. "The immortality comes with that, doesn't it?"

I sigh and lay my head on his shoulder. "Yes. It was never my choice."

"I know." Kai pushes me back slightly but keeps hold of my hands. "I suspect Thyra Winther would prefer to be an ordinary mortal." He smiles. "No, not ordinary. You could never be that, no matter what."

"I would trade it all"—I lift our clasped hands to my breast—"to travel beside you, to attend the university. To study and to learn, with you as my best, my closest, friend."

Kai raises his eyebrows. "Only a friend?"

"I said *closest*." I squeeze his fingers.

Breaking my grip Kai puts his arms around me. His hands slide down my back to my waist. "How close?"

"Very?" I lean in and meet his searching lips.

This kiss melts my bones like sun on ice. I throw my arms about Kai to keep from sliding to the floor. We're pressed so close even the wind can't whisper between us.

Lost in delight, I don't hear the double doors open.

I do hear the gasp and cry of "No!"

Gerda's voice. But she only comes into the Great Hall when it's time to serve a meal, preferring to leave us alone while we work.

Kai pushes me away. He's staring at something over my shoulder, all color drained from his skin.

I turn around slowly, blindly reaching for Kai's hand as I face Gerda. She's standing just inside the doors. Behind her looms the imposing figure of Mael Voss.

"You see, my dear," says Voss, his voice cloying as rancid honey, "everything I told you is true. These two so-called friends of yours have betrayed you. No doubt they'll simply toss you out in the snow once the mirror is complete and they come into their power."

"Liar!" Kai lunges forward but I use my grip on his hand, and a little magic, to keep him anchored next to me. He casts Gerda an imploring gaze. "He's deceiving you, Gerda. Can't you tell?"

I hold out my free hand, coaxing the calm to slow Gerda's thundering heartbeats. "Come to us. Voss only seeks to hurt you, to shatter your love and trust. He can't abide goodness in any form."

Voss's cruel cackle fills the chamber. "She can believe the evidence of her own eyes. The two of you, so closely entwined. That seems like more than friendship to me, does it not, little one?" He grips Gerda's shoulder with his boney fingers.

The sight of Voss's hands on Gerda is too much for Kai. He breaks my grip and flies at the wizard. Gerda stands between the two men—a small, forlorn figure.

Kai halts right before her, the toes of their boots touching. "My dear friend," he says, reaching for her hands. "Come away from this evil. Don't listen to his lies. You know me. I would never harm you."

Gerda lifts her golden head and looks Kai in the eye, wearing an expression that mimics the wraiths' tortured masks. She raises one hand as if to press it in Kai's open palm, then swings and slaps him hard across the face.

Kai rocks back, holding his hand to his cheek.

"I saw you." Gerda's voice is low and laced with venom. "The two of you, kissing like … like that."

"Gerda," Kai pleads, "it doesn't mean I don't care about you. We've always been friends. You're like a sister to me."

I move to Kai's side, shooting him a warning glance. Little as I know about human relations, I know *sister* is the last thing Gerda wants to hear from Kai.

Gerda launches into me, beating her fists against the crossed arms I've thrown up to protect my face. "You witch!" she screams. "You used your magic to steal him from me, sorceress!"

I shove her away. She crumples to the floor, burying her face in her hands, sobs wracking her body. Kai kneels beside her, one hand hovering over her shoulder.

I point a finger at Voss. "You did this."

"Indeed." The mage pulls his black velvet robe about him. The garment's gold embroidery flashes in the light like sparks from a dying fire. "It took very little skill. All I had to do was whisper a few words in the girl's ear while she slept, planting the seed of doubt. Then I waited for the right moment, which I knew I would sense, even from afar. After that it was a simple matter to guide her here to observe your little romantic interlude." Voss's eyes cloud over, as if he's thinking of something, or someone else. "I have proven my point, I believe. All goodness can be corrupted, given the right conditions, and time."

"You had no need to prove your point to me."

"It wasn't you I was trying to convince." Voss's knife-blade smile splits his face. "Or even your little friends. They are but pawns in a greater game."

"Sephia." Of course, Voss is still obsessed with the enchantress. This gambit was a way to prove his theories to her.

"Yes, my dear mentor. Always she taunts me, claiming goodness will triumph, that purity will defeat my power."

I take in a sharp breath. In Voss's crystalline eyes there's a hint of something human. Twisted and bitter, but human nonetheless. A flicker of hurt and loss.

Kai's taken a weeping Gerda into his arms and sits, rocking her gently back and forth. "You have no power. Not in the end, no matter if you lay claim to all the mirror's magic." Kai's dark eyes flash. "I think I wish you to have it, your immortality. You deserve to live with yourself forever."

"Watch your tongue, boy. I'll transform you into an insect if you're not careful."

"You won't." I step between Voss and Kai. "You need his hands, and his mind. Only four pieces remain to be placed. With Kai's help I can manage it, otherwise"—I spread wide my hands—"you know what happens. Yes, I become a wraith, but you lose everything too. Remember what happens to the mirror if I fail."

Kai glances up at me, puzzled. "What do you mean, Thyra? I know he has to create another Snow Queen … "

"And the mirror flies apart. It must be reassembled again, from the beginning. Isn't that right, Master Voss?"

Voss levels an icy glare at me. "True, though I do not know how you discovered that fact."

"I'm rather intelligent, or hadn't you noticed? I put some clues together quite a while ago." I extend my hand to Kai. "Let's take Gerda to her room. She needs some rest."

Kai grabs my hand and uses my leverage to lift Gerda as he rises to his feet. She clings to him, limp as a frost-blighted leaf. "Yes, she's exhausted."

I don't tell Kai it's my magic that's sunk Gerda into a stupor. Although I'm using it to protect her—concerned that in her anger she might say something to trigger Voss—I doubt Kai would understand my motives at this moment.

"Perhaps you"—I address Voss—"should leave us alone from now on. You've played your little game with Gerda, now allow us to finish your precious mirror. It's in your best interest to do so."

Voss bends his head in a mock bow. "And yours, Snow Queen."

"I don't deny it." I move to Gerda's side, placing one of her arms around me as Kai drapes her other arm about his shoulder.

Voss observes us, the cold smile fading from his face. "I do have another journey planned, so I shall leave you for now." He wheels about and heads into the corridor. "I expect the mirror to be complete when I return." His words drift back, winding their way around my temples and tightening like a vise.

I motion for Kai to wait for a moment before we leave the Great Hall. I've no wish to encounter Voss in the corridors.

"What journey must he embark on now?" asks Kai as we make our way to Gerda's room. "Surely he wants to be present when the mirror's completed."

I help him lower Gerda's limp body onto her bed before I answer. "I suspect he's gone to seek out Sephia, the enchantress I mentioned. I think he's still trying to prove her wrong, after all these years."

"But why does he care so much?" Kai drapes a bearskin throw over Gerda and sits on the edge of the bed. He keeps one hand on Gerda's shoulder as he looks up at me.

"Because, once upon a time, I think he loved her." I meet Kai's searching gaze. "Love can make one do foolish things, or so I've been told."

"It can indeed." Kai extends his other hand to me.

I shake my head and back away. "Not now, Kai. We've no time. You must make sure Gerda's all right, and I must return to my appointed task. Only a few days left, remember?" I break my hold on Gerda, allowing her to wake, before I turn and stride into the hall.

Kai's voice follows me. "It isn't over, Thyra. Not till time, or death itself, defeats us."

CHAPTER TWENTY-TWO: WINTER'S END

SHADOWS DANCE AS THE LIGHT flaring across the mirror flickers. I snap my eyes open and grip the edge of the table with both hands, forcing my buckling knees to lock.

"Thyra?" Kai rushes to my side and places his hands on my waist. "You must get some sleep. I think you were sliding to the floor."

"I was." I rub at my aching eyes. "But I can't sleep. We've only three more pieces to place, but tomorrow … "

"I know. Tomorrow's the final day before your birthday." Kai pulls me close. "We'll do it. We must. I can work by myself for a while if you'll sleep."

"And who'll keep the lights blazing?" I shake my head. "Only I can conjure enough light for us to work."

"I know." He sighs deeply. "Let's get back to it, then."

Two shards lie upon the blank section of the mirror. Only three pieces remain to be placed. It should be so easy, but the last fragments have resisted all our efforts thus far.

His dark head bent over the shining mirror, Kai's a picture of concentration. His lips are pressed tight and lines furrow his brow as he places two fingers on one of the shards. I stare at his profile. An observer might say he's rather a handsome young man, but nothing extraordinary. Not the type of person to turn heads as he saunters down the street. But

I know better. I know I'll never see another face that will stop me in my tracks, or speed the beating of my heart. Only this one. Only Kai.

I step closer and lay my fingers over his. "What about this?" As we move our hands together, turning the fragment ever so slightly, it clicks into place.

Kai jumps back, still holding my hand. "Another one!" He pulls me close and kisses me firmly on the lips.

For several minutes I forget all about the mirror. Kai's the one to pull back, planting a final kiss on my forehead before he steps away.

We stare at one another, both breathing hard. There's a look in Kai's eyes that delights and terrifies me at the same time.

Kai averts his eyes. "Sorry, I lost track of myself there for a bit." He clears the hoarseness from his voice. "Now—for the final two shards." He stares at the mirror and frowns. "Hadn't you better retrieve Voss's shard so we have it ready? We've yours, of course, but I wouldn't want to leave his piece until the last minute."

"Of course." I examine the mirror. Only a tiny corner remains dark. "I wanted to wait until he was out of the palace, but I think I saw him leave this afternoon."

"He took off after lunch." Kai shrugs when I cast him an inquiring look. "I saw his sleigh through the windows. The black one, isn't it?"

"Yes, pulled by a snow-white reindeer." I slide my shard around the small space left on the backing board. "Speaking of lunch, or rather food in general, where's Gerda? She never brought us any dinner."

Kai stills all his movements. "No, she didn't." He glances at the reflective blackness of the windows before looking at me. "That isn't like her. You don't think … " His dark eyes widen.

My mind races, evaluating the possibilities. "Luki's with her, so the wraiths won't bother her. And they can't harm her, at any rate. Although perhaps they terrified her enough she's kept to her rooms?"

"Surely Luki would've alerted us if something else was wrong." Kai carefully places my shard in the bin. "I'll go check, just in case."

"I'm coming with you." I brush aside Kai's protestations and follow him out of the Great Hall. We race each other down the corridors.

Kai scans Gerda's empty room. "Her boots are gone."

"And her cloak." I lay my hand on Kai's trembling arm. "She probably decided to step outside for some air."

"In this weather?" Kai dashes out of the room.

I have to run to keep up with him. He's right, of course. A quite natural, but fearful blizzard is raging. It's already dumped several feet of snow around the palace.

When we reach the kitchens a distinctive howl rises from the pantry.

"Luki?" I stride over and toss aside the chair propped up under the knob. Claws scratch wildly at wood. I throw open the door and Luki leaps out, whimpering and panting. He places his forepaws on my breast and licks my chin before dropping to the floor.

"No, no." Kai's voice is as strangled as an animal in a trap.

I turn to see him slumped against the sturdy kitchen table, a piece of paper dangling from his fingers. "What is it?" I reach for Luki's warm body and bury one hand in his fur.

"Gerda's gone." The pain in Kai's face strikes my heart like a dagger.

I cross to the table, Luki at my heels. "Gone? Gone where?"

"Away," says Kai with a harsh laugh. "Home, she says, though how she expects to get there, in this storm … "

Leaning in, I gently pull the note from Kai's fingers. It's written in a childish but very firm hand. "She does say she took Bae. That's something. The reindeer's much more likely to get her home safely than if she were traveling on her own."

Kai swings out one hand, pointing toward the kitchen doors. "Out there? In the dark? Even Bae can't fly through a blizzard."

"I know." I examine the note more carefully. Gerda's words leap out at me—"since you don't love me the way I wish to be loved … "

"Oh, Gerda," I say aloud. "Why couldn't you just wait?"

Kai casts a sharp glance at me. "What do you mean?"

"Well"—I take hold of one of his hands—"you and I know we can't stay together. You said it yourself. In order to survive I must accept immortality as the Snow Queen. Whereas you"—I turn to face him—"must return to your own world, your real life. A life that includes the university, but also family, and friends, and love. Perhaps Gerda's love, in time?"

"No." He grips my shoulder with his free hand. "There's only one girl I love. I told you that."

I smile, knowing he'll read the sadness in my eyes. "You did. But it's a dream, Kai. A beautiful, impossible, dream. Now—we must put all this aside and go and find Gerda and Bae."

"But the mirror." Kai gives me a little shake. "You can't leave the mirror. There's so little time left." He glances at the standing clock. "Only twenty-four hours. You must stay and place the last two pieces. I'll search for Gerda and Bae."

"In the dark?" I lay one hand on his cheek. "In a blizzard?" I release my grip on his fingers. Placing my freed hand on the other side of his face, I lean in until our foreheads are touching. "You'd freeze in hours, no closer to finding Gerda than you are now. No"—I kiss him with great deliberation before drawing back—"only I can control enough of the storm to allow us passage. We go together."

"We should hurry, then." Kai draws me into a tight embrace. "The mirror must be completed. For my sake as well as yours."

I stroke my fingers along his backbone. "It will be. But for now"—I break away from his embrace—"we dress for deadly weather and venture into the storm."

He nods. "I'll meet you in the stables in less than half an hour."

"I'll be there," I reply, watching him dash out of the kitchen. I pat Luki. "It appears we must attempt another rescue, my friend. What do you say? Will you truly follow me anywhere?"

Luki gazes up at me, golden eyes bright, tail wagging. I don't need him to speak to know his answer.

Buffeted by the driving snow, it takes much of my power to maintain a sphere of calm air about our sleigh. Forced to concentrate on our protection, I've handed the reins to Kai, who drives the ponies like he's been doing it all his life.

"I'm good with horses," Kai shouts at me over the whistling of the wind.

I hang onto my hood with one hand and yell back at him. "Turn left, toward the mountains. Bae will seek out a cave, as he did before."

Kai nods and cracks the reins across the ponies' flanks. We spring forward, almost flying through my circle of protection. I redouble my efforts to tame the winds. The amount of magic I'm drawing makes my limbs tingle. I pull off one glove and observe my hand glowing blue against the darkness.

Yanking the glove back over my fingers, I slump into the seat of the sleigh, tuning my mind to pick up any sense of Gerda or Bae. The reindeer's enchantment makes him the better target, and I focus my thoughts on him.

After some time a flicker of Bae's essence crosses my mind. I straighten and direct Kai to one of the peaks rising beside a pass. It's the most direct route to the village, but despite its convenience this passage is rarely used. A narrow path flanked by steep cliffs, it poses the same dangers as the pass my parents attempted to cross before their deaths.

I direct Kai to land the sleigh at the foot of the mountain. "They're somewhere close," I call to him as we drag the ponies and sleigh into a shallow indentation in the rocky cliff. Luki leaps from the sleigh and circles the area, sniffing the air.

Kai leans against me, raising his voice. "How could they survive this? Without your help we'd be dead by now." He puts his arm about me and draws back quickly. "Good God, you're frozen."

I shake my head furiously, knocking back my hood. "No, no. That's just my magic. See?" I pull off the glove and hold out my hand. My illuminated skin casts a pale azure light over the snow.

"It doesn't hurt?" Kai's brown eyes are wide with concern.

His reaction confirms my assessment of our situation. A slight recoil, a tinge of fear. Not something one wishes to see in the eyes of a lover.

"No, not at all." I breathe out and shake my limbs, expelling the power from my body. Only after the glow fades do I move close to Kai and place my arm about his shoulders. "See—all gone."

Kai tentatively touches my bare hand. "Cool, but no longer an icicle," he says before pulling me close to his side.

As we huddle together for a moment a howl pierces through the screams of the wind.

"That's Luki." I spring out into the snow.

Calling forth a globe of cold light, I balance it in my palms, illuminating the area around the cave.

Luki's crouched before me, his ears flattened and his haunches raised. His growls rumble, growing louder as the wind dies down. The blizzard's dissipating, but as I swing the light in an arc I see our troubles haven't disappeared.

The light catches several pairs of phosphorescent eyes. They form a semi-circle before Luki's tense form.

"What is it?" Kai's at my elbow, peering into the darkness. "Wolves? I've encountered plenty before. Loud noise will usually scare them off."

I shake my head. "These aren't natural creatures."

"Then what?" Kai grabs my arm. "They've no real form. Just keep shifting … "

Kai's right. These wolves, white as the snow and twice Luki's size, are as amorphous as the wraiths.

"Some of Voss's creations. Set to guard the pass, I suppose, in case anyone was foolish enough to attempt to venture here."

The snow wolves slink closer, their paws imprinting the snow. Unlike the wraiths, their smoky forms have mass. Their quite solid claws shine like blades.

"Can they harm us?" Kai breathes into my ear.

"I'm afraid so. Those teeth look real enough." I lean against Kai. "Hold me while I muster my strength. I've expended a great deal of magic this evening, but I think I can summon a bit more."

Kai wraps his arm about me. I keep one eye on Luki as I concentrate on marshaling my power. So far my wolf has kept the others at bay but I know this stand-off can't last forever.

A squeal spins us about. The ponies, terrified by the presence of Voss's creatures, have broken free, splintering the tongue of the sleigh. They dash out of the cave and gallop into the darkness. Three of the snow wolves spin with perfect precision and disappear from view.

"No!" I shout, but there's nothing I can do. If I break my concentration to aid them I might endanger Kai or Luki. The horrifying sound of the ponies being brought to ground fills the air. Yoked together, dragging the broken harness, they didn't stand a chance.

Kai buries his face in my shoulder. "My God, they're being slaughtered."

"As we'll be, if I can't defeat these beasts." I meet Kai's gaze as he lifts his head. "Whatever happens, do not step in front of me."

He swallows hard and nods. "What can I do?" he whispers.

"Stay quite still." I break free from his hold and stride forward until the toe of my boot touches Luki's tail. "Luki, get behind me."

The wolf inches backward until his body's parallel to mine.

"Behind me," I say, but he simply looks up at me with eyes glowing golden as the sun. He's shed all trace of domestication. The wild has claimed him as its own.

The two remaining snow wolves split from one another and circle, one to the left, one to the right. Luki's head swivels as he attempts to keep both creatures in view. I hear Kai's labored breathing behind me but don't turn around. Dragging every shred of magic from my body I send a bolt of cold through my arms, displacing the light in my hands with a ball of icy flames. I swing one arm and send the globe of fire hurtling toward the nearest snow wolf.

My missile strikes its target, blowing the wolf back into the night. A loud yelp is followed by a thud and the howls of the other wolves. I hurl more fire balls in the direction of the howls, then send a blast of freezing wind that whips the snow drifts from the ground. The howls grow fainter as the remaining creatures flee my whirlwind of magic.

But there's still one snow wolf left, standing at the edge of the cave. His ice-blue eyes transfix me as I turn to face him. He's crouched back on his haunches, prepared to attack. I sense Kai moving behind me and jump in front of him, sending him sprawling to the ground. The snow wolf flashes its dagger-sharp fangs and springs.

A blur of gray fur leaps in front of me. "Luki, no!" I scream, but it's too late. The two wolves collide in mid-air and fall to the ground, rolling in the snow. Luki's smaller form tangles with the bulk of Voss's minion. Claws flash and teeth sink into skin. Yelps and howls rend the air, but I can't distinguish which wolf is bearing the brunt of the pain.

"Do something!" shouts Kai, stepping up behind me.

I shoot him a fierce glare. "Like what, exactly?"

"Freeze them both," he yells. "Put them to sleep, like with Gerda."

So he guessed that much. I suck in a deep breath of the icy air and clasp Kai's gloved hand for a second before I turn back to the battling animals. As I focus on the wolves, I feel Kai's hands settle about my waist, lending me support. I know my magic is freezing his hands, even through his gloves, but he doesn't let go. I dig my boots into the snow and concentrate.

"They're dropping back." Kai speaks into my ear while giving my body a little shake. "You can stop now, Thyra."

I open my eyes. The snow wolf lies in a drift, its solid form shredding into wisps like wind-driven clouds. Luki is slumped on the ground a little way off.

Luki. I tear myself from Kai's hands and stumble to the wolf's prone body. Kneeling in the snow, I lay my hands on his blood-soaked fur. I feel his heart beating faintly beneath my searching fingers.

Luki. The animal I didn't want, the companion I never encouraged, the pet I wouldn't claim. I bow my head over his crimson-drenched form as full realization hits me. He never hesitated, despite the odds. He threw himself at certain death to save me.

Another howl pierces the air. It takes Kai kneeling by my side for me to recognize these wails are coming from my throat.

"Thyra, Thyra, it's all right." Kai wraps his arms about me.

But it isn't. I lean over Luki, weeping. I, who haven't cried in over nine years, sob inconsolably. Every tear saved over those cold, lonely days finds its way to my eyes.

My hands slide up and down Luki's damaged body. "Back away," I tell Kai. "For your own sake, back away."

Kai releases me and slumps back on his heels. I call forth all the power I can command, demanding more and more, ripping the magic from my bones. My arms shake with the force of the wild magic I conjure from every drop of my blood. Blue light illuminates my hands until they turn translucent. I hold them up to the dark sky.

"Freeze my bones and shatter my heart like a crystal but give my touch life!" I cry, not at all certain who I'm addressing. My fingers flutter like leaves shredded in the wind. I plunge them into Luki's thick fur until I touch skin. Pressing my hands against his trembling body, I allow the tears to slide unheeded from my chin.

"What are you doing?" Kai slips next to me, his voice touched with wonder.

An azure tint radiates from my hands and spreads through Luki's fur, until his entire body glows an icy blue. As swiftly as the illumination spreads it fades away.

Wind ruffles Luki's gray fur. I lift my hands and stroke his ripped muzzle. As my fingers slide away from his nose I notice the marks fading. I cast a frantic gaze over the length of his body. The blood's gone, along with the ragged cuts and slashes. A damp tongue licks the hand cradling Luki's head. I glance down to meet the adoring gaze of those golden eyes.

"You saved him," says Kai in hushed tones. He creeps closer and strokes Luki's head. "How did you do that?"

"I don't know." I sit back as Luki rises to his feet, shaking the snow from his unmarked fur.

Kai stands slowly. He holds his hand and pulls me up beside him. "Your face is frozen." He takes the edge of his knitted scarf and wipes the ice crystals from my cheeks. "You were crying."

"Yes." I throw my arms about Kai and hug him tight. "I was. I was crying."

"I've never seen anyone so happy about that before," says Kai with an indulgent grin. "So, my wonderful, magical queen, what do we do now?" His bright eyes cloud over. "We've lost our sleigh and ponies."

"Yes, that's a problem. But once we find Bae—and we will—perhaps we can figure something out."

"Bae can't transport all of us."

Luki bumps my leg with his snout. I drop one arm and pat his head. "He can safely carry you and Gerda to the palace. Luki and I can make it on foot."

Kai shakes his head. "Not in time to complete the mirror."

"You can finish the mirror. I told you where Voss stores his shard."

"I don't know." Kai's expression is troubled. "You'd be placing your entire future in my hands, Thyra."

"There are no better hands," I reply, giving him a swift kiss. "Now, come—I believe I know where we can find a young girl and a talking reindeer."

CHAPTER TWENTY-THREE: FINAL CALCULATIONS

WE TRUDGE THROUGH WAIST-DEEP SNOW. I haven't enough strength to grant us the power to skim the surface. Luki leaps from drift to drift, disappearing momentarily only to bound up again, shedding snow with every bounce.

"So, not a pet?" Kai peeks from behind the furred edge of his hood.

"Very well, I confess my attachment," I reply, my lips twitching into a brief smile. I glance over at the pass and shiver. "Let's move on. This place makes me nervous."

"Because of your parents?" Kai holds out a hand. He grips my fingers, helping me slog through the drifts obscuring the mouth of another cave.

I close my eyes for a moment, willing the memory to fade. *This does not touch me. Let it fall away.* "Yes," I say shortly. "Help me dig out some of this snow, will you? I sense Bae's very close."

After I give Luki a command to guard the entrance to the cave, Kai and I use our hands to shovel snow, creating a path wide enough to squeeze through. My fingers tingle inside my gloves as we crawl into the cave.

The scent of damp reindeer fur assails my nostrils. I can't create a ball of light but I can call forth a faint illumination in the cave walls. It's enough to show the curve of a reindeer's wide back.

Gerda's tucked between Bae's belly and the far wall of the shallow cave. Huddled in a ball, one hand clutching a handful of fur, she's fast asleep. Bae lifts his heavy head to stare at me. His lids droop over his eyes and I can read the weariness imprinted on his grizzled face.

"The little miss is exhausted, Snow Queen." Bae eyes Kai suspiciously. "She was determined to flee the palace. I felt I had to assist her."

I kneel beside the reindeer. "I'm glad you did, Bae. No one wishes any harm to come to Gerda. But we must wake her. It's time to return to the palace. I promise she'll be safe, and you can carry her home in a day or two."

Bae shakes his shaggy head until his antlers rattle, making me leap to my feet. The reindeer nudges Gerda, who opens her eyes and sits up.

"Kai!" she cries with delight as Bae lumbers to his full height. She rises and moves around the reindeer to face us. "And you," she adds in a much frostier tone.

"We've come to rescue you, Gerda." Kai steps forward and embraces his friend. "Foolish girl, what were you thinking, running headlong into a blizzard?" He brushes back her tousled hair with one hand.

"I just wanted to get away," mutters Gerda, ducking her head.

"You should've talked to me first." Kai taps Gerda lightly on her wind-chapped nose. "We've always been able to talk through our problems, Gerda."

"Not this one." Gerda lifts her head to gaze into Kai's face. Tears drip from her lashes. "I love you, Kai."

Kai sighs. "I know."

"But you don't love me." Gerda dashes away the dampness with the back of her gloved hand.

"I do," says Kai, with perfect sincerity. "I do love you, Gerda, but just not … "

"The way I want," replies the girl. She stares past Kai's shoulder and fixes me with a fierce glare. "You love her. That sorceress. That freak."

"Gerda!" Kai backs away from her. His tone's sharp as a blade.

"It's all right." I know the anger and hurt in Gerda's eyes. I've lived with it for years, eating away at me like frostbite.

"Thyra abandoned the mirror to save you." Kai takes my hand. "Even though she has only a few hours left. She knew I couldn't find you on my own and insisted on accompanying me. You owe her your life."

"Bae saved me." Gerda strokes the reindeer's velvety muzzle. "We would've been fine."

"No." I shake my head. "You would have died before Bae could travel far enough to escape this weather. You'd probably have frozen here, fast asleep, before you knew you were dying."

The reindeer butts his nose gently against Gerda's cupped hands. "The Snow Queen speaks the truth, little miss. I allowed you to sleep, knowing what would happen, knowing you would never wake. Not after enduring a full night of this bitter cold."

Gerda presses her forehead against Bae's head. "Oh, my friend, why didn't you tell me?"

"I did not want you to depart this world in fear," Bae replies.

"Now we must return to the palace, so Thyra and I can complete the mirror before midnight," says Kai firmly. He glances at me. "The only problem is, Bae can't carry all of us. So I'm going to stay behind."

"No, you're not." I tighten my grip on Kai's fingers. "You and Gerda are riding Bae back to the palace. Luki and I are following on foot."

Kai wheels around to stand in front of me, still holding my hand. "That doesn't work for me."

"It must." I face down his implacable stare. "With rest I can conjure enough magic to protect myself and Luki from the worst of the weather. You'll freeze here." I turn to Gerda. "Convince him to go with you."

Gerda's blue eyes are clouded with sorrow. "I don't have such power. Not anymore." She straightens until she's rigid with resolution. "I could stay."

"Bravely spoken, but not an option," I reply. "We didn't risk our lives to save you only to abandon you now. No, it must be as I say."

Bae swings his head around. "The wolf is calling you."

I run to the passage at the mouth of the cave. Luki howls once, followed by a short series of yips. "More snow wolves?" I wipe the fear from my face before turning to Kai and Gerda.

"I don't think so," says Kai, joining me. "He doesn't sound distressed."

"Only one way to find out." I plunge through the snowy passage.

Kai's right at my heels. "You're weakened, Thyra. Be careful."

"I can still protect myself." I stride into the small circle of snow previously flattened by our boots. Luki's ears poke out from behind a small drift. They're pitched forward, as if listening to something.

Then I hear it—the distinctive rattling call of a male reindeer. I follow Luki's gaze and see a great white buck standing on a ledge jutting over the mountain pass, his ghostly outline illuminated by the full moon.

"Oh no." I reach for Kai's hand. "Voss is here. That's his stag."

Kai surveys our surroundings. "But where's the sleigh? I see nothing, and the reindeer's not wearing a harness."

"No, he must have unhitched the sleigh for some reason. If we could find it before he sees us … "

"Over there." Kai points out a distinctive shape silhouetted against the snow, several yards from where we stand. "If the tack is there we could harness Bae and get all of us out of here."

"Stranding Voss in the bargain?" I raise my eyebrows. "I like that plan."

Bae emerges from the cave, Gerda by his side. "Why is the wizard in this place, Snow Queen? You must ask yourself this question."

"It isn't logical," agrees Kai. "But perhaps we've been granted a touch of luck. I, for one, will take my chances."

"Kai"—I take hold of both his hands—"lead Gerda to the sleigh and hitch up Bae, if you can. I will see if I can sense the mage's presence, just in case."

"Join us soon." Kai leans in and kisses me tenderly on the mouth.

"I will." I step back and whistle for Luki. "Go with them," I command the wolf. "Keep watch."

Luki leaps up and licks my face before racing for the sleigh. Bae plows through the deep snow, beating a path as Kai takes Gerda's arm and follows the reindeer's tracks.

I cross to the foot of the pass, staring down its narrow alley of rock and snow. In the distance I spy a dark figure. Tall and supernaturally thin, the figure moves toward me, gliding over the ground. When it reaches a point in the center of the pass it halts.

"Thyra Winther." The familiar, mocking tone is carried on the wind. I realize Voss is amplifying his voice so I can hear him. We stand at some distance, Voss in the center of the pass and I much farther back. I've no interest in moving any closer to the mage or stepping into that narrow passage.

"Master Voss." I project my own voice so my words can reach him. "What brings you out on this cold evening?" Drawing myself up to my full height, I cast one glance over my shoulder to ensure Kai and the others have reached the sleigh.

"I was returning from a journey and thought to check on my guardians of the pass. Alas, they appear to be destroyed or scattered. Your work, Snow Queen?"

"It was." I run a series of calculations—evaluating whether I can hold off Voss long enough for the others to escape, considering whether my thoughts can touch Kai's mind with enough force to convince him to flee with Gerda, Bae, and Luki.

"Pity. They were some of my finest creations." Voss spreads wide his skeletal hands, which are bare of any gloves. "But why are you here, my queen? You have only a few hours remaining before you, too, whirl away with the mist."

"I have time, if you allow me to leave now. There are only two pieces yet to be placed. Mine and yours. If you permit me to travel back to the palace with my friends, I swear I'll complete the mirror before midnight."

"Oh, I'm afraid that won't be possible. Traveling with your friends, I mean. You see, Thyra, I brought my shard with me." He pats the front of his cloak. "Tucked safely inside my robes. Yes, I know I never carry the fragment, but this time I thought it wise."

"You're lying." I bite the inside of my cheek to refrain from screaming. There's no way to tell if Voss has fabricated this story to manipulate me. I only know he's never taken his shard from the palace before.

"You don't know that for certain, Snow Queen. Would it not be best to take me at my word and ride with me back to the palace?"

"Ride?" I glance up at the white buck. "You mean on the back of your reindeer?"

"Yes, he's quite well trained. He'll carry us both easily."

I survey Voss, suspicion tingling the back of my neck. "Let my friends go first. They can use your sleigh. Bae will safely transport them to the village and then return the sleigh to the palace."

"Bae? Ah yes, the talking reindeer. What a curious habit you have developed, naming these creatures." Voss flings out one arm, raising a blast of wind that rolls over the ground, sweeping clean everything in its path. "But I am afraid your companions are going nowhere."

I spin about, my eyes following the path of the wind. It whips the snow off the surface of the ground lying beneath the sleigh. I breathe a sigh of relief that Kai, Gerda, and Luki are already safely seated in the vehicle. Bae, with the wisdom of his kind, has planted his hooves solidly enough to withstand the gale. But then I notice the dark sheen of the ground under the sleigh. It isn't dirt. It's ice.

"Yes, my dear queen. They are standing on a frozen lake. A very deep lake, and so cold one minute of immersion will freeze the blood and bones of any living creature." Voss snaps his fingers, a sound that rings through the clear air. "And, sad to say, the ice has suddenly cracked."

I wheel about to face the mage. My hood flies back and my white hair springs out about my face. "You did this!"

"Why yes, I did." Voss's crystalline eyes sparkle with malice. "And placed a holding spell on them. They cannot move, even if they'd be willing to leave you. There they sit, frozen, while that crack splinters, creating a network of fissures that will soon overtake the sleigh."

"Let them go!"

"I will, the moment you agree to come with me." Voss whistles for the white reindeer. It springs from the ledge and sails to the ground not far from where I stand. "Climb upon my mount, and I will break the enchantment that holds your companions. Delay too long and the sleigh will slip through the ice, dragging them to the depths. And to their death, of course."

I close my eyes and calculate. I know the properties of ice. The crack in the frozen surface of the lake will spread exponentially, too fast for Bae to lift the heavy sleigh from the ground. The pressure expended by his hooves in the take-off will undoubtedly shatter the ice beneath him. Logic tells me Bae cannot pull my friends to safety now, no matter how swiftly I submit to Voss. They are doomed.

Unless I can seal that crack in the ice. It is within my power, if Mael Voss were not standing before me, poised to thwart any magic I deploy.

Of course, he knows they will not survive, even if I obey his commands. He simply wants to watch, fiendishly pleased, as I put my needs first. He wants me to choose my life over theirs. He longs to prove, once again, that goodness will falter in the face of necessity.

Yet, what can I do? Voss claims to hold the final shard. I don't know if he is lying or not. But if he's telling the truth, I must deliver him safe and sound to the Great Hall. I've little time left before my mind and body are ripped away and I'm forced to forever wander as a wraith.

I open my eyes and glance over my shoulder, my gaze resting upon the anguished faces in the sleigh. Gerda, her blue eyes filled with gratitude as well as fear. A brave girl, whose heart holds love like a deep well holds water. Luki, my beloved companion, gazing at me with adoration and trust. And Kai.

Kai, who loves me for what I am.

Kai, whom I love.

I turn away. Lifting my chin I meet Voss's frosty stare and smile. I know ice and I know snow. Voss gave me that power. He imbued me with magic. He created me to serve his purpose, to fulfill his dream. Very well, I will deliver him to his destiny.

I lift my arms, stretching my illuminated fingers to the dark sky. Time has restored my strength, now love will determine my fate.

Voss's words can't touch me. Let them fade.

Whatever pain awaits, let it come.

"Let it all fall away!"

My voice rings through the narrow pass, resonating against the perfectly balanced sheets of snow blanketing the highest ledges. There's a noise like the crack of a whip. Voss flings his head up to see one of the plates of snow split and slide from the mountaintop. His face contorts in fury as his eyes flash with understanding. He lifts his arms to draw upon his magic, but it is too late—a greater power is bearing down upon him. A roar fills my ears and I use my own magic to fling myself back, far from the mountain pass and the snowy billows thundering down the slope. Voss screams, his shrieks piercing the roar of the avalanche. I remember that sound all too well, but this time I feel no pain at the memory. I see one boney hand held up, impotent before a thundering wave of white. It crests and crashes over his body, burying him in the depths of a snowy sea.

The sound of the avalanche coming to rest rumbles behind me as I spin and fling a sheet of ice across the lake. The new surface freezes instantly into a sold mass, sealing the cracks encircling Bae's hooves.

Freed from Voss's enchantment, Kai springs to his feet and leaps from the sleigh. He slides over the smooth surface of the lake with the grace of a skater. Luki follows close upon Kai's heels.

I run to them, lifting my feet on the wind so I can glide softly as a snowflake. When I reach the edge of the lake I drop to the ground. I throw my arms around Kai, who grabs me and spins me about while Luki leaps in a circle around us, yipping wildly.

"How did you do that?" Kai's brown eyes are bright with wonderment. "Is he gone? Voss, I mean?"

"Yes. He was not expecting me to kill him." I stand still. "I surprised him, in the end."

Kai leans over, breathing hard. "I know, but his magic … "

"Could not avail him in time. And nature, you know, is more powerful than any enchantment." I glance over Kai's shoulder and meet Gerda's gaze. "We should go. There's little time to place those last two pieces."

Kai straightens and slides his arm through the crook of my elbow as we walk to the sleigh. "Why didn't he suspect, though? He must've known you hated him and you'd try to save us." Kai leans over and kisses my cheek as he helps me into the sleigh. "Thanks for that, by the way."

"No thanks are needed." I take up the reins as Kai climbs in from the other side. "I found I preferred you alive." I glance back at Gerda and Luki. "All of you."

Gerda smiles faintly and lays one hand on Luki's shoulder blade. "Thanks all the same."

"My pleasure," I laugh when I realize this is true. "As for Voss's miscalculations, well"— my voice sobers—"he thought I wouldn't dare to destroy him, as he claimed he was carrying his shard on his body."

"Thyra!" Kai grabs my arm. "You're not serious. Then how could you bury him? That wipes out your last chance to escape the wraiths."

"It was the only logical choice at the time." I meet Kai's desperate gaze with a warm smile. "Besides, Voss was a notorious liar. I'm sure his shard rests, safe and sound, in his rooms. Off we go," I call to Bae, who clatters over the thick ice and sails into the sky. I spy Voss's white buck, gliding like a ghost beside us as Bae breaches the clouds. "Fly as fast as you can."

"For your sake, Snow Queen," the reindeer replies, "I will outrun the wind."

CHAPTER TWENTY-FOUR:
TEARS AND ROSES

A FLOOD OF ANIMALS FLEES THE palace as we approach, dark and light forms fanning out in all directions, streaking across the snowy landscape. Bears, foxes, owls, rabbits—all of Voss's transformed creatures freed from his spell at his death. I direct Bae to land the sleigh in front of the stables and jump out as soon as we glide to a stop. Dashing to his head, I look the reindeer in the eye.

"Can you still speak?"

"Yes, Snow Queen, because I choose to do so. The others shed their enchantment as soon as they were able. The choice came into my mind the moment you buried Voss under the avalanche but I decided I may still be of use to you, and our other friends, as I am."

"You possess great nobility, Bae." I stroke his velvet nose. "I think you're more a king of reindeer than I am queen of anything."

Bae bows his head. "You've displayed your regal nature today, Snow Queen."

Kai appears at my side, holding Gerda's hand. "We must get inside. Time's ticking away. Bae, do you mind staying in harness for a little while?"

"I'll unhitch him." Gerda pulls away from Kai and takes hold of Bae's harness. "We understand each other, don't we, Bae?"

"Indeed, little miss." The reindeer turns his head and gently butts Gerda's shoulder.

"You go." Gerda motions to Kai and me with her free hand. "I'll join you in the Great Hall when I've taken care of Bae."

Kai shakes his head. "But you must navigate the corridors alone, and the wraiths … "

"Can't harm me, as Thyra says." There's a new steeliness in Gerda's eyes. "Now run and finish that blasted mirror, will you. I'd like to get home someday."

Kai laughs and gives Gerda a swift kiss on the cheek before grabbing my hand. "Come, Thyra, we have our orders."

We race through the kitchens, Luki loping in front of us. Dashing down the corridors, I don't illuminate the walls any more than is necessary and the wraiths are soon trailing us. Their wails resonate within the icy halls. Luki howls in response.

"Leave them," I tell Kai as he swings an arm to chase the former queens away. "If they follow us they won't be swarming Gerda."

"Good point." Kai halts and motions toward a set of open doors. "Look—Voss's chambers."

"The spell on the doors evaporated as well." I draw up beside Kai. "Dash inside and grab the pewter box sitting on the table. I'm going to run to the Great Hall and try to place my shard while you bring Voss's fragment."

Kai nods and gives me a quick kiss before disappearing into the dark room. I call forth more light in the hall to aid his search before I take off at a run.

The wraiths swarm in my wake, their hollow voices chanting a familiar refrain. "The last piece—I will place it. Give it to me."

I don't bother to answer. Reaching the Great Hall, I throw back the double doors and stride inside with Luki, leaving the wraiths clustered in the corridor. They can't cross the threshold, even now. It's not Voss's spells but the mirror's magic that controls them.

"Soon, soon," they howl and hiss. "Soon you'll be one of us."

I block their cries from my mind and grab my shard from the bin. Leaning over the mirror, I turn the fragment by tiny increments. I don't attempt to think, I strive only to experience the feel of the sharp glass under my fingers and the warmth of Luki's body pressed against my leg. The wraiths' wails are muted as I concentrate on those things I refuse to lose—my mind, the essence of my being, and the memory of Kai's smile.

Kai runs into the chamber, holding the pewter box aloft. "I have it, but it's locked."

Behind him, Gerda slides past the wraiths without flinching. "Bae's comfortably settled." She follows Kai across the room.

I feel my shard click into place just as Kai places his arm about my waist.

"Done!" he exclaims, hugging me to his side. "Now for Voss's piece." He hands me the box.

"Midnight hour, no time left," chant the wraiths. "Soon you'll be one of us. Soon."

Luki slinks toward the doors and crouches, growling.

I slide my fingers under the latches on the box, calling forth enough magic to spring the locks. Holding the box before me, I slowly open its domed lid.

The interior is lined with black velvet. Soft as a snowflake, dark as a starless night.

And empty.

I close the lid and cradle the box to my breast. "For once in his life"—my voice is fragile as an ice crystal—"Voss didn't lie."

Kai yanks the pewter casket from my hands and flings open the lid. Every trace of color drains from his face. "No. No, it can't be."

"Midnight hour, midnight hour." The wraiths' words thrum inside my head. "Ding, ding … "

"No!" The box slips from Kai's fingers and crashes to the floor.

"Clang, clang, clang," cry the wraiths.

Gerda gasps and leans over the mirror, pressing her hand against the glass, her fingers outlining that one small, dark spot. "No." Tears well in her eyes. "It isn't right."

The wraiths' voices ring out like a ghostly choir. "The bells chime. Six, seven, eight … "

Kai takes me in his arms. He covers my face with kisses. When he reaches my mouth, his lips linger until I pull away.

"Nine … "

I will fade. I will disappear. My body will melt to mist, my mind will shatter like ice hit with a hammer. I will cease to be Thyra Winther.

I tilt my head back and gaze into Kai's eyes. I read his love there, beneath the terror and despair.

"Ten … "

I will become a wraith. But in this last moment I hold one precious thought—that in these past months I've finally lived. For so many years I was a ghost, every emotion muted, my heart frozen. Long before Voss brought me to this icy kingdom, I'd rejected my feelings. A necessity perhaps, for self-preservation, for survival, but sad and lonely all the same.

"Eleven … "

Smiling, I take Kai's face in my hands. I utter the final words he should hear, the last words I'll ever speak as Thyra Winther. "I love you."

I bow my head, prepared for whatever comes. Gerda's sobs break the silence and I glance at her just as a tear trembling on her lower lashes slides and falls, striking the mirror.

"Twelve. The hour has struck. Come to us, Snow Queen. It is time."

Nothing happens. As the wraiths' voices fade away like dying chimes, I lift my head and meet Kai's astonished gaze. He touches my face and gently turns me to the mirror.

It gleams smooth as a lake newly sheathed in ice. Where the empty space had blemished its purity, light refracts from an unbroken surface. I touch the spot where the final fragment was to be placed. Cool glass slides beneath my fingers. "How is this possible?"

Kai lays his hand over my fingers. "Gerda's tear. It fell on the empty space and filled it."

"But it's turned to glass. The mirror's whole." I straighten and gaze at the girl who stands next to us, her cheeks still damp with tears.

Gerda lifts her chin and meets my stare. The familiar look is back in her blue eyes—that look of love and compassion I remember from long ago, on another face. My mother's look.

"But I don't possess any magic. I simply wept."

I take hold of Gerda's hands. "You cried for me. Even though you had no reason to care, even if your life might be better with me gone, you cried for me."

Kai laughs and pulls us both into an embrace. "We did it! Together! We conquered the mirror and saved Thyra." He kisses Gerda on the forehead before kissing me in a much less brotherly fashion.

I feel Gerda break Kai's hold and step away. "The wraiths," she says, her voice suffused with wonder. Luki's low growl turns into a whimper.

Kai and I turn as one to face the open doors. The wraiths are drifting into the room. As they cross the threshold their wispy forms solidify, until they stand before us, a semi-circle of young women. Their mode of dress varies, indicating the span of time, but their faces are all alike in beauty, and radiate joy and calm.

I step out of Kai's arms and approach them. "Are you free then? Free to depart in peace?"

They do not speak but curtsey in unison, bending low before me. As they rise their solid forms fade, thinning to translucence before they disappear. A soft breeze wafts through the room, filling the chamber with the scent of roses.

"Now you are the last, the eternal Snow Queen." Kai's voice pierces my reverie.

No. Recalling Bae's recent words, I spin about and stride to the mirror, placing my hands on its cool surface. I bend my head over that reflective pool, gazing into my own crystalline eyes. "Give me my chance." My words ring throughout the chamber. "The choice must be mine and mine alone."

The mirror vibrates beneath my fingers. I press my palms against the glass and feel the hard surface quiver and give way, until my hands are plunged wrist-deep into icy water. Ignoring the gasps and exclamations from Gerda and Kai, I cry out. "I renounce immortality and all the powers of the Snow Queen. I choose to remain mortal. I choose to be myself, Thyra Winther, a girl like any other." I pull back my damp hands as a tremor races through my body. Shaking, I step away, watching the mirror solidify.

Kai catches me before I slide to the floor. "What have you done?"

I lean back against his chest as he wraps his arms around me. "Given myself a future." I concentrate, calling forth the magic I've summoned so easily for many years. "Nothing," I say after a moment. "Nothing there." I laugh and turn in Kai's arms until we're face-to-face. "I've given it up, Kai. I've no more power, no magic. I'm simply human. I'm just another girl."

"No." Kai's index finger traces the contours of my face. "Never that. Thyra Winther is never just another girl." He leans in and kisses me until Luki wiggles between us, yipping and licking at our hands.

"You"—I pat the wolf's head—"must learn some manners." I lean closer and whisper in Kai's ear. "As should we. We've left Gerda just standing there."

A flush reddens Kai's cheeks. "So we have." He turns to the girl. "Time for all of us to get some rest. Tomorrow we take you back to the village, Gerda. Back home."

Gerda smiles, but I detect the sorrow in her eyes. Yes, a very brave child—destined to become a remarkable woman.

"I can't light the halls anymore," I say, as the three of us leave the Great Hall. "It may be difficult to find our way."

"Not with Luki leading the charge." Kai motions toward the wolf, who trots before us, tail swinging. "Wolves can see in the dark."

"So they can." I link one arm through the crook of Kai's elbow and extend my other hand to Gerda. "Come, let's retreat to our respective rooms. We can talk more tomorrow."

"Oh," Kai whispers in my ear, "are we sleeping apart?"

"We are." I jab his ribs with my elbow. "I may have lost my magic, Kai Thorsen, but I haven't lost my mind."

He throws back his head and laughs. The merry sound rings through the icy halls like silver bells. A chuckle rises in my throat. I fight to keep it contained, to no avail. Gerda glances at my face and giggles.

"You're red as a rose," she sputters.

Kai peers into my face. "Yes, you are. Bright crimson, just like a rose."

I sniff and lift my chin, choking back a laugh. "Just because I'm no longer a queen doesn't give you leave to tease me unmercifully."

"Oh yes, it does." Kai winks at Gerda.

"Here are my rooms." I fling open the door and cast Kai and Gerda a fierce look that doesn't quite hide my smile. "You two head off now. I need some sleep." I allow Luki to slip through the door before I close it, defeating Kai's attempt to grab me. Running across the room, I fling myself on my bed. I recall Kai's astonished face and dissolve into a fit of laughter.

CHAPTER TWENTY-FIVE:
A SINGLE CROCUS

MORNING SUN SPILLS THROUGH THE tall windows of the Great Hall, spreading fingers of light across the surface of the mirror. I rose early today, waking when Luki left my rooms for his first run. I dressed quickly and dashed outside behind the wolf. After completing a necessary task, I returned inside, only stopping by Voss's old rooms to rip the heavy drapes from the window and drag them with me to the Great Hall. Now I contemplate the mirror, and wait.

Kai and Gerda stumble into the room, their eyelids drooping.

"What are you doing?" asks Kai, crossing to my side. He gives me a quick kiss before turning his attention to the fabric piled upon the mirror.

"Waiting for you. I need your help." I direct Kai and Gerda to assist me in lifting the mirror just enough to slide the swathe of material beneath it.

"What's this for?" Gerda tugs at the fabric, pulling it to the edge of the table. Her cheeks are pink with exertion.

"I've sent a message. I hope to receive a reply soon." I meet Gerda's questioning look with a frown. "You're exhausted. Didn't you sleep?"

"Not much." The girl tosses her golden braids and shoots a glance toward Kai. "We stayed up for many hours, talking."

Kai lifts his head and offers me a reassuring smile. "We did indeed. All about the mill, and what should be done going forward."

"Kai"—Gerda's voice is very firm—"has promised to teach me the business. Before he heads off to the university, of course. I convinced him our mothers and I are perfectly capable of running a mill." An unexpected grin lights up Gerda's face. "We'll just hire a few more burly men to help with the heavy lifting."

I eye Kai with interest. "Oh, you worked this out last night? You and Gerda?"

Kai smiles sheepishly. "Well, really it was more Gerda telling me how it was going to go. Considering this new side of her, I've no doubt she can run any business."

I smother a laugh. "No doubt. So you're off to the university after all?" I give Gerda a nod. "I knew you could bring him around."

"It wasn't that difficult," says Gerda as a bird flies through the open door.

"It's the falcon." Kai's tired eyes widen, his gaze following the bird's spiraling flight.

It sails upward to the rafters before turning and plummeting down, straight to my waiting arm.

"This was my messenger." I unscrew the cap off the cylinder fastened about the falcon's leg. "Now let's see whether I received any reply."

My heart leaps as I pull a small roll of paper from the metal tube. So I didn't kill him that day. "It's from Holger," I say to Kai, who turns and tells Gerda he'll explain later. "He's agreed to my request."

Kai moves closer, trying to read the scroll. "What request was that?"

"Watch," I reply, tucking the paper in my pocket.

In an instant the chamber is flooded with birds. Falcons, geese, doves, even two eagles. Their wings fill the room with the sound of a great rush of wind.

Gerda runs to us and huddles at Kai's left side while he puts his right arm about me. "What are they doing?" she asks, her blue eyes wide with awe.

"Watch," I say again.

The birds hover over the table, forming a circle that surrounds the frame, then fly down and grip the loose fabric lying beneath the mirror with beaks and claws. They pull the heavy tapestry material taut, creating a cradle for the mirror.

"They're carrying it off?" Kai turns to me in amazement. "But where?"

"Back where it belongs." I lean into Kai and give him a knowing smile.

"Ah … " Kai's eyes follow the progress of the mirror as the birds lift it from the table and swiftly maneuver it toward the double doors. "To the cave where Voss discovered it."

"Yes, where it will rest, safe from anyone who wants to wield its wild magic."

I watch the flock of birds and the swaddled mirror disappear into the hall.

"Protected by Holger, of course." Kai strokes my shoulder gently. "I'm glad he lived."

"So am I," I reply fervently. Kai raises his eyebrows, but I shake my head. "Someday I'll tell you why. But not today."

"You've given it all up." Gerda steps away from Kai to face me. "Every bit of magic. I didn't expect that, Thyra."

"Nor did I expect you to save me." I extend my hand. "Thank you, by the way. I don't think I thanked you properly last night."

Gerda takes my hand and gives it a firm shake before releasing it. "I did it for Kai as much as for you. But—" Her eyes shrewdly assess me—"you're not so bad, all in all. Kai could do worse."

"Now, wait a minute." Kai steps between us. "What exactly are you two plotting?"

"Your life, of course." Gerda flashes him a cheeky grin. "But before we can settle all that we must leave this dreadful place. Thyra, you said we could travel to the village today?"

"Yes, of course. Go and pack your things and dress for the weather. Bundle up—I can't protect you from the cold anymore." I motion for both Gerda and Kai to leave the room.

Gerda bobs me a swift curtsey. "Yes, your grace." Her tone is merry enough to lighten her mockery. She leaves the room with one backward glance at Kai.

"You're coming with us?" Kai takes hold of my shoulders and turns me about.

"Of course. There's nothing for me here. This place"—I wave my hand—"will fall in upon itself over time. Soon no one will find anything here but empty caverns and great piles of ice."

"Good." Kai pulls me close and kisses me.

This time it's me that pulls away. "Go and get ready to travel." I infuse my words with a trace of my old haughtiness. "Meet me in the stables in half an hour."

Kai executes a sketchy bow. "Always at your command." His grin belies his words.

"I only wish that were true. Go now." I push him out the doors and into the hall. Standing in the dark corridor we share one glance before we both take off, racing each other to our respective rooms.

Luki returns from his run just as I finish harnessing Bae to Voss's sleigh. The wolf gazes expectantly at me. "Jump on in," I tell him as I walk around to the reindeer's head. "You're coming too." He leaps into the back of the sleigh, tail swishing.

"And you," I say to Bae. "What do you desire, my friend? I know you mean to carry us to the village, but after that, what's your wish?"

Bae's glossy eyes regard me with great solemnity. "I'd like to stay with the little miss, if I may." He bobs his head and I turn to see Gerda and Kai approaching.

"You don't want your freedom? Because I believe I can still grant you that." I stare into those wise eyes, trying to read his true feelings.

"No. Others can lead the reindeer of these lands." Bae lifts his head and stares toward the mountains.

I follow his gaze. A large reindeer stands upon a ridge not far from the paddock, its ghostly silhouette melting into the snowy landscape. Voss's white stag.

"Bae, you'll stay with me?" Gerda rushes forward to stroke the reindeer's grizzled muzzle.

"Yes, little miss. I assume a mill owner could always use another reindeer. I am old"—Bae gently blows his warm breath into Gerda's cupped hands—"but there is strength in me yet."

Gerda leans forward to kiss Bae on the nose before she hurries around the sleigh and climbs in the back, beside Luki.

"No, no." I walk into the stables, where Freya waits, already saddled and bridled. The few items I own are bundled in my saddlebags. The bags only bulge where I packed the illuminated manuscript I stole from Voss's rooms. I know I do not require the book, but such beauty should not be left to rot. "Sit up front, Gerda. And Kai, you must drive. I'm going to ride Freya. I think she retains enough magic to fly beside you, at least until we cross out of this kingdom." I pat the mare's sleek neck. "I can't just leave her here."

"No, of course not." Kai gives me a sharp look as he climbs into the sleigh. "So we should land outside the village?"

"Yes, and dispose of Voss's sleigh. I don't want anyone to use it after today." I mount quickly and direct Freya to move alongside the sleigh. "We'll have to walk the last little way."

"Or run," says Gerda, as she settles beside Kai. "I may want to run all the way home."

"So may I." Kai glances at me. "We can have a race."

I turn my gaze away. "We'll talk again when we reach the village." Digging my heels into Freya's flanks, I send her on one final flight.

We land behind the mill, and after unhitching Bae, Gerda and Kai help me destroy Voss's sleigh. We dig in our heels and push it toward the water. The force of our combined shove glides the sleigh to the center of the lake. It sits there for only a moment before the thin ice cracks and plunges the dark form into deep water. Kai tosses the harness so it skids and drops into the black hole just as the sleigh disappears from sight.

"Now we walk." Kai wipes his hands on his breeches.

"You do." I dismount but stay close to Freya, gripping her bridle.

Kai turns to me, his dark eyes clouding over. "What do you mean?"

Before I can reply Gerda steps forward and gives me a quick hug. "I hope we can be friends, but you must allow me some time. I've loved Kai for so long it will take a while to change my way of thinking."

I clasp her hands. "I've no doubt there'll be many young men vying for your love now that you aren't spoken for."

"Indeed." Kai flashes a grin. "They've been circling about for a while. She just never paid any attention."

"And you can still love Kai, if only as a sister." I touch Gerda on the arm, willing her to look into my eyes. "He'll need a good friend."

Gerda glances from my face to Freya and the saddlebags. Her blue eyes widen with comprehension. "I'll walk on ahead," she says as she turns away. "Come, Bae. Our home awaits."

Kai watches Gerda and the reindeer disappear beyond a bend in the path before he takes me in his arms.

I attempt to wriggle free from his embrace. "Follow them. Freya and Luki and I must take another path."

"Whatever are you talking about? You're fully human now. You can come back to the village with me ... "

"And do what?" I regard his anxious face calmly. "Sit in a little cottage while you trot off to the university? Take up some trade or perhaps help Gerda at the mill? No, I don't think so."

"But we would be together." Kai presses his forehead against mine. "I love you, Thyra."

"And I love you." I tilt my head back. "But you have much to learn, and so do I. You need to go to the university by yourself, not with some wife or sweetheart dragging at your coattails. And I must find my own education." I yank off one glove and stroke the side of his face with my bare fingers. "You know they won't allow me to attend classes with you or receive any training at your university."

"I could teach you." Kai grabs my hand and presses it to his chest. "Every night. I could teach you what I've learned that day."

"No." I curl my fingers tightly about his hand. "I won't be your pupil, Kai. I must be able to meet you, mind to mind as well as heart to heart." I release my grip and step back. "So I've decided to travel, to use the world as my university. Don't you see? I want to go to those far-off lands I've only heard about, to learn new languages and customs, to perhaps find a place where someone will agree to teach me. A university that allows women a chance to learn as much as men. I don't know if that exists, but if it does, I must search until I find it."

Kai stands in silence, examining me with his brilliant, beautiful eyes. I can see the genius lying behind them, the fine mind working, puzzling out this problem, and arriving at a solution.

"Very well." He sighs deeply. "But you must write. You must write me from every place you travel."

"I will." I move toward him, walking into his open arms.

"You'll know where to send the letters. I'll be in the village until the fall ..."

"And then at the university. Yes, I know." I kiss his lips before I speak again. "And you must write back to the addresses I send you."

"Only if you promise you won't move from each place until you receive at least one letter from me." Kai takes hold of my hands and steps back, looking me over as if to memorize every inch of my face and form. "I intend to include some very difficult equations with my letters." He smiles. "We'll see if you can solve them."

"Hah, let's see if you can conquer the challenges I send to you." I bow my head for a moment. "I should go now. The longer we linger, the harder it becomes."

"A valid conclusion, as always." Kai clutches me to his chest and buries his face in my hair. "Don't forget me."

"It's not logical I would," I reply before he leans in for one last kiss.

This kiss almost shatters my resolve. When we break apart I turn on my heel and stride to Freya, swinging myself up into the saddle before I can speak, or think, again.

"I won't say farewell, Kai." I tap my heels against the mare's flanks. "It's not as final as all that."

"You bet it's not," Kai calls after me. "I'll be seeing you again, Thyra Winther, if I have to track you to the ends of the earth."

I don't turn around. There's no sense in that. I ride on, dashing away tears with one hand. Luki trots before me, glancing back every now and again to make certain I'm following his lead.

The village lies far behind me by the time I slow Freya to a walk. I rub my bleary eyes and see we have traveled to a place where a thaw has already touched the land. The trees lining the dirt road are covered in swollen buds, ready to burst into green. As I look around a flash of color catches my eye.

Dismounting, I cross to the bright splash of purple nestled amid the melting snow. I bend down and touch one finger to the velvety petals. A single crocus blooms, heralding spring.

Luki yips, making me lift my head. When I follow his gaze I spy a tall, slender figure standing by a nearby oak tree. Wrapped in a spring-green cloak, her auburn hair loose, Sephia smiles as I approach her.

"Thyra Winther. I thought I might meet you on the road."

I rise to my feet and order Luki to sit by Freya. "You helped me more than I knew, didn't you?" I stride closer to the enchantress.

"I did. For my sake as well as yours. I knew you'd choose the right path in the end." Sephia's emerald eyes survey me with interest. "So you tossed aside the mantle of the Snow Queen. Did power not entice you?"

I rub my hands together. Now that I can feel the cold, really feel it, I long for warmer skies. "I want to travel, to learn. I couldn't do that and remain Queen."

"A wise choice."

I look her over, noting the embroidery decorating her cloak—tendrils of vines and brilliant flowers. "Why did you help me, truly? I never gave you reason."

Sephia's smile blooms like a rose. "I sensed the seed within you, buried beneath the snow. I knew someday, given the right conditions, it would grow and flower."

I duck my head, ashamed of my memories. I never saw her clearly in the past. "The mirror's safe, at least for now. Holger guards it."

"Ah, Holger." A wistful expression flits over Sephia's face. "Yes, he will guard it well."

She stares over my shoulder, down the road I've already traveled. "But you left him? Your friend, I mean. I did not think you would abandon Kai Thorsen so readily."

I lift my head and meet her steady gaze. "I haven't abandoned him. We've promised to stay in touch, to write often."

"And you plan to return?" Sephia reaches out and lays her soft hand on my arm.

As I've traveled farther from Kai, my thoughts have chased themselves in circles over this topic, always settling in the same place. "When I can teach Kai as much as he can teach me. When we can work together again, as equals. I must seek out my own education if I hope to achieve that."

Sephia tightens her fingers on my arm. "Ah, I understand. You wait for a sign."

"Yes. One day, when he writes to tell me he's done with his studies and is teaching students of his own—be they children or university scholars—I will return. I'll enter his classroom and ask him one question. His answer will determine my future from that point forward."

Sephia's grip loosens as her gentle smile envelopes me. "He will answer the same then as he would today. You have much to learn, Thyra."

I straighten and lift my chin. "I know."

"I trust you will. Perhaps more than I can imagine. So you travel far?"

"As far as Freya can take me," I reply, gesturing toward the mare.

Sephia's green eyes grow clouded. "It may be dangerous, traveling alone."

"I'm not alone." I whistle and Luki bounds toward us. "Few people will tangle with a girl protected by a wolf."

"You have a point." Sephia casts Luki an approving glance. "Now I have something for you. My final gift." She whips off her cloak and holds it out to me.

"What is this?"

"Give me your furs. They will not serve you well in warmer climes. Trade them for my cloak." Sephia strokes the soft wool with one graceful hand. "It will keep you warm, despite its lightness. Or cool, if that is your desire. And it can keep you dry when storms assail you."

I shrug my heavy cloak from my shoulders and pass it to Sephia, taking her woolen garment in return. She's right—it's light as milkweed floss. As I pull the cloak about me I feel warmed as if by a summer sun.

Sephia surveys me with a smile. "Green suits you." She tosses my furs over one arm. "I may need this. I would like to visit an old friend."

"Holger?" I know this is the answer as soon as the question leaves my mouth. "But I thought you couldn't venture into the lands of ice and snow?"

"Only because Mael Voss held them under his control. I am free now to journey where I wish."

I extend my hand. "It occurs to me I haven't yet thanked you properly, Sephia."

The enchantress clasps my fingers for a moment. "There is no need. Follow your path into the world and learn all you can. Then return and visit me one day. Tell me tales of every place your feet have trod. That will be my thanks."

"I'll do that." I smile and squeeze Sephia's hand.

She lifts our clasped fingers to her breast before releasing her grip. "I wish you safe journeys."

I honor her with a sincere, if awkward, curtsey before I turn and walk back to Freya. "I hope to have some wonderful stories to share," I say as I swing up onto the mare's back and take up the reins.

Sephia calls to me as Freya trots past her, "I am certain you will."

AVAILABLE NOW

SCEPTER OF FIRE

Book Two in *THE MIRROR OF IMMORTALITY* Series

She's the ugly duckling in a family of swans. But eighteen-year-old Varna Lund is determined to become someone who matters.

Ridiculed by the young men of her village, Varna vows to live a useful life—as a healer. The skills she's learned from her ancient mentor prove vital when she encounters Erik Stahl, a young soldier who deserted the battlefield to carry an injured friend to safety. Aided by her sister Gerda, she cares for the soldiers in secret.

When betrayal catapults the four young people into life on the run, Varna encounters her former mentor—now revealed as the sorcerer, Sten Rask. Seeking an enchanted mirror that offers unlimited power, Rask seems intent on seducing Varna to his side.

To protect their country, Varna and her companions form an alliance with a former Snow Queen, a scholar, and an enchantress. But when Rask tempts her with beauty and power, Varna's heart becomes a battlefield. Caught between loyalty to her companions and a man whose kisses ignite a fire on her lips, Varna must choose—embrace her own desires, or fight for a society that's always spurned her.

ABOUT THE AUTHOR

Victoria Gilbert turned an early obsession with reading into a dual career as an author and librarian. An avid reader who appreciates good writing in all genres, Victoria has been known to read seven books in as many days. When not writing or reading, she likes to spend her time watching films, listening to music, gardening, or traveling. She lives in North Carolina with her husband, son, and some very spoiled cats.

Through Snowy Wings Publishing, Victoria is the author of The Mirror of Immortality series (Crown of Ice, 2017; Scepter of Fire, 2017), a YA fantasy series adapting Hans Christian Andersen's classic fairy tales. Her short story, The Cat and the Conjurers, is part of the 2019 Snowy Wings anthology, A Touch of Magic.

Victoria also writes mysteries. Her Blue Ridge Library Mystery series -- which includes A Murder for the Books (2017), Shelved Under Murder (2018), Past Due for Murder (2019), Bound for Murder (Jan. 2020), and a fifth book in 2021 – is published by Crooked Lane Books. She is also writing a new series for Crooked Lane, the first book of which, BOOKED FOR DEATH, will be published in June 2020.